Love Me Endlessly

ELLIE HARPER SMITH

First paperback edition November 2025

Cover Design by Lyssa at Booked Forever Shop

ISBN 979-8-9928013-4-7 (paperback)

ISBN 979-8-9928013-1-6 (ebook)

Contents

This one is for little me and all the others with childhoods like mine. I'm sorry you had to be so strong. We're safe and healing now, baby-girl.

Author's Note

Includes Content Warnings

DEAR READER,

Thank you for picking up Love Me Endlessly. Emery and Oliver began as side character in my debut, Love Me Softly, and demanded their own story. This book overlaps timelines with Riley and Matt's book but can be read as a standalone. Their story contains several subjects that may be triggering for some and I have detailed them in this note.

Emery and I both live with a condition known as Polycystic Ovarian Syndrome – PCOS for short. This condition affects the endocrine system and can vary from person to person. I have written her experience based on my own and that of people close to me. Please note that due to her condition this book includes content that may be triggering to some readers including: infertility, past miscarriage, negative body image, weight gain, mentions of harmful diet behaviors. She also has a past experience with an abusive relationship that is discussed on page.

Oliver has a traumatic childhood that was inspired by my own experience growing up in a religious household with an alcoholic father. I have heavily changed details and done my best to handle his trauma with care. I have mostly kept details vague for the sake of my own mental health, but please note that this book contains the following triggers: alcoholic parent, homophobia, biphobia, domestic violence, religious trauma.

This book is dual timeline and Oliver's grandparents pass away during the time that the two are seperated. While writing this book I lost my own grandfather after a long battle with his health. I poured my own grief during his time in hospice care and after losing him into these pages. Oliver is heavily grieving their loss during the present timeline and this may be triggering for some.

Please take care of your mental health! Writing this book was a difficult journey for me that ultimately ended up being far more healing than I expected. I understand if you need to pass on this one because of the heavy subject matter.

This book also contains several open door scenes between two consenting adults and is not intended for readers under 18.

Chapter 1

Emery

October Now

The espresso machine hissed filling my kitchen with the aroma of fresh coffee. I carefully measured out the pumpkin pie seasoning. I'd perfected the amount over the years. Having as many food allergies as I did made making things as simple as my own lattes a necessity. I'd always felt left out seeing my friends going to the chain coffee shops, getting to order whatever they wanted off the menu. My brother and sister often suffered along with me growing up because my parents were so afraid of how sensitive my allergies were, but eventually I had to watch them transition to enjoying things I never could.

Today was my favorite day of the year – the Apple Festival in the nearby mountain town of Fairview. The Georgia weather had finally started to transition to cooler fall temps just in time for our trip. I couldn't wait to be surrounded by the beautiful fall foliage and cool breeze.

The front door opened, and voices filled the living room. "Em, hurry up, they're here."

They?

I poked my head around and my breath caught when I saw the man with freshly cut dark hair just long enough on top to show a slight curl and a short neatly trimmed beard standing behind my sister's boyfriend – well not boyfriend according to her – Matt. The man's hands were shoved in the pockets of his jeans as he took in all the fall décor that covered the room. It looked like the fall section of Home Goods had thrown up in our living room, just the way I liked it. He wore a dark green button down open over a white t-shirt; the sleeves were bunched around the top of his wrists from his pockets. *That outfit always looked better when he rolled those sleeves up.* The silver chain around his neck that disappeared under the collar of his shirt was new.

Matt passed my sister a bouquet of sunflowers and pulled her in for a kiss.

"Riley, can you come help me for a second?" I said with a forced smile.

Riley dropped the flowers into the waiting vase on the coffee table before joining me in the kitchen. Matt was always bringing her flowers, way more than necessary, so she always had a vase ready for them now-a-days. I gestured to the three lattes in paper to-go cups decorated with fall leaves. Those cups had brought me so much joy when I saw them at the store last week, but right now looking at them made my stomach burn. "I only made three," I told her. "You didn't tell me that someone else was coming with us."

"Oh yeah, I thought we could make this a double date. I know you probably get tired of third wheeling with us all the time. Just make another one."

I sighed and started the espresso machine while I prepped another cup with my homemade pumpkin sauce. "That's not the point."

She twisted the bottom button of the cropped corduroy shirt I told her to wear over her berry-colored plaid dress. "I thought it was time for us to play matchmaker for you." The natural downturn of her lips was exaggerated by her worry and her cool brown eyes were wide. The wild curls that framed her face fell over her eyes.

Our features were nearly identical, some people thought we were twins, and I wondered if the look on my face was the same. We didn't look as much alike now as we used to since I constantly changed my hair style, and we styled our makeup differently. Her's was softer while I preferred full coverage with bold lipstick. We weren't total opposites when it came to our styles, never had been, but there were enough differences. Our mannerisms, on the other hand, have always been identical.

I rolled my eyes, knowing she must be thinking about what I had said to her during the summer while pushing her to use dating apps. *"Break your curse so I break mine."*

I needed help, we both knew it, but I wasn't ready yet.

I had been testing the waters, but she didn't know that. There were a lot of things my sister didn't know about my dating history, even if she was my best friend. The most important thing she didn't know was that the man standing in our living room wasn't a stranger.

He was the only man that had ever been good to me.

I poured oat milk into the milk steamer.

Riley looked into the living room and then back at me. "Just play along. If you don't like him, that's fine. Just be nice, okay? He's a friend of Matt's."

Shit. Had they figured it out and were fucking with me?

I schooled my face into a neutral expression as flashes of memories washed over me. I had known Matt looked familiar when I had shown him to Riley on the dating app back in June, but I thought he just had one of those faces. In August when we met him again at the district meeting hearing his last name had made all the stories Oliver told me about his best friend connected with a jolt in my brain.

At the time it only made me more convinced that Matt was the perfect match for my sister. I managed to convince myself that it wouldn't mean my path would ever cross with Oliver's. The potential of my sister getting her much deserved happy ever after was more important to me.

I'd never been more wrong in my life.

Well, except for maybe when I broke his heart.

My hand shook trying to snap the lid onto the cup. Rising steam curled around my hand and stung my skin. The lid finally snapped into place. I lifted two cups, a bit of coffee sloshing out of the top of one, and handed them to my sister, who stood there with a guilty look on her face. I picked up the other two and made my way to where the guys stood in front of the TV stand. Matt's friend pressed the button on the front of the musical haunted house figure. He jumped back in surprise as lights flashed, and it started to play creepy music overlayed with monster noises.

Matt shook his head at him, "I told you not to touch anything."

"Matt, aren't you going to introduce us?" I asked, coming up behind them.

Both men turned to face me. His friend's eyes widened, but I gave him a quick shake of my head. His eyes dipped and fixed on the deep purple mini skirt I wore over semi-sheer black tights with a cropped light weight cream sweater that slouched off one shoulder showing off my tattoos there. I wondered if he was thinking about how much he used to like this skirt. His eyes move lower and take in the new tattoos covering my legs that were just barely visible through the tights. I had been slowly covering myself in them since before we met, but in the last year I had started to run out of blank skin.

Matt stared behind me at Riley and didn't seem to notice the movement. "Yeah, um, Emery, this is Oliver. Oliver, this is Riley's sister Emery," he said with a quick wave of his hand between us. He moved around me to get to my sister. I didn't even need to look back at them to know they were probably eye fucking again.

Oliver stuck out a hand ready to shake on our faux introduction but noticed my full hands. He transitioned to a small wave. "Hi, Matt's told me a lot about you," he said.

I rolled my eyes and then glanced at Matt. "Don't listen to anything he says. I promise I'm not as bad as he probably told you." I was probably worse than anything Matt had said about me, and Oliver knew it.

I started to offer a cup to him, but stopped, remembering the question I always ask every new person. My sister may be distracted, but I still couldn't risk her noticing. "Any food allergies?" I asked him. Most people never consider checking for allergies before offering anyone food, but for me it was a given. It was a courtesy I wish more people would give me. Maybe it would have been more believable if I asked before making the drink, but it was too late.

He paused, stunned by my question. We both knew that I knew the answer. I motioned with one of the cups over my shoulder at Matt and Riley. "Please," I mouthed at him.

I studied his thick dark brows and deep brown eyes while I waited for his answer. Those eyes had haunted my memories for two years.

"No food allergies," he finally responded. His voice came out steady and clear, his accent controlled the way it always was when he was trying to stay calm. The bastard was using his customer service voice on me.

I passed him a latte. "It's dairy free. If you don't like it, I don't want to hear it." He'd had this drink before – hell, he had helped me perfect it. Again, it was a statement meant more for the others in the room. I reached for my keys and a large crossbody bag hanging on the hook by the door. I normally preferred a smaller bag, one just big enough for my wallet and EpiPen case but today required a bag large enough to hold emergency snacks.

"I'm driving," I told them all. I pointed at Matt before adding, "I'm not going to be in a wreck on my favorite day of the year because you're too busy eye fucking my sister."

Riley flicked her eyes to me for a silent check in. She knew I had to drive so I wouldn't get car sick, or at least that's what I always told her. I tried to avoid Oliver's eyes. He knew the truth that I had never found the courage to tell my sister.

Matt threw an arm around Riley, "That's fine. We could use some time in the backseat being chauffeured around."

I made a gagging noise as I walked through the front door.

***

I tugged the wagon full of my purchases around to my side of the picnic table while my eyes stayed fixed on Riley and Matt walking away until they were swallowed up by the crowd at the apple festival. Oliver leaned forward on the opposite side and folded his hands on the tabletop. His hands were rough with calluses, scars, small cuts in various stages of healing, and a spot that looked like a burn.

We spent all morning with him following me around pulling the wagon while I did my best to pretend he wasn't there. "Still not wearing gloves when you work on cars?" I asked him as if I hadn't been ignoring him for hours.

"I didn't know it was you until you walked out of the kitchen," he blurted out. He scrubbed a hand over his beard and then moved it to rub the back of his head. "I know Emery isn't a common name, but he didn't really tell me enough details to make me certain it was you. You've moved since before."

I wondered if he'd had any suspicions when he saw Riley.

I reached for the small pumpkin shaped pendant on my necklace and slid it back and forth over the chain. "I didn't know anything about this until you guys showed up." I looked up to his eyes and searched for any sign of what he was thinking.

He drummed his hands on the table and glanced back to where Matt and Riley had wandered off to find a food truck for lunch. "So, your sister doesn't know about me?"

I looked down at my lap as I shook my head. "She doesn't know a lot about any of my past relationships." His hand crept into my field of vision, and he rubbed his thumb over the back of my hand. My skin prickled at the touch. My head shot up as I narrowed my eyes at him. "Would you just go ahead and get this over with?"

"Get what over with?"

"Yell at me, tell me you hate me. Whatever it is you need to say to me." I pulled my hand away from him, crossing my arms over my chest.

He snorted. "Em, I'm not going to yell at you."

Of course he wasn't going to, he never did. Even when I deserved it. Even when I was so scared I ruined everything because I was tired of waiting for the other shoe to drop.

In the sea of abuse and toxicity that had been my past, Oliver was the only bright spot. The one I didn't deserve.

"But what I did to you was -"

"Very shitty," he finished for me.

"I'm trying to get better," I told him. It was too little, too late. I knew that. My therapist knew that. Hurting Oliver Franklin would always be at the top of my list of mistakes.

"Your sister makes Matt happier than I've ever seen him," Oliver said, pulling me from my thoughts.

"He does the same for her."

"He told me that he thinks she's the one." He bounced his knee against mine. "He's my best friend, so I imagine that we're going to keep crossing paths."

I shook my head. "No, I can find a way to make sure you don't have to see me anymore. There's no reason for us to be stuck in each others' lives."

"Look, Em, you hurt me, and I understand why you did it, but it still hurt. All I'm saying is "I can play nice if you can."

Play nice, I could do that, right? It was the least I could do.

He worked his jaw and rubbed the thumb of his right hand over the burn on the back of his left. There were lines on his forehead and between his eyebrows that weren't there two years ago, the type of lines that come from carrying extra stress and worry. He had always been so serious about work, so focused, now he looked like the years had taken their toll.

"How are Granny and Pop?" I asked.

His hand went to the chain around his neck tucked under his shirt and then he pulled it away quickly. "I don't want to talk about them."

I looked back down at my hands on the table. Ollie had never shied away from talking about things when I asked, even the hard things he didn't like talking about.

"I like your hair like this," he said.

I looked up at him and smiled softly as I tucked the highlighted front pieces of my short shaggy bob behind my ears. I had gone through several different styles in the short time we knew each other, and a few more after. I had decided to go back to my natural ash brown last year but added highlights over the summer. I don't think he had ever seen it this close to natural. "You always said that no matter what I did to it."

For a moment his face softened, and his mouth lifted in a smile. It was like we had slipped back into the past. "You look beautiful no matter what." Just like that he was the man that cheered me on every time I started scrolling through hair inspiration because I was bored and wanted a change. He was the man that handed me a pair of clippers the day that I got frustrated and said I was going to just shave it all off and told me I would look badass with a buzz cut.

Then his jaw tensed, and his brows knitted together as he cleared his throat. "You look happier now."

I shrugged my shoulders. I was happier for the most part. In the two years since I last saw him, I had been putting in the work. I was in a place where I felt like I was starting to figure things out. After all that work, I still felt like there was a piece missing.

A piece that was now sitting next to me.

I swallowed back the "I missed you" that threatened to slip from my lips.

Chapter 2

Oliver

October Now

E MERY JUMPED OUT OF her car as soon as she threw it in park, pressing the ignition button to shut it off when she was already out and snatching the keys from the cupholder. She left her purse on the floor next to my feet. That short purple skirt rode up her full thighs as she sprinted inside. Matt tapped my shoulder from where he sat in the back seat with Riley. His keys appeared over my shoulder.

"I'm going to walk Riley in, I'll be right back," he said.

I nodded and took the keys from him and passed him Emery's forgotten bag. He got out of the car and pulled Riley out behind him. They opened the trunk to pull out the bounty of things Emery had picked out. The two kept their heads together, whispering to each other, their hands brushing together like magnets.They had been like that all day, two adults acting like teenagers that couldn't keep their hands off each other. As happy as I was to see my best friend so happy, the way they looked at each other made me sick today.

The fear that flashed across Emery's eyes sat heavily in my chest. I never wanted to be responsible for that look on her face again. I should have figured it out when Matt showed me photos of Riley. They looked so similar, more like twins if you didn't know them well. Riley's features were softer, her expressions lighter. Emery's features were sharper, but her jawline and chin were rounder. They had the same roman nose and brown eyes. In the photos it had been easy to overlook the similarities because of the way Riley posed differently than Emery, but in person it had been more noticeable. Their body language was so similar, even if everything about Emery was more animated.

Emery looked different than she did two years ago. Something in her eyes was different, the way she carried herself. She was still the same firecracker, but she didn't seem as weighted down. I wondered if this is what she had been like before she had been hurt by the ex before me.

I wanted nothing more than for her to get to live her best life – I just thought I would get to be by her side while she did.

After moving to Matt's car I pulled out my phone. My thumb swiped frantically to navigate straight to the album of photos I couldn't bear to delete, scrolling until I found my favorite one. My hand went to the chain around my neck, sliding the rings along it as I looked at the three smiling faces.

Emery, Pop, and Granny. Emery held a tray of cupcakes, one hand out offering me one, while they all laughed at a joke Granny had made. I couldn't remember what she had said, but I could hear their laughter mixing like they were all in the car with me. Emery's loud high-pitched gasps punctuated with snorts, Granny's a devious cackle, and Pop's a low boom.

The things I would give to hear those tones together again.

"I found her, Pop. She's happier without me," I whispered.

I regretted all the things I didn't say to her today.

The car door slammed, and I looked over to see Matt in the driver's seat staring at my phone. I flipped it over attempting to hide the picture a little too late. He pushed his glasses up his nose with one knuckle and ran his other hand through his messy blond hair.

"Alright, Oliver, no more secrets," he said, starting the car.

"She's the one that got away," I answered. There was no use beating around the bush. Matt could read me better than both my siblings. The only person that knew me better than him was Emery. He already knew someone had broken my heart. I had never needed to tell him her name. When Liz left him around the same time that everything between Emery and I fell apart we had spent a lot of time reconnecting and catching each other up on our lives while avoiding talking about the women that broke our hearts.

"Did I ever tell you that Granny called me once to tell me about her?" he asked softly. Granny had taken him in the same way she took in everyone when we were kids, the same way his own family had taken me in. While he was close to his own parents, sometimes he needed to get away from all his sisters. He had become another brother to Drew and I, another grandson for Granny and Pop.

I knew they still talked even after he had moved away. Sometimes she would tell me about their calls to tease me that she knew more about his life than I did.

"No, I didn't know that," I choked out.

He tapped his fingers against the steering wheel. "The first time I met her, I thought it might be her, but I convinced myself there was no way. This town is small, but it's not that small." He chuckled. "It makes sense now. She's just like Granny."

My chest ached in the hollow way I'd grown too used to in recent months. "What am I supposed to do now, Matt? I didn't think I would ever see her again."

He smirked and reached for the radio. "Just see what happens, man. If there is one thing I've learned about those two, it's that you've just got to let them drive the bus and be ready to take the long way around."

I unlocked my phone, the picture filling the screen. I could do that. I had spent the last two years throwing myself into work, never able to forget her. I could keep going the same way until we figured this out.

Chapter 3

Emery

July Then

I DOUBLE CHECKED THE building in front of me against the photos on Google. The cinderblock walls in person looked like they were a decade overdue for a power wash and the blue paint across the top of the building declaring this Franklin Auto Shop was chipped. The white garage doors were covered in grease smudges. The building may have looked worse for wear, but the parking lot was jam packed with cars.

I chewed my bottom lip and pulled up my hairdresser's contact on my phone. I pressed the button to start a video call and tapped my fingers against the back of my phone while I waited for her to answer.

"Hey, Em, what's up?" Ava's face popped up on my screen. Loose pieces of dark hair with purple ends hung around her face from under a black ball cap and it looked like she was walking around the salon as she took a bite of a sandwich.

"Sorry to bug you, it looks like you're busy. I'm at that shop you said your family owns. Are you sure I didn't need an appointment? They look busy." I flipped the camera on my phone to show her the crowded parking lot.

Ava had been my hairdresser for a couple of years now, but we hadn't really talked much outside of the typical conversations of how I wanted my hair. Last week I showed up to my appointment and told her I didn't care what she did, but I needed a major change. I'd had the same long hair with simple layers and my natural color for seven years. Every time I looked in the mirror all I could hear was my ex.

"Your hair looks better, long and straight like this, Emery. Why would you want to ruin it?" he would ask anytime I mentioned wanting to change it up. "I'm the one that has to be seen with you. Why would you want to embarrass me by doing your hair that way?"

I had straightened my hair every day for four years for that bastard. My hair was so heat damaged I couldn't even wear my natural waves if I wanted to.

Ava had pried until I broke down and told her the truth behind why I needed the change. Then while she worked her magic, I had told her about how he used to handle all the maintenance for my car and now there was a light telling me it needed an oil change. It was something so simple but with everything I'd been through recently it felt like a giant weight. I was too embarrassed to ask my dad or brother where to take it.

I left the salon with my hair cut to just below my shoulders with shaggy layers and dyed an auburn so deep it was almost burgundy. She had also written down the name of this shop. "Pop and Granny will make sure you're taken care of," she told me.

"You're fine. I already told them to be on the lookout for you. Pop said they had a lot of cars waiting around for parts that won't be in for a couple days." The last of her words were almost drowned out by a hairdryer as she walked around.

"Okay. I just don't want to be a burden if they're busy."

Ava flashed a soft smile that made her round cheeks pop and adjusted her crooked septum ring. She shook her head and then looked over her shoulder as someone in the background called her name. "I promise it's fine. Just tell them that I sent you. Gotta go. See you later." She practically shoved the entire sandwich in her mouth before hanging up.

I walked through the entrance door and into a waiting room that looked like it wasn't meant for much waiting. The cramped space held a handful of chairs against the wall and a table covered with old, faded magazines. Behind the front counter there was a man close to my age in a deep navy uniform with a dark brown beard and hair a shade lighter just long enough to curl out from the edges of his backwards cap. His hands and arms were smeared with faded grease that looked like he had tried to scrub off but had given up . His arms were stretched out in front of him with his palms braced on top of the counter as the middle-aged man on the other side yelled at him. The man I assumed was a customer was red in the face and waving his hands around as he yelled.

I stepped up behind him and cleared my throat. Both men ignored me.

"Sir, you heard what the parts guy said, the part you need is on back order until next month. If you want, I can try to make some calls to see if we can find a used one to get you by, but if you want us to use new parts only, we won't be able to get it until they have one in stock." The employee was short, but his voice was deeper than I expected. He spoke slowly like he was struggling to keep his voice even.

The middle-aged man shook his head. "I don't understand why this is so damn hard. The last place I went to already put in a salvage part. I just want a running car. I don't want to wait another fucking month to get my car back." He crossed his arms and turned to me. "Don't bother with this place, young lady, they don't know what they're doing."

I raised my eyebrows and crossed my arms right back at him. "Sounds to me like he is trying to do exactly what you're asking him to, but you can't get your head out of your ass long enough to see it."

The employee dipped his head and brought a hand to his mouth to cover the smile that teased across his lips. The older man's face turned a deeper shade of red that had me worried about his blood pressure. My heart raced against my chest under the weight of his glare.

I shouldn't have said that.

"Why do you always have to say whatever pops in your head? Your mouth is going to get you in trouble, Emery."

An older couple walked in from the door that led out to the shop. That must have been Pop and Granny. Pop put his arm around the customer and led him off to the side while Granny sat at a chair behind the counter. She patted the employee on the hand. "Son, you should have let me deal with him. You know I like getting to put the dumbasses in their place," she said sweetly.

I rolled my lips between my teeth to hold back a laugh.

The employee lifted his cap off and ran a hand through his hair before placing it back on. He looked up to where I stood. I tugged at the hem of the short summer dress I wore, suddenly not sure if it was too short even if the mid-summer heatwave called for it.

Don't you think you're a little too big for that short of a dress?

"How can we help you?" he asked. I could get a better look at him now without the other man blocking my view. He may have been short, but he had the kind of stocky build I'd heard people refer to as being built like a tank. His chest and shoulders were broad and his stomach was thick enough it stuck out over his belt some. My eyes went to the name patch on his uniform. Oliver. It suited him.

"Hi, um, Ava told me to come by. I think my car needs an oil change." I chewed my lip and tried to remember what else Ava told me it may need. My hands shook as my confidence deflated and I clutched the strap of my crossbody bag. "Maybe rotate the tires?" I added quickly.

"Oh, you must be Emery," the older lady said. She smiled softly and motioned for me to step closer. "Ava said she texted you everything her car would need," she said to Oliver.

Oliver pulled out his phone and started scrolling, his thick dark brows knitted together as he looked at the screen.

"Yes, ma'am, that's me." I flicked my eyes between the two of them, not sure which one I needed to talk to.

"Call me Granny, everyone does." She held a clipboard out to me. "Just need some information from you."

My eyes scanned over the page. I tried not to wince at all the information they needed about my car that I didn't know. Her hand patted the one I had rested on the counter. "Just fill out what you can, dear. Most of that we can get when they pull your car in."

I filled out the contact information portions along with the make, model, and year of my car but left everything else blank.

"Looks like Ava thinks we should just go ahead and give everything a good look over," Oliver finally said. His voice sounded different now, lazier with his southern drawl stronger, less forced. He looked at me like he was waiting for me to ask what that meant.

"Okay, that's fine. I haven't noticed anything different about it, no strange sounds. The only light on is the one for the oil change." I tapped the pen against the clipboard. "I think she only said something about the tires because I wasn't sure when the last time was that they were rotated." I handed the clipboard back to Granny.

"There's no extra charge for them to give it a thorough check for you, dear. If Oliver finds anything wrong, we'll let you know if it's something that you need to make a priority to fix or if you can wait on it. I won't let these boys pressure you into anything and you're welcome to get a second opinion about anything we recommend."

Granny's voice made me feel so calm I was starting to feel like I'd trust this woman with my life.

Oliver took the clipboard and looked over it. When he looked back at me the crooked smile on his face was the same as Ava's, the right side lifting just a little more than the left. The anger that had been all over his face while dealing with the other customer was gone and replaced with the same charm Ava had worn while she made me spill my guts to her last week. "Feel free to call my sister if I do anything to make you not trust us. She's always looking for a reason to beat me up," he said.

On Ava, that look had made me feel like we had been best friends for life. On Oliver, it made me want to do whatever I needed to see it again. I smiled back at him and chuckled at the mental image of his petite sister beating him up.

He was cute. His teeth were just slightly crooked, like he hadn't bothered to wear his retainer after he had braces. His top lip was thin, almost covered by his facial hair, but his bottom lip was full. There was a spot in the middle of his nose that looked like he had broken it once upon a time.

His smile dropped. Red started to creep up his neck and over the parts of his cheeks above his beard. Shit, I had been staring for too long. I blinked and smiled back as I handed over my keys.

***

Oliver sat down in the chair next to me. He held a clipboard between us and pointed to the notes he had made in small, blocky handwriting. He lifted his hat, and I noticed the tips of his ears were red when he ran his hand through his hair. His eyes stayed on the clipboard. Great, I openly ogled him and made him uncomfortable at his place of work. Now I needed a new mechanic and a new hairdresser.

"That looks bad," I said.

"It's not, I just tend to make a lot of notes. The tread on your tires is getting close to wear indicator, where the manufacturer suggests replacing them. You don't need them right away but need to keep that in mind. We'll check them again the next time you come in. Based on the mileage of your car Ford recommends a few maintenance items. We'll give you an estimate of those to look over, get back to us if you want any of them. Feel free to do your own research. I didn't see anything that I was really concerned about today. Your oil was a little low, but I couldn't find any leaks. I recommend keeping a check on it. If it gets low before you're due back just go ahead and bring it back early for me to look at."

My brain scrambled trying to remember when my dad had shown me how to check the oil in my car when I first started driving. I don't think I had ever actually checked it by myself. It sounded like I would be doing a lot of Googling when I got home.

"I can show you how to check the oil, if you want."

I looked up to see Oliver's eyes fixed on me instead of the paperwork. His brows were drawn down like he could hear how much my thoughts were spiraling.

"He's not just offering because you're a woman," Granny yelled from where she sat at the counter. "We get a lot of people in here that have no idea how to check it."

Oliver nodded and lifted one corner of his mouth in a half smile. His eyes dropped back to the clipboard. "Even men. I had a guy that overfilled his oil one time because he thought he should be able to see it when he opened the fill cap. He had no idea there was a dipstick. Then there was another guy that didn't understand how to read the dipstick and kept insisting that we underfilled it. He cussed us out for half an hour over that. Granny had a field day with him."

I looked over to Granny. She was laughing so hard she had to swipe a tear from the corner of her eye. I wished I had been able to see that.

Oliver motioned with his head toward the door that led out to the shop. I could see my car still sitting there through the window. He stood and handed the clipboard over to Granny. "Come on, I'll give you a quick tutorial while she gets everything written up for you. I'll show you what I mean about your tires, too." He flashed his crooked smile again and met my gaze for a millisecond.

I wondered how any customer wouldn't trust what he was saying. I'd made him uncomfortable, and he was still willing to help me understand everything he was saying about my car. An embarrassed blush heated my face while I followed him out, making sure to keep ample space between us.

He popped the hood and pointed to what I knew was the dipstick. He pulled a rag out of his pocket and wiped the end of it off before sticking it back in the car. "It's really important that you make sure you insert it all the way like this so it's accurate. I've had people make that mistake too." He pulled it back out and showed it to me. "If it's at the top of the cross-hatches it's full. If it's at the bottom it's a quart low."

I tried to focus on what he said and not the way standing this close to him made my body heat. I caught my eyes drifting to his left hand as he held the dipstick. No ring or tan line.

Don't do this, I told myself. *He's just being nice.*

He pointed to a cap and told me that if I needed to add any oil that was where it went. There was something about checking the owner's manual.

"So, Ava did your hair?" he asked as he closed the hood.

"Huh?" I asked, not realizing he had stopped talking about my car. My cheeks grew even hotter. Thank God for full-coverage foundation or I'd probably look like a tomato right about now. "Yeah, I needed a change. She did a good job."

He nodded and cleared his throat. "Yeah, it looks good." His eyes moved to my shoulders and then over my arms. He opened his mouth like he was going to say something about the tattoos that started at my collar bones before winding over my shoulders and stopping at my elbows. His eyes dropped to the ground, and he adjusted his cap.

I wished he would say whatever else he was thinking. I liked the tattoos I'd spent so much time and money having inked into my skin over the past few months and always appreciated a compliment on them. There were more hidden by my dress and shorts.

Was he one of those men that thought women shouldn't be covered in tattoos? If he was, I needed him to say it now so I could get the ick and stop checking him out.

He dropped into a squat next to the driver's side front tire and pulled something out of his pocket. I squatted down next to him, tugging at the bottom of my dress. I was thankful I'd worn shorts under it, not just because it kept my thick thighs from chaffing but because I would be mortified if I accidentally flashed him. I still didn't want the dress to ride up enough for him to know that the shorts were the only thing in the way of a slip up. His left hand hovered just behind my back as I steadied myself in the squat.

He used a gauge to show me how to measure the depth of the tread on my tires. I think there was one of those floating around somewhere in my car. This was another thing my dad had shown me how to do. "Like I said, they're getting low but they're okay for now. It might be a good idea to get some new ones for winter just in case we get any snow this year. It'll be a little safer."

I bit back a laugh. Snow. Yeah, right. This was north Georgia, we might get snow once every few years in January or February. Maybe if we were in the mountains instead of the valley, we would see a little more. Just once I would like to have snow on Christmas.

He held the door to the lobby open for me. "Any other questions?" I shook my head as I walked through the door. He dipped his head a little and adjusted his cap again. "Alright, well if you have any concerns feel free to call me – us."

Granny rang me up and explained the list of things Oliver had mentioned she would print out for me. I noticed on the receipt she handed me there was a family discount applied. I wondered what Ava had told her family about me. They probably felt bad for me. That would explain why they were being so nice.

"You're all set, dear. There's a sticker on the windshield of your car that'll tell you the mileage you need to come back in at. Let us know if you have any questions or concerns." She looked toward the glass front door and watched as Oliver pulled my car up in front of it.

I thanked Granny and said goodbye.

Oliver opened the shop door for me and then rushed over to open my car door.

Ava must have told them something. A blush crept up my neck and face as I imagined how sorry they all felt for me. He patted the top of my car as he opened and closed his mouth like he wanted to say something. He adjusted his cap once again before muttering bye and closing my door.

I picked up my phone to pick a playlist to listen to and was met with a new message from Ava.

Ava

Granny says my brother likes you.

Chapter 4

Emery

October Now

MY GRIP ON THE steering tightened at the shop came into view. I pulled into the parking lot before I could change my mind. The last time I'd been here was before Oliver and I broke up. Switching mechanics was a no brainer because I was too afraid to look any of his family in the eye after what I did. I hadn't even been able to keep letting Ava do my hair.

I still hadn't been able to find a mechanic or hairdresser I trusted as much as them.

The building had been cleaned up since the last time I was here. The cinderblock was painted white, and the garage doors were blue. The name had been repainted across the building in the same shade of blue as the doors.

A tall man approached me after I jumped out of my still running car parked sideways in front of the lobby door. His inky black hair was pulled back in a ponytail. I didn't recognize him from when I had been here before.

"Ma'am, you can't park there," he said.

I glanced at the name patch on his uniform, but it was covered up by a flashlight sticking out of the chest pocket. "Hi, sorry, I'll be quick. I just needed to drop something off." I held up a covered foil pan. "Is, um, Oliver here today?" Of course he was here, he was always here. The man didn't know how to take a day off.

He blocked my path toward the building. "That's not a parking spot."

I slammed my car door and pushed my way past him toward the lobby door ignoring what he had to say. He took a few steps after me and then detoured to one of the doors that led straight into the shop. This wouldn't take long. Oliver probably didn't even want to see me. A girl with blonde hair sat at the counter. Her round face and blue eyes looked familiar, but I couldn't place why. She was petite, but not as short as Ava, and midsized.

"Hi, welcome to Franklin Auto Shop. How can I help you?" She smiled brightly at me showing all her teeth. Again, that smile looked familiar.

I looked around for Granny but didn't see her anywhere. My eyes moved to the window in the wall between the lobby and the shop. She wasn't there either. I could see a familiar redhead and the employee I had met in the parking lot. There was a third employee with their back to me.

"I'm looking for Oliver and um, Pop and Granny." I held up the pan. "I wanted to drop something off for them."

Her smile dropped and her eyes widened. "I'm sorry, has it been a while since you've been here? Pop and Granny –" She was cut off by the door to the shop swinging open and Oliver stepping through. There was a smudge of grease on his forehead and another on his cheek. He lifted his ball cap and scratched the top of his head before dropping it back down. His arms were covered in black like he had been in the middle of working on a car and had stopped to come in here without washing up. The sight made my heart race while remembering how he used to get so excited to see me he'd drop whatever he was doing and run straight to me without stopping to clean up.

Oliver's brows drew together when he saw me, and he crossed his arms. My heart raced faster. He wasn't excited to see me. He was probably just rushing up here to handle what he expected to be an irate customer. "What are you doing Emery?" His voice was stern and measured. Was that the anger I was looking for last Saturday?

"I made some cinnamon apple rolls and thought I would drop off a batch. Matt and Riley can only eat so many of these things." Out of the corner of my eye I could see a look of confusion wash over the face of the blonde at the counter.

"Trying to beg for forgiveness with sweets?" The corners of his mouth twitched, his customer service voice dropping to let his normal voice through. My heart skipped a beat at finally hearing the teasing tone he used to use all the time with me. Not upset to see me.

I shrugged. "I made you pull that wagon around all day. It only seemed fair that you got to enjoy some of the spoils." My hands started to shake, prompting me to sit the pan on the counter before I dropped it.

Oliver stepped closer, his arms still crossed, and the other three employees I had seen through the window filed in. I recognized the redhead as Ava's wife, Aubrey, triggering a blush I tried to fight back. I wondered if Oliver had ever told her what I said. She had never mentioned it during our handful of interactions before. The third person that'd had his back to me I now recognized as Oliver's younger brother Drew.

Still no Pop or Granny.

Did they retire? I knew they had been planning for it, or at least said they had been planning for it. We had all doubted that they would.

"You probably remember Drew and Aubrey," Oliver said, motioning to them. He pointed at the employee from the parking lot, "That's my cousin Wade." His finger moved toward the blonde. "That's Shelby."

"I'm Matt's younger sister," she added.

My mouth dropped open. Shit. I took in her face, the familiar features now making sense. I needed to get better at remembering people's faces. "Can you do me a favor and not tell Matt about this?"

"Depends on how good those are and how often you bring them by." Definitely Matt's sister.

I pushed the pan closer to her. She rubbed her hands together and started pulling the foil from the top. "Where are Pop and Granny? I was hoping to see them too," I questioned Oliver.

Everyone's eyes dropped to the floor. Oliver grabbed my arm and pulled me out into the shop. He adjusted his ball cap and rubbed the back of this neck, the nervous tic of his making my palms sweat. His hand shook as he lifted it to the chain around his neck, and he pulled it out from under his shirt. There were two rings hanging from it.

Wedding bands. They were plain gold wedding bands.

Why would he be wearing a necklace with wedding bands?

Shit. Shit. Shit.

No.

He ran his fingers over the rings as he took a deep breath. "They passed away within a few days of each other last year. She went first. He gave me their rings at her funeral and told me to get my head out of my ass and find you." He paused and held my gaze with his. His eyes were filled with unshed tears. My heart pounded and my body felt numb. "He never gave up on me and you." He paused again to take a deep breath. His voice raised, not a yell, but loud enough I could feel his anger. "When he passed, I stared at my phone for hours wanting to call you. All I could think about for weeks was calling you, Emery. When I finally did, I found out you had changed your number. I took that as my sign that I missed my chance."

I backed over to a rolling chair beside his toolbox. I ran my hands through my hair trying to process his words, my eyes focused on a spot of some sort of car fluid on the concrete floor.

They were gone. They were gone and I never got to say goodbye.

Six months. That's all the time I had gotten with them, and it was all my fault.

Gone.

They remembered me. They still wanted me for their grandson even after I broke his heart.

Oliver tried to call me.

He tried to tell me.

Tried to give me another chance.

He just raised his voice at me. For the first time ever, Oliver just raised his voice at me.

My stomach flipped and my throat burned. I stood up so fast the chair went flying, rolling back to collide with the toolbox, sprinting to the closest trash can. I felt Oliver's fingers brush over my neck as I threw up.

He rubbed my back until I was done. My skin and shirt were going to be covered in grease, and I didn't care. I leaned over the trash can and sobbed, not looking up as I accepted the clean rag he handed me to wipe my mouth with. Time stood still while hunched over the trash and lost myself in the crashing waves of grief.

"Oliver," I finally managed to say. My hand trembled around the cloth rag.

He still held my hair, his fingers rubbing the base of my skull. "I know, Em, I know." He wrapped his arms around me in a hug from behind. For a moment I almost forgot how long it had been since his arms were around me. I almost forgot the anger in his words. One of my hands gripped his arm and I relished the familiar way the hair there tickled my skin. I turned around to face him, throwing my arms around his neck as he pulled me closer and buried my face in his shoulder. One hand stroked my back; the other my hair. I still couldn't bring myself to care how ruined my clothes were.

His arms were the only thing keeping me from crashing onto the floor.

"I'm so sorry, Ollie," I whispered.

"I should have tried harder to find you. I should have told you sooner," his chin trembled against the top of my head.

"I shouldn't have left." I changed my number. I moved. I made myself hard to find. It didn't matter how much he tried if I made sure he couldn't.

He pulled back, lifting my chin until I looked at him. His eyes were red, and tears had streaked down his face, droplets gathering in his beard. "You did what you had to do."

I shook my head. I've learned a lot about myself in the past couple of years, spent a lot of time in therapy working through my trauma. It hadn't taken long for me to conclude that what I had done hadn't been the right choice, even if in the moment it had felt right. I was too embarrassed to come crawling back, to admit to him how wrong I had been.

So I just kept moving forward. I went through the motions of trying to date again while pretending that my heart didn't ache to have him back. Convinced myself that he was better off without me and I deserved to be unhappy.

His hands held my face as I whispered apologies over and over until he finally cut me off. "You and your sister both apologize way too much."

I sniffled and stepped back, putting space between us so I could think again. "What do you mean?"

"Her and Matt showed up to my apartment with their own baked goods a couple days ago." He scuffed the toe of his boot against the concrete. "Why are you here, Emery?"

Why was I here? I didn't know, it was an old habit, I guess. An olive branch. An apology for the past and how I spent our time together at the festival ignoring him.

Because I missed him.

I held out the rag I still clutched in my hand and waved it for him to take. My feet took another step back away from him. I shrugged. "Just wanted to apologize and drop off the rolls. I'll get out of your hair. I sort of parked right in front of the door and Wade was pretty upset with me over it."

"I'll talk to him about it. He's kind of a stickler for rules, but he's a good kid."

I shook my head. "Don't worry about it. I won't bother you again." I marched to the side door, there was no way I was going to walk through the audience in the lobby. I swung around to yell across the shop, "you're allowed to be mad at me Oliver. Stop trying to hide it."

The left side of his mouth lifted in a slight smile. His tears spilled over leaving tracks in the black smudges on his face.

Coming here was a stupid decision.

Chapter 5

Oliver

October Now

I STARED AT THE rag in my hand as she disappeared outside. *Go, Oliver, don't let her leave this time. Tell her how you feel.* It felt like my boots were glued to the floor. I wasn't mad at her, at least I wasn't before whatever just happened. She went from hot to cold so fast I couldn't keep up.

I knew I shouldn't have told her all that, but it came pouring out before I could stop. I had been bottling it up, rehearsing the conversation in my head in case we ever had the chance to have it. None of that was supposed to come out that way. I was going to ease her in, break the news and then comfort her. Get her to let me back into her life. I was going to be patient until she was ready to hear everything.

It came pouring out before I knew what was happening like steam from the pressure cooker of my emotions finally releasing. It had taken everything in me not to tell her during the double date, to act indifferent about the situation we were in. Seeing her here in the shop felt like stepping back to a time when things were easier, a time when we had told each other everything.

She needed to know. I needed her to know. It didn't matter if she wasn't ready. I had been holding it in for too long, my patience was too thin for whatever game she wanted to play, my heart too raw.

My blood boiled as I watched through the windows in the bay doors to see her car leave the parking lot. My pulse roared in my ears.

I didn't know if I was angrier at myself, her, or the situation. Would the timing for us ever be right?

How could she just come in here and say I was pretending not to be mad at her? I had forgiven her a long time ago. I knew she did what she had to do, even if she hurt me in the process.

A hand clapped on my shoulder. My eyes focused on Drew standing in front of me. For a moment he morphed into the kid with sad eyes waiting for me to tell him everything would be okay. "I'm sorry," he said.

I blew out a rough exhale. "She had no idea they were gone." My shoulders slumped.

He nodded and took his hat off, scratching the side of his head in the way we had both picked up from Pop and he studied my face. "I thought Pop made you promise to tell her."

I shrugged his hand off my shoulder. "She made that hard to do." I grabbed his shoulders and gave him a shove. "Get back to work. We still have a lot to do today."

We always had a lot to do. My to do list never got any smaller, the cars never stopped coming, the phones never stopped ringing. Everyone had known Pop, the whole town had been loyal to him when it came to their mechanic needs. We weren't the only shop in town, but we were the last locally owned one. People around here made it clear that they would rather support us over the chain shops. No one was going to let the place fade away just because Pop and Granny were gone.

It didn't matter how hard we worked, how many hours we put in, it still always felt like we were drowning in work. A good problem to have, I guess. It made me feel like a failure to not be able to live up to what Pop had built.

He pursed his lips at me over his shoulder. "You should have gone after her just now."

Wade appeared beside me. "You don't have much room to talk, Mr. Friend Zone," he said to Drew. I raised an eyebrow, weighing the thought of asking for details, but decided I didn't have the energy for wherever that conversation was going. "You should have gone after her," Wade tossed over his shoulder as he went back to the car he had been working on.

Wade shouldn't be here. He had a big future ahead of him, plans after college that didn't happen. Working here was supposed to be a steppingstone for him, something to do while he found his own path. A favor to me. How much longer until he figured out his future? I knew he wouldn't leave us behind while we were struggling. The kid would stay here forever out of loyalty.

Drew was the same. He was past the struggles that brought him here now, had been for a while. He had dreams he should be chasing.

I was failing them both by holding them back.

I needed to move hiring a few more hands up on my to-do list.

I swiped the back of my arm over my face to knock away the tears I didn't have the energy to hide, succeeding only in smearing more grease on my face. My feet dragged the ground as I pushed myself toward Pop's – *my* – office. The worn desk chair creaked at the force of my weight dropping down on it. I propped my elbows on the desk and rested my head in my hands.

By its own accord one hand went to the top right drawer, pushed aside all the junk accumulated inside, fingers scraped around until I felt the crumpled envelope. I pulled it out, smoothing it out on the desk in front of me with trembling hands. My fingers traced over the looping letters of Emery's name in Granny's handwriting. She had written it when her health started to decline, just a few months after Emery walked out of our lives, pressing it into my hands on a sunny Monday morning making me promise that I would give it to Emery one day.

The paper was covered in my fingerprints from all the times I pulled it out, usually late in the evening after everyone else had left for the day. I always stayed behind, working myself to exhaustion, the need to make Pop proud the only thing fueling me. Going home meant thinking about losing them. About losing Emery. About how I was a failure of a son, grandson, and brother.

I didn't know what was in the letter, what Granny had thought was so important to tell the love of my life.

I wanted to read it.

I wanted to tear it up.

I wanted to run after Emery and force her to take it.

Would it be about their will? Would it be about her leaving us?

Like I had done all the times in the past fourteen months I shoved the envelope back into the desk drawer, burying it under everything until I couldn't see it. I would give it to her one day. I was a man of my word.

Today though, I was a man slowly being crushed under the weight of my responsibilities.

Chapter 6

Emery

August Then

AVA SECURED THE CAPE around me and pressed the pedal to pump up the salon chair. "Your hair grows fast," she said. "You're right at four weeks and the amount of new growth you have is impressive." She ran her hands through my hair looking at the roots. She wore her usual uniform of ripped black jeans that hugged her plus size body and a fitted t-shirt under her apron. Her winged liner and brick red lipstick were perfectly applied.

I nodded; it was easier than explaining why it grew so fast. I took a lot of hair growth vitamins to try to help with the thinning I had from PCOS. Polycystic Ovarian Syndrome was an endocrine disorder that I'd been fighting since puberty. There was no cure, only ways to try to manage my body's fucked up hormones level. The disorder stole a lot of things from me over the years, my confidence in my body being one of the things I was finally overcoming.

My hair was naturally thick, and people loved to tell me how much hair I had. Even with that I had sparse areas around the front and crown that I was self-conscious about.

"What are you thinking today? Are we keeping the red or do you want to try something else?"

"Let's keep the red a little longer, I think. Can we go a little shorter on the cut? I'm thinking maybe adding bangs and just above my shoulders?"

Her eyes met mine in the mirror and she squinted. "I'm all for embracing the breakup hair cliches, but I'm going to have to save you from yourself on this one." She pinched a few pieces of hair and pulled them up to my forehead to mimic bangs. "You really don't have the forehead for bangs."

She was right, my forehead was on the small side. Even growing up my mom never let me, or my sister have bangs because she said it wouldn't suit our faces. She always told us we would thank her for it in the future.

"I can do some face framing pieces, maybe give the appearance of long curtain bangs." She tapped a finger against her lips as she moved pieces of my hair around with the other hand.

I smiled at her in the mirror. "You're the expert, Ava. Please, do your magic and make me look pretty."

She laughed. "You don't need my magic for that." She patted the back of the chair. "I'm going to go mix up your color."

I pulled out my phone to start scrolling while I waited for her. Out of the corner of my eye I caught the movement of someone walking by and sitting in the next empty chair.

"Emery?" a deep voice asked from the station next to mine.

I closed my eyes and tried to place how I knew the voice before I looked over. Oliver sat in the chair of the empty station next to Ava's wearing a black T-shirt and worn-out jeans. He held his ballcap in his lap, so I got a better look at his shaggy hair, a mix of straight and curly. The pieces around his ears curled forward and brushed against his beard.

"Hi, Oliver," I said a little too loud. I fought the urge to cringe at how I sounded.

He looked down at his lap. The red tips of his ears were just barely visible through his hair.

"What are the odds of running into each other here?" I blurted.

The corners of his mouth twitched. Was he fighting a smile? He probably thought I was stupid. "Well, my sister is doing your hair, so I guess that makes for pretty good odds." He rubbed the back of his neck, the sleeve of his shirt riding up just enough I could see the line where the tan on his arms ended and changed to pale skin. "She keeps telling me I'm past overdue for a haircut."

Ava walked up behind him and kicked his chair, spinning him a little. "He likes to wait until it gets long enough that his hat won't fit on his big head anymore. I keep telling him he would look better if he would keep it short."

The shaggy hair did take away from his face, or rather it hid it. He was probably hiding a killer bone structure behind all that hair.

"Tell Emery she's already pretty, no magic required," Ava said with another kick to Oliver's chair.

He looked back at his lap, his hair falling to hide his face more. "Ava is right," he said and then cleared his throat.

Ava made eye contact with me. "Damn, I should have recorded that. It's not every day that he admits I'm right." She leaned forward and lowered her voice, "I don't know why he's being so shy. He's usually not like this. Usually, he's in here flirting with anything that moves."

I looked over to where Oliver slumped back in the chair with a ballcap now pulled low over his face. My face was on fire remembering how blatantly I had checked him out at the shop. "That's my fault. I sort of made him uncomfortable the other day."

She snorted as she turned my head back toward the mirror. "Nah, I told you he likes you." In the mirror she winked at me. "I've never seen him shy with anyone, so he must really like you." She started sectioning it with a comb. I tried to look back towards Oliver without moving my head. He pulled the ballcap lower over his face. "I think I'm just going to go home and cut my own hair," he groaned.

In the mirror I saw Ava point the comb at him. "Don't you dare. The last time you did that you gave yourself a buzz cut, and it looked awful." Ava was shorter than both of us, just barely five feet, but she gave off mom vibes that had me shrinking in my chair.

"You said it looks better short."

She rolled her eyes. "Stop being dumb. A buzz cut and a short cut are two different things." She dipped a brush in the bowl of color and started painting it onto my hair. "You're going to sit right there and wait."

Ava talked the whole time she worked on applying the color. I didn't hear a word she said. All I could focus on was the man stretched out in the chair beside me hiding his face behind his hat. Was he watching me? Was he as aware of me as I was of him?

My brain flashed to that day at the shop. The way he had smiled at me, had walked me through everything about my car. The laugh he tried to hide after I smarted off to the angry customer.

Out of the corner of my eye I caught the movement when he stood and walked toward the back of the salon.

"Ava, did you tell your family about my ex?" I blurted in a low voice once he was gone.

Ava narrowed her eyes at me in the mirror. "Honey, no, what is said in this chair is strictly between us. Stylist and client confidentiality. I just told them I had a friend that needed some help with her car."

I scrunched up my face. "They were so nice to me. I thought they felt sorry for me."

Ava smiled and tapped the brush against my head. "Don't be silly, they're just good people. Granny makes sure everyone that walks in their shop feels like family." She stopped talking while she applied more dye. "They did like you, though. Something about you standing up to a difficult customer."

I blushed. "That guy was being an asshole."

The chair next to us squeaked as Oliver sat back down in it. "Pop told him not to come back," he muttered and then laughed. "He told him we're a family establishment and can't have customers in there with less manners than a toddler."

I laughed so hard I earned a light smack on the back of my head from Ava as she ordered me to keep still. It only made me laugh harder.

"All done," she huffed as she pulled off her gloves. "Trade places with Oliver while your hair processes."

I shifted subtly as I stood, trying to make sure my dress wasn't pushed up too high. Oliver held the other chair steady for me to sit down. The tips of his fingers grazed over my shoulder as he moved away. I tried to hide the way it made me shiver.

Ava pulled Oliver's hat off and tossed it onto her station. "I'm trimming the beard too. You can't even see what your face looks like anymore."

Oliver shook his head. "I can do that at home. You always go too short."

Ava pulled a pair of clippers out of a drawer along with a container of guards. She sat the guards in his lap with a roll of her eyes. "Tell me which one to use on it."

He sighed as he dug around in the container. He held one up to her. "Go any shorter than that on my beard and I'll be doing DIY buzz cuts from now on."

She worked quickly on his hair. The amount hitting the floor made me wonder how there was any hair left on his head. She left the top just long enough for it to start to curl and then did a fade down the sides and back. She grumbled at him anytime he argued with what she was doing, sounding more like his mother than sister.

She brushed away the stray hairs and spun his chair to face me when she was finished. "What do you think, Emery?"

He was cute with shaggy hair and a scruffy beard but cleaned up he was flat out hot. Sharp cheek bones peeked out over the top of his beard, the hair still long and thick but short enough to see the shape of his mouth and jaw. His jaw and brows were strong. His upper lip was visible and didn't look as thin as I had thought it was. He smiled shyly when my eyes locked with his.

I cleared my throat. "You clean up well," I replied.

Ava's eyes sparkled, flicking between the two of us. Oliver looked down at the floor, a blush creeping up his neck, but his mouth lifted into a crooked smile that spread across his face My heart skipped a beat.

Damn. That smile was even better now that I could see more of it.

Ava undid the cape around Oliver and shook it out. Even more hair joined the pile on the floor. He jumped up and grabbed the broom that leaned against her station, sweeping the pile over to a container that sucked the hair up.

Ava crossed her arms and shook her head as she watched him. Then she picked up the color bowl that was still on her station and walked toward the back without a word.

Oliver opened a drawer and pulled out a jar of styling paste. He leaned toward the mirror and smoothed some onto his hair and beard. He picked up the comb Ava left out and combed the product through. My eyes focused on the way his forearms flexed as he worked. With them scrubbed clean of grease I could see the bulge of veins under the tanned skin and dark hair. His eyes flicked to me, and I blushed at being caught watching him.

"Don't trust Ava to style it for you?" I asked him.

He raked his fingers through the top of his hair making it just a little messy. "Don't tell her I said this, but she always slicks it back too much. She's great when it comes to the clients she's not related to, but the older sister programming kicks in when it comes to mine."

"It's our secret."

He leaned against the station and crossed his arms over his chest. His eyes raked over me, the shyness from earlier gone. Heat rushed to my cheeks as I remembered that I was still wrapped in the cape and my hair slicked back with dye. I fought the urge to look toward the mirror, knowing I probably looked crazy while he stood in front of me with the audacity to look so hot.

"It was good to see you again," he said.

"Yeah, you too," I blurted too fast.

He uncrossed the arms and tapped his knuckles against the top of the station. "Maybe I could see you again sometime soon?"

My brain whirled. That was a question, not a statement. Was he asking me out?

"You're lucky I think you're attractive, no one else will."

I pushed my ex's voice out of my head. I was pretty, I shouldn't be surprised he was interested. Ava had even told me he liked me.

Six months of freedom.

Was I ready to put myself out there again?

Maybe.

No. No, my heart said. *We weren't ready for this yet.*

"You're broken, Emery. How can you expect anyone to stick around when you're this broken?" The voice of my ex continued to haunt me.

I twisted the edge of the cape in my fingers. The word no twisted up in my mouth along with all the explanations for why. No was a complete answer, I knew that, but it wasn't the answer I wanted to give. "Um, maybe," I managed to say.

He swallowed, his jaw clenching as he heard my answer. He knocked his knuckles again. "I guess we'll see then," he mumbled. Maybe he sensed the no I was holding back. His eyes locked with mine. "You know where to find me when the answer is yes," his voice was clearer and lower, his accent dragging the words out slowly.

I broke our eye contact and shifted to focus on the dollop of dye that had dripped onto the cape right above my chest. At the edge of my field of vision I could see Oliver scoop up his cap, fingers tensing as he clutched it, and spun to leave. I held my breath while I waited for the bell over the door to ding, exhaling and looking up once I heard it.

Chapter 7

Oliver

October Now

How late are you working tonight?

Why does it matter?

How late are you staying at Riley's tonight?

Did you eat dinner yet?

You stalking me or something?

Dude your brother is worried about you.

We're all worried about you.

I'm working as late as I need to. Stop worrying about me.

My phone landed with a clatter on my toolbox. I gave Drew access to the security cameras after they all insisted they were worried about me being at the shop by myself with the possibility of getting hurt. My hand added a fresh black smudge to my Bluetooth speaker as I turned up the volume, Taylor Swift singing about doing it with a broken heart filling the empty shop. Through the window in the bay door I could see the lights of the coffee shop across the street turn off. Shit. It must be later than I thought. I should probably stop and eat something but the weight in the pit of my stomach made it hard to want to.

I could worry about food later.

The bay door behind me rattled like someone was lifting it up. The hairs on the back of my neck stood up, my fingers tightening around the breaker bar in my hand ready to swing. I grunted as I turned around, arm swinging up and out ready to catch the intruder before they could get me.

"Holy fucking shit, Ollie, it's me," someone screamed over the music. A blur of highlighted hair filled my vision as she dropped to the floor. My arm swung over her head expecting to come into contact with someone taller.

My chest heaved and my eyes dropped to the woman on the floor. Emery's eyes were wide with fear, a canvas bag on the concrete next to her. I dropped to her side, more guilt eating at my stomach. "The fuck are you doing here?" I grunted over the blasting music.

I wrapped my hands around her arms and pulled her up. My hands went to her skirt, tugging it down and dusting any shop debris from her ass, without thinking. Her fingers wrapped around my wrists pushing them away. "Why the hell did you just take a swing at me?" she yelled.

My body deflated, the adrenaline leaving me and the realization of what I almost did taking its place. "I thought you were someone breaking in."

"You shouldn't have left the door unlocked."

Emery pushed past me toward my toolbox, shutting off the music. She dug through the bag pulling out something wrapped in tin foil, a bag of chips, and a bottle of Gatorade. "Matt texted me. For some reason, he thinks I'm the only one you will listen to."

I crossed my arms over my chest. "I'm going to kill him."

She blew out her breath. "Let's not resort to that yet. Right now, my sister is pretty attached to him, so I'd like to keep him alive for her sake."

I couldn't help the gruff laugh that pushed out of me. "Interesting that's the only reason you have for me to not kill him."

Emery kicked the rolling chair next to my toolbox, sending it careening across the space between us and knocking against my shins. I fought back a wince at the impact. She held up one final item from the bag and shook it in the air while her other hand gestured to the chair. "Eat your dinner and I'll let you have dessert." She tapped a finger against her chin. "Actually, eat your dinner, go home, and then I'll let you have dessert."

It took everything in me to fight back the crude comment about only wanting dessert if she was on the menu. Two years ago, the line would have been an easy part of whatever this exchange was, but we weren't those two people anymore.

"Go home, Emery. I don't need someone to babysit me."

"I'm not babysitting you. I am bringing you dinner, so Matt doesn't have to leave my sister to do it." She nudged the tin foil toward me. "Bologna on white bread with mayo and cheese, your favorite. I even brought chips for some extra crunch."

The mention of cheese sent a fresh wave of panic through me. "Emery, why would you bring me cheese? That shit could kill you. Should you even be touching it?"

Her body shook with the force of her laughter, one finger swiping under her eye to wipe away a tear. "What's it matter? It's not like we're kissing anymore."

It was an arrow straight through the heart and a sucker punch to the gut. I knew that. Of course I knew that. It killed me every day that we weren't kissing anymore. Along with all the other things we weren't doing anymore. "Low blow, Em."

She cocked a brow. "Oh, now you're mad."

"Isn't that why you're rubbing it in, because you want to make me mad?" I scratched my beard. "Why are you here Emery?"

Whatever the fuck was happening was exhausting. Things were never like this between us before. We used to be able to talk to each other so easily. We'd never even fought before the day that everything fell apart.

Why couldn't I just have the Emery I used to know back instead of this woman that insisted on pushing me away?

"Damn, Ollie, way to let me know you don't want to see me." She dropped the dessert onto my toolbox next to the rest of the food. Her shoulder caught mine on her way back out the door. My fingers caught her wrist on her way by, pulling her against me and turning us so her back pressed against the support of the rack.

I opened and closed my mouth a few times, grinding my teeth each time I closed it. The muscles of my jaw bulged. Her eyes were heavy and focused on my mouth, her chest rising rapidly against my own. "It's always nice to see you again, Emery," the words were ragged as they slipped out. "Maybe we'll see each other again sometime soon?" I asked her, fighting back the hope of getting to see her. I loosened my grip and took a step back.

She lingered against the rack, one hand gripping the straps of the bag on her shoulder. The heavy silence stretched for what felt like hours but couldn't have been more than a couple of minutes. At last, she shook her head and scurried out the door.

"You know where to find me when the answer is yes," I hollered after her, echoing the words I said to her a lifetime ago.

Chapter 8

Emery

August Then

I wiggled in the driver's seat of my car pulling my dress down before I got out so I wouldn't have to do it with an audience. All the bay doors were open to the shop with cars on the racks. Sounds of various power tools flowed from the open doors. My eyes caught on Oliver as he pulled the back tire off a car. I couldn't believe I had gotten this far into life without noticing how hot mechanics were.

Maybe not mechanics in general. Just one mechanic.

Those forearms I noticed in the salon popped even more as he lifted the tire. His shirt tightened around his bicep. Heat flooded my entire body watching him. I wonder just how strong he was. I was a big girl and the idea that he might be strong enough to toss me around crossed my mind. It was something I'd never had the opportunity to experience before.

I flipped my visor down to check my lipstick in the mirror. It was faded to a sheer red stain, but I was too close to the doors to get away with reapplying without anyone noticing. I pushed the mirror back up and climbed out of my car, the black floral print dress swirling perfectly around my thighs as I did. The door slammed behind me a little too hard as I made my way to the passenger side to retrieve the tray of cupcakes.

It was late morning, but the August air was already hot and thick with humidity. It felt like this summer was never going to end. I ran home after wrapping up my morning bus runs to change and grab the cupcakes. I didn't have long before I would need to rush back home to get ready for the afternoon drop offs. My favorite part of my hours as a school bus driver was that I had a few hours of down time between the runs, but it also sometimes made it difficult to go back in the afternoon.

I almost collided with someone as I turned around with the tray. Hands wrapped around my wrists to steady me and the tray. His touch made my heart flutter in my chest. My eyes lifted from where one of the cupcakes had smushed against the side to meet a crooked smile. "Hi," I breathed out.

The smile widened. "You remembered where to find me," he said. His eyes dropped to where he still held my wrists, the now familiar blush flooded his face and neck. Never in my life had I thought that a man who blushes could be so attractive.

"I, um, wanted to bring these by. Just a, um, thank you for how nice...um...all of you were to me." I stammered. His hands dropped from my wrists. "Does anyone here have food allergies? They're dairy and eggs free just in case, but I have an ingredient list." I nodded to the piece of paper I had taped to the lid.

"No food allergies here that I'm aware of," he dropped his eyes to the paper. "Do you have food allergies?"

"Yeah, a few." I gave a small shrug, not ready to start listing everything off. "These are lemon cupcakes with blueberry frosting. The blueberries are from a local farm."

He took the tray from my hands and motioned with his head for me to follow him through the front door. He shifted the cupcakes to one hand so he could hold the door open for me with the other.

"Emery!" Granny greeted me from the front counter.

"She brought us cupcakes," Oliver said as he sat the tray on the counter. "I'm going to go get Drew and Pop." He slipped out of the door to the shop leaving me with Granny.

She gave me a soft knowing smile, ignoring the cupcakes in front of her.

"What?" I asked even though I knew what she was thinking.

I had been trying to think of an excuse to come by for the past few days since running into Oliver at the salon. I knew I could show up and just tell him yes, he had practically told me to, but it felt too forward. I had been thinking about bringing a little something as a thank you since that first day. I kept talking myself out of it because I thought they felt sorry for me. Now that I knew they didn't, it felt easier.

Food was always a great way to say things that felt too hard to say. Sharing it was practically my love language. Not that this was a situation that called for love languages, just that it was what was easy for me.

Granny motioned with her eyes to the cupcakes and then to the men out in the shop gathered around a sink scrubbing their hands. Oliver's face was red as the one I assumed was his brother Drew elbowed him. Pop laughed with his head thrown back.

"The way to a man's heart is through his stomach," she said with a laugh.

My face heated. "I just wanted to say thank you for how nice y'all were to me," I told her.

"Sure, dear," Her eyes narrowed and she gave a slight nod. "That's why you're here." She popped the lid off the container as the men walked in.

Oliver walked straight to my side while he wiped his hands with a wad of paper towels. He pointed to the man that walked in behind Pop. He was taller than Oliver with longish hair like Oliver's had been when we first met. He was clean shaven so I could see the bone structure that most likely hid under Oliver's facial hair. He looked a few years younger, maybe in his early twenties. "That's my baby brother Drew," he explained.

He lifted a hand in a wave but went straight for the cupcakes without a word.

Oliver turned toward me, the paper towels rustling in his calloused hand. He urged me to the other side of the lobby as far away from the others as possible. "I'm going to go on my break soon. Want to grab lunch with me?" His mouth tensed as I blinked at him. "Not a date, just lunch," he said. He adjusted his hat as his ears turned red. "I'd like to take you on a date sometime too," he added. "Just want to make that clear."

Fuck. Why was him being so forward so hot?

"Um, food allergies," was all I could say. "I have food allergies, and it makes going out to eat difficult," I clarified for him. There were a handful of places I trusted if I was able to catch certain employees there. Aside from the struggle of making sure that the food I was eating was safe, it was downright embarrassing sometimes. I almost always felt like I was being too difficult.

"Oh, um." He rubbed the back of his neck. "I'm game for whatever you're comfortable with."

"I kind of just got out of a relationship," I whispered for only him to hear. He was putting himself out there for me. I couldn't handle the thought of not being at least a little honest with him. "I'm not sure if I'm ready to get back out there yet."

He nodded. "Okay, okay. Well, if you change your mind, you know where to find me." He gestured vaguely to the lobby we stood in.

"What about friends?" I offered.

He pulled his eyebrows together.

"We could get to know each other just as friends for now," I elaborated. "Not like, sticking you in the friend zone or anything. I just want to get to know you better and –" I clamped my mouth shut to stop the words from tumbling out. That day at the salon Ava had said he normally would be flirting with anything that moved, something I still couldn't reconcile with the Oliver I knew, and it made me question if I was doing the right thing. He probably had no interest in being just friends with someone he had now attempted to ask out twice. He probably also had no interest in trying to pursue someone that rejected him both times when he had other options.

"Okay, whatever you need," he answered.

I leaned forward and plucked a pen from his chest pocket. I took a deep breath as I wrapped a hand around his wrist to bring his forearm up toward me. I couldn't believe I was doing this. I pushed down the doubts that crowded my head as I scribbled my number on the inside of his arm. "Text me," I whispered as I slid the pen back into his pocket.

I tried to hold my head up and keep my pace steady as I walked out the front door.

Chapter 9

Emery

November Now

I knocked on the apartment door. This was stupid. He probably didn't even live here anymore. I crossed my fingers and hoped a stranger would open the door. I waited with my breath held.

The door didn't open.

I ran my hands through my hair and sighed. No one opened doors if they weren't expecting anyone nowadays. Or maybe he wasn't even home. Knowing him, he was working late again tonight. I clutched the strap of my purse and turned to walk away. *I had tried,* I told myself, *all I had to do was try.*

I didn't have his number anymore and I sure as hell wasn't asking Matt for it, especially not after the shit Matt pulled last week.

I was not going to go to the shop to check. That would be embarrassing for both of us.

He had a shop to run, he didn't need a crazy ex showing up and picking fights. But that's what I wanted, what I needed. We were going to fight this out once and for all. It would be good for both of us.

Closure.

I turned to leave.

"Emery?" a voice called out when I was halfway down the hall. I turned around to see Oliver leaning out of his open door. His hair was messy and wet, almost time for a haircut. He wore grey sweatpants and a grey thermal shirt. He must have just gotten out of his after-work shower.

I walked back to him, head down, trying to remember the words I came here to say. He didn't move to let me through the door. "Can we talk?" I asked.

He leaned against the door frame and crossed his arms. "I don't know. Are you going to talk to me?"

"Are you going to yell at me?"

He scrubbed a hand over his face. "God, Emery, I'm sorry I raised my voice at you."

"I don't want you to be sorry." I exhaled sharply. "We're going to talk. We're going to fight. We're going to yell if we need to."

He shook his head, still not moving to let me in. "We're not going to yell. If you want to talk like two mature adults, we will do that. But if I let you in here there will be no yelling. That's the rule. Break the rule and you leave."

I tapped my fingers against the strap digging into my palm. We'd had a lot of rules in the past, most of them were mine. This one was new. He was finally telling me something he needed, and I could respect that.

I could be mature about this.

"Okay," I agreed.

He shifted out the way to let me in. My eyes flicked between the couch and the table to choose a place to sit. The couch felt too intimate. I pulled out a chair at the table. Oliver disappeared and returned with coloring books and a pencil case. I laughed at the sight of them. Were they the same ones that I left here?

"To help you think," he said as he dropped them on the table in front of me. He pulled out the chair next to me and crossed his arms.

I lifted the corner of the book on top to peek inside. Sure enough, there were pages that we already colored in. "I can't believe you kept these," I whispered.

"I couldn't bring myself to throw them away."

Anger flooded my veins. My throat burned as my heartbeat filled my ears. I asked him to let me go and it was clear he never had.

I opened the book to a fresh page and popped open the lid of the pencil case. I pressed the pencil so hard against the page the tip broke. Oliver plucked the sharpener from the case and dropped it in front of me. He pulled one of the other coloring books from underneath mine as I sharpened the pencil.

We colored in silence. The tension in the room grew as we filled the silence with the scratch of pencils against paper. I couldn't remember why I was here, what I needed to say. I just felt angry.

Angry that he had held onto this piece of me for so long.

Angry that we could sit in silence when there was so much to say.

Angry that he didn't hate me when he should.

Oliver dropped the pencil he held against the page and crossed his arms, leaning back in his chair. His page was full, all the small details of the mandala colored in. He had even shaded in the background of the page. He waited as I finished mine. I worked slowly trying to ignore the way his gaze burned into me.

"You wanted to talk?" he said once I leaned back in my chair.

"I'm sorry," I said.

"You've said that already."

I took a deep breath, closed my eyes, and counted to ten. "It makes me mad that you don't hate me," I said with my eyes still closed.

"I told you that I could never hate you." The air shifted and I could feel him leaning closer to me.

I popped one eye open. Oliver leaned forward in his chair with his elbows resting on his knees. There was hardly any space left between us. "Are you at least mad at me?"

His jaw worked slowly. "Yes."

That was something. I could be happy with that. I closed my eyes tighter. "I thought I had gotten over you. I was going to move on. Then you just popped back into my life. It makes me mad that seeing you reminded me how much I missed you."

Oliver tapped one finger against my leg and then pulled his hand away. "If you're that mad about seeing me, why are you here?" Did he want to run his hand over my leg as much as I wanted him to?

"I need you to be mad at me," my voice shook despite my effort to keep it steady.

"Why?" He tapped my leg again. "Look at me and tell me why."

I opened my eyes, wincing as I made eye contact with him. I thought back to my conversation with my therapist yesterday and how much she stressed I needed to be honest with Oliver. "Because I hate myself for what I did."

His face was tense, the corners of his mouth pulled down. I wanted to reach out and cup his cheek, smooth my thumb over the corner of his mouth until it relaxed. "You did what you did because you needed to, mistake or not. You have to live with the choice you made. I have to live with the choices I made. You don't get to come here and tell me I have to hate you for it just because you hate yourself."

"I want to go back and change things." I busied my hands with adding the pencils we had scattered between us one at a time back into the pencil case. "I don't want to have to live with regrets."

Oliver dropped his head into his hands. "That's the hard part of life, baby."

I nodded and wiped the tears pooling in my eyes with the backs of my hands. "I should go."

I couldn't be here anymore. The memories of our time together surrounded me. Ghosts of our past covered every inch of this place. They danced in the eyes of a man that still looked at me the same way he did then.

Oliver reached out a hand and brushed against my arm as I moved past him. "Talk to me," he pleaded.

I swallowed back my tears. "I will, one day. I will. I thought I was ready but I'm not."

***

Two days later I dropped one of the heavy grocery bags by my feet so I could knock on Oliver's door. I focused on the handles of the other bag digging into my hand to keep me grounded while I waited for him to answer. He was fresh out of the shower again. This time I couldn't fight the feeling that he had been expecting me and that was why he wasn't working late. I pushed down the urge to breathe in his familiar scent. He still used all the same products.

"If you're here to talk, you better actually talk this time." His eyes narrowed as they caught on the grocery bags. "What's all this?"

I bent down to retrieve the bag I had dropped. My V-neck sweater slid off my shoulder with the movement. Oliver couldn't hide the way his breath hitched. "Matt and Riley are at my house and quite frankly, I'm not in the mood to be around their gooey-ness."

"I don't understand how that leads to you being here with food." God he was grumpy today. The lines I had noticed on his face at the apple festival looked deeper, his eyes colder.

"Who peed in your cheerios this morning?" I retorted as I pushed past him into the apartment. I sped to the kitchen to drop the bags on the counter.

"You did." The words were a punch to the gut, colder than he had ever been toward me.

I braced my arms on the counter and held my head up high, my back toward him. I focused my eyes on the glowing clock of his microwave, counting to ten as I steadied myself. "I guess you're finally mad at me."

"What are you doing, Emery?" His customer service voice was back, and it felt like a blade to my heart.

"I'm cooking us dinner. If you're lucky I'll even clean up after myself this time." My hands shook as I pulled ingredients from the bag.

"Emery."

Why did he keep saying my name like I was a wild animal that just waltzed into his home, and he was trying not to startle me? It was infuriating. My thumb pierced through the packaging of the chicken I held. I dropped it on the counter and rushed to the sink to wash my hands.

"Emery."

Holy fucking hell. "Stop saying my name like that, Oliver." My voice shook. My hands shook.

One.

You're okay.

Two.

You can do this.

Three.

You wanted him mad at you.

Four.

He's just giving you what you wanted.

Five.

You keep fucking it all up.

Six.

Breathe.

Seven.

Breathe.

Eight.

Fucking breathe, Emery.

Nine.

It's all going to be okay.

Ten.

You can do this.

"Then talk to me," he pleaded with me, the edge gone from his voice. I looked over my shoulder to see his throat bob and his fists clenched by his side. He dug his nails into his palms. He looked so tired. So done.

"Let me cook for you, please. You once told me that I could cook for you every night for the rest of your life. I know that's off the table now, okay?" A sob slipped from me. "I know that. But just one more time, please? I can't be at my house watching my sister and Matt dance around each other like two happy idiots."

"Why don't you tell them to go to Matt's?"

I slumped over the sink and sucked back my tears. "Because it's my sister's house too. Being there makes her feel safe. You know me, you know I will always put my sister's needs above my own."

Oliver joined me by the sink and pushed up his sleeves to wash his hands. "One more time. You'll cook and I'll clean."

I dried my hands with a paper towel, letting the material scrape against my skin until the back of my hand turned red. "Just one more time." I pressed the paper towel against my skin until it tore. "I was wrong. You being mad at me hurts more."

"I know, Em, I know."

I've never cooked slower in my life. Never obsessed more over getting the seasoning just right. The plating perfect. I felt like I was cooking for my life.

We ate in silence. Oliver brought out the coloring supplies and I colored while he washed the dishes. Once the kitchen was cleaned, he joined me at the table and pulled a coloring book toward himself.

I accidentally tore the page twice. He broke pencil after pencil. One page each done and then we both glanced at each other. Without a word we each flipped to a fresh page to keep going.

I couldn't stop yawning and my whole arm ached when I finally closed mine. I pressed my face onto the table. I felt Oliver's hand hover over the back of my head, but it dropped away before he touched me. I missed the way his hands felt on me.

"Are you going to talk to me?" he asked.

I looked over to see he had his elbows rested on the table and his head cradled in his hands. My breath came out as a quiver. "I almost called you so many times after that day. I knew as soon as I walked away how much I messed up. I missed you so much."

"Why didn't you?"

"I convinced myself that you were better off without me. I was a mess, Ollie. I'm still a mess. You didn't need that dragging you down." I reached for his arm but transitioned to putting away the pencils that lay beside it.

"Messes don't scare me. I'm a mess too." He stopped himself. I knew where he was going. His whole family was a mess. He had been dealing with messes his whole life. Now, with his grandparents gone he was more of a mess than ever. It was hard to reconcile the man next to me with the one I knew before.

I'm one of the reasons he's like this.

"Can we be friends again?"

He dropped his hands to the table and lifted his eyes to meet mine. "I really don't know."

I couldn't get out of his apartment fast enough. My hands shook while I scrambled for my purse and canvas grocery bags. It took every cell in my body to hold back the hot tears stinging my eyes. I kept my head down to hide my face from him. Oliver didn't say a word or lift a hand to stop me this time.

Chapter 10

Oliver

November Now

"HEY BOSS MAN, EMERY is back," Shelby's voice cut through my concentration. I swore as the bolt I had been trying to line up slipped from my fingers and fell into the darkness of the engine bay.. Great, I was never going to find that.

"What does she want?" I tore the gloves off my hands and tossed them on top of my tool cart. Those things were useless. I don't know why I kept trying to wear them.

Shelby had a mischievous grin on her face. Most days she was just like Matt, all sunshine and kindness, but she had a sneaky side of her that loved drama. While that side was usually directed toward Wade, occasionally she would slip up with the rest of us. It was fucking annoying.

Sometimes it felt like she was my little sister too.

"She brought more apology baked goods."

"Okay, put me some aside. I'm busy." My feet dragged as I walked to my office and sank into my desk chair. I needed to take a break and get some admin work done, with my focus already broken from the car on the rack this was as good a time as any.

I wanted to go up front to see Emery. I wanted to slide my arm around her back and listen to her present whatever she had brought by for the day like I used to do. Sneak a kiss when no one else was watching. But every time I saw her it stirred up so much inside me. I couldn't keep doing this to myself.

She was supposed to be mine, but I had let her walk out of my life without a fight. We both needed to move on. Constantly seeing each other was making things harder than they needed to be.

"Knock, knock," a soft voice said. My eyes lifted to where Emery stood in the open doorway of my office holding something wrapped in a napkin. She wore one of those short black skirts that hugged her curves with tights just sheer enough to let her tattoos show through. Her sweater was cropped, showing a strip of inked skin between it and the skirt. "I didn't want you to miss out on your favorite." I don't know if she was talking about the food she held or the outfit.

She stepped in and placed it on my desk. It was a pumpkin cinnamon roll with maple frosting. My mouth watered as the smell of it hit me. It was one of my favorites. Hell, the maple frosting had been my suggestion. I fought the urge to reach for it.

"I'm sorry I ran away from you the other night." She nudged the pastry toward me.

"Emery," I said, locking my eyes with hers, my words coming out in a boom that caught us both off guard. I took a breath and tried to steady myself. I should just give up control already, yell enough to make her too scared to come back. It would fix all our problems. Her light brown eyes widened as she took her own deep breath, holding it in. "We can't keep doing this. Either we talk or we stay out of each other's lives. You're giving me whiplash."

She closed the door behind her and twisted the lock. I could hear muffled sounds of tools as Drew and Wade got back to work. Emery leaned against the door and crossed her arms over her chest. "I don't know how to talk to you anymore, Ollie."

The nickname slipping from her lips made my mind tumble back to before. She was the only one that ever called me that. It started one day out of the blue and had quickly turned into her favorite thing to call me. One slip of the tongue sent me wanting to press her against that door, touching her in all the ways I knew she loved, until she was screaming it again for me.

I backed the desk chair against the opposite wall putting more space between us. "Me either, Em. Talking to you used to be so easy, but now I feel like all I do is say the wrong things." It was still the wrong thing. I should tell her all the ways she kept hurting me, all the ways she piled on to the weight that was crushing me just like everyone else did.

She twisted the sleeve of her sweater in one hand. The motion made her sweater slip down over her shoulder showing new ink there. "You scared me that night when you told me you loved me. You knew everything I had been through; you knew how broken I was, but you still pushed me for more than I was ready for." Her bottom lip trembled the way it had that night, and her eyes moved to focus on the wall behind me.

Memories of that night flashed through my mind. Her on my lap shaking, her shutting me out in a way she had never done. Her refusing to listen to what I had to say.

"You made it really hard not to fall in love with you," I offered weakly.

"You wanted to save me, just like you save everyone in your life. You're a good man, Oliver, you have such a good heart. But I didn't need to be saved. I needed you to let me save myself."

I fisted my hands, the skin on my knuckles stretching until the fresh scratches from today burned. "I didn't want to save you. I wanted to be by your side."

"You tried to give me a building for my restaurant." The volume of her voice started to climb. She took a few deep breaths, her lips moving as she silently counted.

"It wasn't doing any good just sitting there empty. It wasn't just me; my whole family was in on that." I stood up and planted my hands on the desk, leaning forward. "You were so passionate about it. I just wanted you to be able to have anything you needed to make your dreams come true."

She met me at the desk, planting her own hands on the surface and leaning forward until the space between us was so small I could feel her breath against my face. "I didn't need your help. I was going to figure it out on my own."

I wanted to pull her onto this desk and remind her how much she loved it when I took care of her. She rolled her eyes at me. I shook my head "That's all you had to say. You could have told me to back off. I would have let you figure it out. You didn't have to leave."

She lifted her hands and dug her nails into her palms. "I didn't know how long it would take me to be able to meet you where you were. Did you want me to drag you around like Riley is doing to Matt until you got sick of waiting?" She slammed her hands down. The loud thud of her palms against the surface startled both of us. "I had to leave before you could, Oliver. I couldn't stick around until you told me I was broken. I couldn't hear you tell me that I couldn't give you what you needed. I couldn't let you hurt me, Oliver!" Her voice broke on my name. Tears filled her eyes and she tilted her head up toward the ceiling to stop them from falling.

"So, it doesn't even matter to you that you hurt me, Emery? I loved you, and I thought you loved me." My hands clenched the loose papers scattered across my desk as the volume of my voice climbed. I was yelling and didn't have it in me to care anymore. She had no idea what she put me through, no idea that her leaving had been the start of my world crumbling. All she cared about was protecting herself from an imaginary situation. "You left me, Emery! Then months later my grandparents left me too. Granny's decline was so slow and then one day she was just gone. Pop couldn't take it. He was gone within days. I didn't even get to tell them goodbye because I was here just like I always am." My jaw clenched as a sob overcame me. It was the first time I'd cried since they died.

I wiped a mix of snot and tears from around my mouth with the back of my arm. I'd been running away from all this as hard as I could. My dad nursed his pain at the bottom of a bottle. Ava bottled hers up and nursed the pain of others instead. Drew and my mom stuck their heads in the sand.

Me? I worked my ass off until I was too numb for the pain to touch me. Fuck, this hurt so much. "My dad is drinking again because of it and we're all ignoring it because we don't fucking talk about that shit. No one in my family talks about shit. We're all just going on like nothing is wrong. I spend every fucking day here working my ass off and I still feel like I'm drowning, Emery. I don't fucking want to hear that you thought I might call you broken or leave you. You left me! I'm the one that's broken!" My fist slammed against my chest.

Emery wrapped her arms around herself. Her whole body shook as her tears spilled over. Fuck. Fuck. Fuck. Seeing her cry just made it all hurt worse. I rounded the desk, unwrapped her arms, and hugged her tight against me. She shook in my arms, resting her face against my shoulder as she sucked back her tears. Instead of melting against me she pushed away from me, wrapping her arms around herself again.

I shouldn't have done that. I knew what that would do to her. She wanted me to be mad at her, had begged me to be mad at her. It wasn't what she really needed, and we both knew that. I took the bait anyway.

"I'm so mad that you're back in my life. I'm so mad that seeing you again brings back all these old feelings. I was doing better; I was moving on. Now I feel like I'm right back to being that broken girl I was then." She looked up at the ceiling as she chewed on her bottom lip. Her lipstick smeared on her teeth. "You told me before that there was no yelling allowed."

I held my hands out, silently pleading for her to be back in my arms. "I changed my mind. Let it out, baby. Yell at me. Tell me how much I suck. Tell me I'm an asshole." I backed off as she tightened her arms around herself. My tear-filled eyes dropped to the pumpkin cinnamon roll on my desk, and I knocked my hand against the surface next to it. "You remember when you said you would teach me how to make those?"

I needed the Emery back that didn't want to talk about what happened. I needed her to stop crying. I needed to stop crying.

She sniffled and laughed. "Yeah, but that may have been a selfish offer." Her eyes met mine for a moment before dropping down to my arms. "I liked watching you in the kitchen. It was way hotter than it should have been." I knew that. Watching her get all hot and bothered watching me had been one of my favorite parts of cooking for her.

I took a deep breath to steady my voice before I spoke, "I'm not mad you're back in my life, but I am mad you can't make up your mind. You can keep hating me if that's what makes you happy. Or we can try to be friends again. I can't handle this back and forth anymore." That was a lie. I couldn't be friends with her, never could. I gestured around the office and then toward the door out to the shop. "A lot has changed in the past couple of years. I've got a lot on my plate."

"I thought you said you didn't know if we could be friends."

"I'll be whatever you need me to be." I cocked an eyebrow at her wishing she would call me on the bullshit. I would do whatever it took to keep her in my life this time. I didn't have a lot left in me to give but she could have it all if she wanted.

She ran her tongue over her bottom lip smearing her lipstick even more. "Tell me what you need, Ollie."

Her. I needed her. I needed Granny and Pop back. I needed things to just go back to what they were two years ago.

I didn't know what to tell her. Everyone had been asking me what I needed. Ava, Aubrey, Drew, Wade, Shelby, Matt – every single one of them had asked me how they could help. They all saw me drowning, but I couldn't tell them. We don't talk about that kind of stuff.

I needed my parents. I needed the man that was supposed to be my hero. But where were they? They weren't here at the shop. They just acted like nothing happened, just like they always did. But we don't talk about that kind of stuff. The only time I talked to them now was during the occasional text check in where we all lied and said we were okay.

I only knew dad was drinking again because I saw him at the grocery store with bottles of his wine of choice tucked at the bottom under their weekly groceries like he was trying to hide it. It always started with the wine. I hadn't told anyone. I hadn't checked on him, hadn't checked on Mom. Because we don't talk about that kind of stuff.

I collapsed back in my chair and banged a fist against the desk. The drawer with the letter popped open, the envelope was right there on top. It didn't matter how many times I tried to bury it under everything. It was always right there at the top every time I didn't want to see it. With shaking hands, I picked it up. I held it out to Emery. "You can start by taking this and getting it out of my shop," I said in a voice so low I could barely hear myself.

"What is it?"

"I don't know." My shoulders slumped forward as I shook it at her. "I don't fucking know, and I don't want to know."

Emery stepped closer, her eyes flicking between me and the letter. Her hands fell to my shoulders and pushed me back to sit up straight so she could step between my legs. I stared at the strip of tattooed skin on her stomach. Once upon a time I would have smoothed my hands over that bare skin, would have let my hands wander up under the sweater as I pulled her down in my lap. Emery's arms wrapped around my head and pulled me to her. My body froze up. I couldn't even hug her back.

"I'm here, Ollie, I'm here." She scraped her nails lightly over the back of my head. I couldn't stop myself from melting into her. I breathed in her familiar vanilla scent.

"I can't keep doing this."

"I'll figure it out. Okay? I'll figure it out this time." Her arms left me.

I dropped my face against my hands. I couldn't watch her walk away from me again. I wanted her to stay and fix it all for me. For once there was something I couldn't fix for myself.

The door clicked shut softly behind her.

Chapter 11

Oliver

November Now

A knock on the door frame of the office broke my focus on the wiring diagram in front of me. I rubbed a hand over my face. My eyes burned from looking at the computer screen for so long. There was a throbbing ache in my temple.

"We're headed out for night," Drew said. He shifted his weight from one foot to the other and pushed his hands into his pockets. "Do you need anything before I go?"

My gaze dropped to the clock on the computer screen. It was an hour past closing time already. They should have all been long gone by now. "I'm fine. Go home. Don't you and Wade have plans tonight?"

He shrugged his shoulders and stepped further into the office. "It's not a big deal. I can stay here so you're not alone. Or maybe you could come with us? You might like Dungeons and Dragons if you give it a chance."

I used to promise him all the time that I would join in on a campaign one day. Our parents used to hate how interested he was in it because of the magic. When I moved out of our parents' house and into Granny and Pop's at eighteen I started storing all his supplies for the game in my room. The best part about being so much older than him was that I could help him sneak around mom and dad.

I smiled half heartedly up at him. "I need to find the short in this car tonight. How about another time?" It was too easy to feed him excuses despite the guilt pooling in the bit of my stomach.

"Wade and I were talking about going to Dragon Con next year. Do you want to come with us?"

The three of us used to go to the massive convention in Atlanta every year when they were teenagers. Then after everything happened and Drew had to leave college I promised I would take him again when he got better. I kept my promise and the last time we went was the summer I met Emery. I had even let him talk me into cosplaying that year. All I cared about then was getting to see him happy again.

Here we were now and it almost felt like everything was reversed. He spent everyday checking up on me like he was waiting for me to finally fall apart.

The tears I'd been holding in since Emery left earlier in the day stung my sensitive eyes. I looked up to the ceiling and tried my best to blink them away.

Drew moved from his spot by the door until he was right in front of the desk. His eyes fell to the framed photo of Granny and Pop that I kept next to the computer. He reached for it and lifted it up. The whites of his eyes turned red while he smoothed a finger over the photo. "They're proud of you, you know that right? But they would be pissed if they knew how you've been treating yourself lately."

When he looked back at me I noticed for the first time how grown up he looked. This was the little boy that I held when things were bad at home or the shy teenager stuck at home still trying to find himself. He wasn't the broken twenty-one year old I rescued from college and took to rehab. Somewhere along the way he had grown into a man that was a little too wise for his age and I had missed it happening.

"You mean they were proud. They're gone now, Drew," I grumbled.

He flinched at my words. His trembling hand placed the frame back on my desk. Then his gaze sharpened on me. "They are proud, Oliver. I know you were the closest to them out of all of us and that losing them was the hardest on you. It's time to let yourself grieve. Speaking from experience I know exactly what you're doing and it's not healthy. If you keep trying to bury your feelings it's going to hurt worse when they finally break through."

I covered my face with my hands to hide the tears threatening to spill over. The honesty and love behind his words stung.

"Remember when you made me promise to work through my shit and get better?"

Of course I remembered. I made it him promise me a thousand times while he worked on getting sober. I wasn't sure he remembered most of those times.

"It's your turn," he said, his voice sounding closer.

I undercovered my face to find him right in front of me now. He crossed his arms over his chest and a stern expression that reminded me of Granny when she was disappointed — not angry — covered his face. A heavy weight settled in my chest.

"It's time for you start going to therapy again. I need you to get better, Oliver."

I tried therapy once upon a time in my early twenties when I started to notice all the ways my parents fucked me up were starting to spill over into my life. I couldn't even remember making the decision to stop going. Little by little the shop became the most important thing in my life until it consumed all my time. Then Emery came into my life and eclipsed everything. The time I spent with her was the last time I ever did something just for me.

"Okay." I scrubbed a hand over my beard. "Yeah, okay. I'll call my therapist in the morning," I agreed. I didn't know how I would find the time to go, but I would figure it out.

Shit, maybe that was a sign of just how much I needed to talk to someone.

Chapter 12

Oliver

August Then

> Hi.

> It's Oliver.

> From the shop.

Emery

Hi, Oliver from the shop. Thank you for clarifying. I know a lot of Olivers.

> Really?

No lol You're the only Oliver I know.

> Oh ok

> Thank you again for the cupcakes. Can I bring you back your tray?

I can swing by the shop and pick it up.

You don't have to do that. I can bring it to you.

It's no big deal, I'll come get it.

Emery I'm telling you that I'm bringing it to you. Tell me where to go.

Tell me what you want to eat while you're at it. I'll bring dinner with me.

Or we can meet somewhere.

Please

I don't like being told what to do.

I sat back in the driver seat of my truck and looked down at my messages with Emery. I sounded like such an idiot. And also kind of like an asshole. I didn't understand what this woman was doing to me. Something about her made it hard to keep my head on straight.

She said we could get to know each other as friends and gave me her number. Texting wasn't over stepping was it? All I could think about after she left today was seeing her again. Maybe it was uncool to not wait at least a day before texting her, but I couldn't help myself.

I've spent my whole life trying to be the cool tough guy. Just once I wanted to be like my best friend Matt and just un-apologetically wear my heart on my sleeve. My heart wanted this sharp-tongued puzzle of a woman that told off angry men in one breath and then folded in on herself in the next.

If I was going to make an idiot of myself, I might as well go all in. I pressed the call button on the screen.

"You're pushy," she laughed in lieu of hello. Damn that laugh was cute. Calling was the right choice.

"I'm not telling you what to do, I'm telling you what I'm going to do," I tried to keep my voice stern, but a chuckle broke through.

"You told me to tell you where to go and tell you what I wanted to eat. That's telling me what to do." She was right, it was a little bossy of me. I just couldn't help it. Some part of me needed to bring her food in repayment for the cupcake, and for being willing to give me whatever chance she could.

"I also said please." I covered my mouth to hide my smile even though she couldn't see me. The image of her in her car in front of the shop today checking herself out in the mirror before she noticed me noticing her flashed through my head. Then there was the way that little sundress fluttered around her legs when she got out of the car. I almost lost my mind seeing her bend over and the flash of spandex shorts covering her thick thighs.

I could still feel the ghost of her writing her number on my skin and how her fingers had lingered just a little longer than needed on my forearm. There was the whiff of vanilla that flooded my nose when she pushed my pen back in my pocket.

"I told you I have food allergies."

I let out an exasperated sigh. She had mentioned that, but she also hadn't told me what those allergies were. I didn't care if I had to drive forty-five minutes to the closest bigger city to get her some extra special complicated order. "I understand that, woman. Tell me what to get you that you can have and whatever I need to do to make sure it's safe." I didn't know where this caveman urge to keep her safe came from, but it had been there from the moment I caught her checking me out that first day she came to the shop.

"You realize I could send you on an embarrassing wild goose chase right now, right? Gotta get my revenge for you telling me what to do." I didn't miss how hard she fought to keep her voice serious. An uncontrolled laugh cut off her words. It was a glorious uninhibited laugh— loud, shrill and punctuated with snorts. Damn , I wanted to hear that sound forever.

"Emery," I said slowly. "Do what you must do. If it makes you laugh like that, I'll do anything." I should just cut my losses and tell her I couldn't be just friends with her, not in any shape of the word.

"Friends, Oliver, friends only," she said in a stern tone that sent my head spinning. I wanted the silly tone she had been using back.

"I'm a very good friend. I can provide references if you want. I'll do anything for my friends."

Holy hell, I was terrible at this friend thing. I defaulted to flirting even though it was the wrong choice right now.

"I expect a written list of at least five references with multiple forms of contact when you get here." I heard Emery's phone shift and the tapping of her short nails against the screen. "No food. I'm cooking."

"I think you're overestimating how many friends I have. You already made me cupcakes; you're not cooking me dinner too." I wanted to beg her to let me do something for her. Anything, I would do anything. I would go to the grocery store right now, get whatever she could eat, and cook it for her myself. All she had to do was tell me what she couldn't eat.

My phone vibrated against my head. I pulled it away to glance at the screen. Staring back at me was a message with Emery's address.

It was also my address, just a different apartment number. I couldn't believe I'd been living so close to this gorgeous woman and had no idea. "We're neighbors," I said under my breath.

"What?"

"You live a floor above me, Emery."

How many times had we passed by each other in the building? In the parking lot? How many times had I been too blind to notice her? The truth was, it couldn't have been that many times. There was no way I had ever been in the proximity of this woman and not noticed her.

It was well known to everyone in my life that I was a total flirt and playboy. I'd come close to flirting with everyone in Edward County that I wasn't related to at this point. I couldn't help myself. I liked flirting and hooking up. Gender didn't even matter to me, though that detail wasn't as well known to many. I was only out to a select few people.

"Well, I guess I don't have to feel bad about your commute here to bring me back a tray," Emery replied.

"I'm not just bringing back your tray. I'm coming to hang out with my new friend." The word friend felt all wrong in my mouth.

There was a pause, and I could picture the look on her face while she thought about it. I bet it was the same thinking face she'd made before she decided to give me her number. "Fine. You're cleaning the kitchen after dinner. Fair warning, I'm a messy cook."

"I guess it's a good thing that cleaning the kitchen is my favorite chore." It was a lie. I hated washing dishes and cleaning the kitchen with a fiery passion. I would rather do literally any other chore. But for Emery, I would do it if it meant getting just one more chance to see her.

***

I stopped by my apartment to take the quickest shower I could to scrub all the grease and sweat off. I loved my job, but the mess drove me crazy sometimes.

"I already washed it," I said as soon as Emery opened her door. I held up the clean tray. "Sorry I took so long. I didn't want to show up all gross from work." I had also put too much thought into finding a t-shirt and pair of jeans that didn't look like I was trying too hard, but that also looked nice. The shirt clung to my chest and biceps showing off the muscles I had caught her staring at before.

Her eyes lingered just the way I wanted them to. I fought back a smug smile watching her. I took the time to enjoy the view of her in a tight pair of athletic shorts with an oversized wide neck shirt that slipped off one shoulder and a purple apron over top. Her makeup was just as flawless as it had been earlier in the day. She visibly shook herself out of staring and reached for the tray. I spun to the side to keep her from reaching it. "Tell me where it goes, and I'll put it up."

Emery frowned and held her hands out. She leaned forward, getting close enough to make me suck in an involuntary breath.

"Emery," I said slowly, my accent growing stronger, "if I'm cleaning the kitchen I need to know where things go. Now tell me where this goes."

She rolled her eyes and turned her back to me finally moving out of the way to let me in. I followed her to the kitchen and opened the cabinet she pointed at. Inside there was an assortment of other trays and containers. I don't think I'd ever seen a collection this big. "What's for dinner?" I asked.

"I thought about being mean and making something weird, but I decided to be nice." She pointed to the small dining table already set with food waiting to be served. "Sesame chicken with fried rice and stir fry veggies."

I narrowed my eyes. "What would something weird be?" I wish she would just stop being so coy and tell me what she was allergic to. I'm sure it wasn't actually that big of a deal. I mean, yeah it was a big deal because it could hurt her, but not a big deal in it being something I would be weird about.

"Tomato-free chili is usually at the top of that list."

Tomato free chili? I've had my fair share of different chilis in my life, even been to a few chili cook offs. There were a lot of different recipes out there. "Like white chicken chili?" I asked.

Emery shook her head.

My brain was blanking on what she could mean. "I'm not creative enough to imagine what that could be, but I'm game to try anything once." I stopped to think for a second and noticed the blush on Emery's face. Tomatoes. No one makes chili without tomatoes and looks that shy about it without there being a reason. "Are you allergic to tomatoes? I haven't heard that one before, but that doesn't sound as bad as you made it out to be."

None of my family or friends had any food allergies. In fact, we all were the least picky eaters to exist. I really didn't have any experience with them aside from hearing about kids in school being allergic to peanuts. My younger brother had a friend that had to eat at a separate lunch table because of his allergy and sometimes Drew would sit with him.

"Tomatoes, avocado, and dairy. There used to be more, but after a lot of allergy treatments and reintroductions that's what we were able to get the list down to."

I nodded trying to play it off the best I could. "Still not that bad. I could learn to get you food without those." The avocado would be easy. Tomatoes may be a little more difficult but still not bad. But dairy, well, that was going to be difficult. Every recipe Granny ever taught me was loaded with butter, cheese, or milk. Sometimes all three. What about eggs? Did those count as dairy? They were in the dairy department of the grocery store.

"I'm highly sensitive to cross contamination. If a restaurant preps tomatoes and then another veggie in the same space without proper cleaning, I can have a reaction just from that." Emery twisted the ties of her apron around her fingers. "I've had to use an EpiPen in public more times than I care to admit."

Cross-contamination and having to use an EpiPen sounded serious. The way she looked down and let her hair fall in front of her face made me realize how sensitive she was about it. I had so much research to do when I got home tonight. I felt my face soften and the teasing look I'd been wearing faded away. I rubbed the back of my neck and then leaned against the counter. "Okay. I can learn. I'm a great learner when I want to be." I pointed at the crooked spot in my nose from the time it had been broken. "I'm also not afraid to make a scene for my friends if I need to."

The tension pushing Emery's shoulders up eased and she let them relax. Her fingers tugged the ties she twisted around her fingers loose and she pulled the apron over her head. She tossed it onto the counter. "I want to hear this story." She took a seat at the table and started serving the food.

"It's a pretty short story." I sat down in the other chair. The table was tucked into the corner of her kitchen meaning we had to sit next to each other. I tried not to stare at how her movements made her shirt slip further down her arm. "My best friend is a great guy. Probably the nicest person you could ever meet."

"One of those that wouldn't hurt a fly and gently relocates spiders in his house back outside?"

I shook my head. "More like the kind of guy that would find a spider in his house and make a space for it to stay because even spiders deserve a safe home." Matt was a precious soul I've protected with my life from day one of kindergarten. I stopped talking to take a bite of food. It seemed like a fairly simple meal, but this was the best thing I'd ever tasted. I could actually taste how much love Emery clearly put into her cooking, just like I had been able to taste in the cupcakes earlier in the day.

I didn't know what look was on my face. Probably something wide eyed and dumb. Emery's eyes sparkled watching me taste the food and that was all that mattered. She held her hands in front of her mouth hiding her bright smile. I wanted to reach over and pull them away so I could bask in the look of pure joy on her face.

"Okay, never mind, we're never going out to eat ever. You cook like this every night, and I'll clean your messy kitchen for the rest of my life." I looked over to the trail of dishes that covered her counter and led to a sink piled high. There were various spills dotting the counter tops. "You could use more dishes than an industrial sized kitchen and I would happily wash them." I wish I was exaggerating for her benefit, but I wasn't. It didn't matter what I had to do as long as I got to see her eyes sparkle like that again.

Emery blushed and dropped her eyes down to her plate. "I think you're being a little dramatic." She kicked my leg under the table. "Finish your story."

"Okay, so he's super nice and kind of a nerd. Like most middle schoolers he went through an awkward stage. I'm talking as awkward as it gets. Kids used to pick on him relentlessly. One day in eighth grade we were in band class and the teacher had to step out.

Matt was lost in his own little world practicing like the teacher told us to. These boys started picking on him and he wouldn't stand up for himself." I shrugged. It was the way most of the fights I used to get into started. "So, I took care of them. Ended up taking a trombone to the nose." It wasn't one of my finer moments and was one of the only fights that I lost.

Emery coughed and patted her chest. I pushed her water glass closer to her and waited for her to pull herself together. "I have so many questions." She pushed her food around her plate. I knew what she was wondering. Everyone always had the same questions when they heard that story.

"Yes, I was in band. I played percussion for very dumb middle school boy reasons. It was the slide of the trombone, and it hurt like hell. No, I didn't get in fights all the time in school and every single one I was in was because I was defending someone." I rattled off my well rehearsed answers but downplayed how many fights I used to get in. She didn't need to know that it actually was all of the time. I still don't know how I never got expelled.

"Was it worth it?" She asked me. "And were all the fights defending Matt?"

"Hell yeah, it was worth it. Some of them were also for defending Ava and Drew." I stabbed a piece of chicken harder than necessary with my fork. Defending Matt and my siblings would always be worth it. Then everything happened with my dad and people used to whisper about it behind my back. It didn't matter that everyone helped cover it up, people still talked in small towns. "And my dad," I added in a voice so low I wasn't sure if Emery heard me.

Emery looked like she wanted to ask me for more details but thought better of it. Silence settled over us as we finished our food.

I sat back and stretched after cleaning my plate. I pointed to the serving bowls still on the table with plenty of food left in them. "You do know you were only cooking for two people, right?"

Emery laughed, the sound more reserved this time. "I learned to cook for a family of five. I've never been able to cook for less. I always have a ton of leftovers." She stood and walked to the cabinet full of storage containers. "You want to take some with you?"

I couldn't help the way I smiled. "Guess I'll have another excuse to come back," I answered.

"I believe you already promised to wash my dishes for the rest of your life. Or are you going to admit you were just being dramatic?"

"That may have been my stomach talking, but I never break my promises."

We moved around each other putting away the leftovers and carrying the dishes to the sink. Emery rested her back against the counter watching me work.

I looked over my shoulder and held up the handful of spoons from the bottom of the sink. "Did you purposely use as many dishes as you could? There's like twelve spoons in here. Why do you even own this many spoons?"

She chuckled. "I always taste every step."

I waved the spoons around before scrubbing them clean, my shoulders shaking with laughter letting her know I was messing with her. "But twelve spoons? Are there even that many steps to what you made? I kind of feel like this was a punishment."

"Someone is doing an awful lot of complaining after how profusely you were declaring your love for my food earlier."

I choked on my spit when she knelt next to me, her shoulder brushing against my leg. She opened the cabinet under the sink and pulled out a disinfectant cleaner. I pulled the spray bottle from her hand. "I told you to tell me where everything is so I can do it myself."

She pulled the bottle back from me and let it dangle from her fingers as she crossed her arms. "I told you not to tell me what to do."

I unhooked the bottle from her hand, careful not to brush my fingers against her skin, and then opened cabinets until I found microfiber cleaning cloths. I held them up as if asking if that was the right choice. "If this friendship is going to work, you're going to have to get used to being told what to do sometimes, Emery."

"You can try but that doesn't mean I'm going to listen."

Chapter 13

Emery

November Now

Dear Emery,

Oliver refuses to tell me what happened between the two of you but I'm a smart old woman, so I have my suspicions. I could drag this out and give you all the pretty words about how much better my grandson is with you. You and I both know that's not my style.

You remind me a lot of myself when I was younger. I'm sure everyone else has told you the same thing. I say this will all my love, dear, because it's the only way anyone would have gotten it through my thick skull if I were in your position:

Get your shit together. Throw whatever tantrum you need to and figure out whatever is going on in that head of yours. Then get your ass back here where you belong. Oliver and the restaurant are yours.

Don't make me haunt you when I'm dead.

Leave it to Granny to break my heart with so few words. I read the letter so many times I lost count. Each time made my regret over how I left them grow until it took up all the space inside me. All the time I missed out on haunted me. There were a lot of could'ves and should'ves about how I handled the situation. If I could, I would turn back time and ask for the space I needed without cutting them all out of my life completely.

Turning back time wasn't an option, but I could make things right now. Somehow my choices over the summer with Riley had orchestrated this second chance without meaning to. I'd been fumbling that second chance every step.

Damn, I was such an idiot.

There was still time. I could fix it. Oliver probably wasn't mine anymore.

He yelled at me.

It was safe to say that I had royally fucked this up. He wasn't my Ollie from before anymore. Today he had finally let me see just how much I'd broken him, how much life had broken him. Even with him in front of me showing me all his broken pieces I pushed him away. He was never the asshole, I was.

Next to me my phone vibrated on my bed. The screen showed a message from Ava to Matt, Drew, two numbers I didn't know, and me.

Ava

hey, oliver is at the shop again and won't answer my calls to check on him. who wants to swing by this time?

(unknown number)

We're at Dungeons and Dragons night.

(unknown number)

> if i have to drag him out of there one more time he'll probably fire me

Drew

> Matt?

From my spot in my room, I could hear Matt and Riley in our living room. I'd been listening to the obnoxious sound of Riley trying to learn to play his saxophone all evening.

Emery

> He's with Riley.

Matt

> It's no big deal, we can run over there really quick.

> NO

> I'll do it.

***

"It's Emery," I announced before I walked through the open bay door in hopes of not getting a tool swung at me this time. There was a car on the rack lifted in the air, parts scattered around the floor underneath. Oliver wasn't anywhere in sight. My eyes scanned around looking for him and caught on the soft glow of the computer in the dark lobby.

Oliver didn't turn around when I walked up behind him. "I told y'all to stop checking on me," he grumbled. On the computer he scrolled through a list of parts and selected one. He picked up something small and held it next to the image on the screen, tilting his head to the side comparing them. In the dim light he looked even more tired than he had earlier in the day.

"If you don't want anyone checking on you maybe you should answer your phone," I admonished. I slid onto the stool next to him and nudged the container of leftovers I brought him. "No cheese this time," I whispered.

For a split second he froze, his whole body went rigid like he'd seen a ghost, before he turned from the screen to look at me. The right side of his mouth lifted in that crooked smile that always made my heart flutter. "You could have told me the cheese on that sandwich was the dairy free shit."

His eyes dropped down to the hoodie I wore halfway zipped over a tank top and leggings. I didn't think about the hoodie when I put it on. It's a favorite of mine, just the right weight for the slight early November chill and perfectly oversized. There were a thousand stains on the light grey fabric I'd given up on trying to get out. I watched his face scrunch while he studied it.

Then it hit me. This was his hoodie. Well, the oversized hoodie he bought and wore with the intention of me stealing since none of his clothes would be oversized on me. I can't believe I ever forgot that was where it came from. Oliver lifted his hat to rub the back of his head and his Adam's apple bobbed with a swallow.

"Hey, that dairy free shit isn't that bad." I feigned a shocked expression. I'd never had real cheese, so I didn't know how the two compared to each other. Riley made sure to tell me that they tasted nothing alike.

"That's because you don't know any better." Just like that it felt like something between us shifted. Time turned back and we were the two people from before. My Ollie was in front of me teasing me with that glint in his eyes. I wore his hoodie even though it didn't smell like him anymore.

The letter in the pocket of the hoodie burned against my hip. Reality crashed back in reminding me that we weren't them anymore. "I read the letter."

Oliver's smile dropped. He lifted his ballcap and scratched the back of his head. I couldn't help watching the way his bicep flexed with the movement. "And?"

I wanted to hand it to him and just let him read it for himself. Would he tell me that Granny was wrong? Would he confirm for a final time that he wasn't mine? "She said I needed to get my shit together and come back."

"Come back to what?" His tired eyes held mine with an intensity that set every cell in my body on fire. He knew. He had to know. "Come back to what, Em?"

Gravity pulled us together, both of us leaning toward each other as far as we could. I caught myself and froze. Ollie kept leaning forward, close enough that he was barely balanced on his stool now. His eyes dropped to my mouth and then down further. I held my breath while he traced a path down my neck and over my shoulder to where the hoodie drooped down over my arm.

The heat of his gaze felt like he dragged his fingers over my bare skin. I didn't just miss his touch, I needed it.

"To all of you. She told me to come back because the restaurant was mine." I swallowed the lump forming in my throat.

His eyes stayed on my exposed skin and his hand on the counter inched closer to mine next to the container of food. "Is that all, baby? You're just coming back for the restaurant?" Dammit of course he knew. Oliver could always read me like an open book.

"Well, that cranky old woman is sort of forcing me from the grave."

Oliver's whole body shook with laughter. Tears streaked down his face leaving paths through the dirt and grease on his skin. I didn't know if they were from laughing or something else. "They left it to me and you in the will. We've been trying to find you to tell you."

I wanted him to ask me again what I came back for. I wanted to tell him. His fingers grazed mine and it felt like he was trying to tell me that whatever happened earlier today was a mistake. He wasn't really mad at me.

"I'm sorry I yelled at you," he said. All the hard lines that had formed on his face were gone. I noticed a sprinkling of grey hairs in his beard and couldn't decide if it was just a trick of the blue light from the computer screen or if he had aged that much in two years.

"I'm sorry I've been so mean to you," I apologized. I flipped my hand over on the counter.

We sat in silence with his fingers tracing my palm. The touch soothed my racing heart. His features twisted in concentration. I wished he would tell me everything he was thinking. I wished he could rely on me for support the way that I relied on him before.

"I have one condition," I blurted. "I'll take the restaurant, but you have to help me."

I didn't know how long it would take to remodel the small diner to be the place I had been dreaming of for my whole life. We'd need to narrow down the menu, perfect the recipes. It would take a lot of work to take the jumbled mess of ideas I had for the place and shape them into something real. Maybe somewhere along the way we could figure out the pieces of what we were to each other now, find out if maybe things were on our side this time.

"I wouldn't have it any other way," Oliver beamed at me. His fingers wrapped around my hand. Maybe there was hope after all that I could fix all my mistakes.

Chapter 14

Emery

Emery

What's your favorite kind of sandwich?

Oliver

I'm not picky.

I didn't ask if you're picky, I asked what your favorite is. Big difference.

Baloney

As in the sandwich meat or as in you're calling my statement baloney?

The sandwich meat is Bologna.

A good old fashioned baloney, mayo, and cheese on white bread. Sometimes with plain potato chips added for some crunch.

> WTF is wrong with you?

> I think I just threw up in my mouth a little.

> I'm all for eating whatever you want but I'm very concerned about your palette.

Damn are you always this judgmental about food?

> Yes. You're going to eat whatever I bring.

> Spoiler alert, it's not bologna and cheese.

What

Woman what does that mean?

EMERY

Are you bringing me lunch?

> Stop texting me. I'm trying to drive.

ALL OF THE SHOP doors were wide open when I pulled into the parking lot. At the sound of my tires on the pavement the man bent over the car on the first rack looked up. He had black smeared up both arms, his neck, and little on his nose. The tool cart next to him was covered in parts and tools. He lifted a hand in a wave.

I fought back a smile as I parked. Oliver was at my window before I could shut the car off. I rolled it down.

"Whatcha doing?" he asked.

I shrugged as I pushed my sunglasses on top of my head. "It's a pretty day and I'm kind of in the mood for a picnic. I thought I'd drive around and see if I could find someone to join me."

He pulled his cap off and rubbed the back of his head. "Is that an invite?" He flashed that crooked smile. Each time we saw each other over the past few days he relaxed more around me and I loved it. He was cute when he was clearly overthinking everything he said, but I enjoyed how wanted he made me feel when he openly turned on the charm.

Just friends.

"I'll think about it."

He narrowed his eyes as he lifted the right side of his mouth a little higher. "Alright, but you better make a decision soon. I have this strange hankering for a baloney and cheese sandwich."

I wrinkled my nose and flicked my sunglasses back down on my face. "Well I'll leave you to it then. I need to go find someone to share this turkey bacon club on sourdough with pesto aioli with." I pretended to reach for the button to roll my window up.

Oliver reached through the window and wrapped his hand around mm wrist. "Shit, sorry, my hands are nasty," he said as he yanked it back.

I was supposed to care that his hands were nasty, but I just couldn't bring myself to. My wrist tingled from the brief touch of his skin against mine. My eyes caught the bloody scrapes on the back of his left hand. "What happened?" I asked without thinking.

He followed my eyes to his hand and made a face that told me he didn't know it was there. "There was a bolt that was a bitch to get to. Must have scrapped it then." He took a step back. "I'm going to go wash up and let Pop know I'm going to lunch. You want me to show you where the break room is?"

I shook my head and stuck out my bottom lip. "I really had my heart set on a picnic."

"Alright, there's a park right down the road. I'll be right back." He knocked his knuckles on my door as he took another step back. He walked backwards a few more steps before turning around to jog back in. The hand he had touched still tingled while I watched him.

Friends, I reminded myself. *That's all we were going to be.* I turned the volume on my radio up and pressed play on the playlist on my phone to drown out where my thoughts were trying to go.

The passenger side door popped open, and Oliver dropped into the seat.

"Are you cool with me driving?" I braced myself for him to insist on driving like my ex used to do.

His eyebrows scrunched together as he buckled his seatbelt. "Yeah," he said slowly.

"Okay, good. I'm not a passenger princess." I shifted the car into reverse. The song playing through the speakers switched to one of my favorites. "Also, I can't sing," I said just before I launched into singing along.

I wasn't lying. I couldn't even carry a tune. I had been so self-conscious about it growing up I wouldn't even let my closest friends hear me sing along to anything. One day my sister caught me humming along to a song instead of belting it out with everyone else. She had elbowed me in the ribs and started singing even louder off key. "Come on, Em, be silly with me," she had pleaded.

My ex hated it when I sang. He always let me know how embarrassing it was, even when it was just the two of us.

I looked out the corner of my eye to gauge Oliver's reaction. His grin spread wide as he watched me. Then, he caught me off guard by joining in. His deep voice boomed over mine, matching my enthusiasm and lack of any musical ability. He stumbled over the words, making half of them up, making it clear he had no idea what the song was.

We were both laughing so hard we couldn't finish the song.

Since day one I'd been teetering on the edge of knowing just being friends with this man wasn't an option. Listening to his rumbling laugh mingling with the sound of off key singing solidified the fact. In such a short time Oliver had already half stolen my heart, a heart that was still shattered into pieces by someone else's cruelty. Could I trust him to put those pieces back together when I didn't even know what the finished picture should look like anymore?

"Finally, something you're not good at," he said, turning the volume down and pulling me from my thoughts. It sounded like a compliment. "I was starting to think that you were too perfect to be real."

"I mean, I could still be a figment of your imagination."

"No way, my imagination isn't creative enough to come up with something like pesto aioli."

I glanced over his way as I turned right into the park. "Maybe your imagination is trying to tell you that it's time to expand your palette."

Oliver stuck out his tongue. It was incredibly distracting the way the thought of that tongue on my skin crashed into my brain. I was thankful I still had my eyes covered by my oversized sunglasses so he couldn't see the way they widened.

He jumped out of the car as soon as I parked and opened the back door to pull out the picnic basket from the back seat. "Emery, can I ask you a question?" he asked, still leaning in the car.

I pushed down the urge to point out that he just did but nodded instead.

"What's this?" He held up the coloring book I forgot I tossed back there.

I looked out the windshield as I pulled my sunglasses off. My first instinct was to brush it off as belonging to a non-existent niece or nephew, one that I quickly pushed away due to the contents of the coloring book. The cover was boldly titled "Calm the Fuck Down" and all the pages contained various profanity. Someone had told me that coloring was a great way to relax and so I had picked it up. It had quickly become my favorite coping strategy to pull myself out of a panic attack.

"It's fun. You should try it sometime," I finally answered. I turned to pull my cross-body bag from behind the passenger seat. I kept my eyes away from his face so I wouldn't be able to see the judgment it must have been covered in.

"Cool. Wanna color while we eat?"

My mouth legit dropped as he spoke. I blinked as I tried to recalibrate my brain. That reaction hadn't even been on the long list of options I had expected him to pick from. "Um, yeah, sure," I stammered out. I forced my eyes up to see that crooked smile. "I have crayons in my bag," I added.

Jesus, Emery, really? I was so embarrassing.

"Is it the 64 pack with the built-in sharpener?" He tucked the coloring book into the basket and then pulled it out of the car.

"Sorry, I left that one at home. This bag just isn't big enough for that." I jiggled my small purse as I followed him toward a picnic table under the shade.

He snapped his fingers in an aw-shucks motion. "Damn, you were about to make my deepest childhood dream come true"

I laughed hard enough to snort, earning a bigger smile as he opened the basket. He rubbed his hands together before pulling things out like he was opening a treasure chest. Two sandwiches, plain potato chips, and Gatorade were spread over the table. He reached for the container at the very bottom, but I cut him off. "No dessert until you eat your lunch."

"Yes, ma'am."

I let the front of my hair fall across my face as I tilted it down to focus on the food in front of me to hide the blush across my cheeks. Wow, it was really hot today. Oliver sat down next to me and opened the coloring book between us. There were a few inches between us, but I could feel the heat radiating from his skin. My arm tingled as I thought about shifting just a little so we would brush against each other.

Get yourself together.

Just friends. I told him we could only be friends.

I waited patiently, not touching my food, for him to take his first bite. My mom and I had been making this sandwich for years. The pesto aioli was something I had recently learned to make vegan while experimenting with making more recipes top eight allergen friendly. Today's sandwich featured two other new experiments, and I was interested to see how he would react. Instead of the typical tomato that most people would add I had opted for thinly sliced apples. The bread was gluten free sourdough I had made fresh last night.

I watched his face carefully and he chewed, waiting to see if he noticed anything strange. "Emery, I think this might be the best sandwich I've ever had," he said between bites.

"Notice anything weird about the bread?"

He closed his eyes in thought as he chewed. "Maybe something different about the texture?" Those beautiful deep brown eyes popped open questioning if he was on the right track.

"It's gluten free," I elaborated.

He raised his eyebrows and went in for another bite. "If you say so." He polished off his sandwich before I took more than a couple bites from mine. "So, what is it that you do? Are you some kind of celebrity chef?"

I covered my mouth as I chewed and shook my head. "I'm a school bus driver," I answered after I swallowed.

His eyes narrowed like he didn't believe me. "So, it's a secret? Like after you trust me, you'll surprise me by taking me to your fancy restaurant. It'll turn out that you're just in this little, small town because you need a break from fancy chef life to get some inspiration or some shit."

I choked on my food because of the laughter that forced its way up my throat. I alternated between coughing and chugging Gatorade, fighting for my life, while Oliver gently rubbed my back. When I could breathe again, I started laughing so hard that tears gathered in the corners of my eyes. Oliver's hand kept rubbing circles over the middle of my back, almost making me loose the ability to breathe again. I dreaded the moment he moved it away. "You're so dramatic," I wheezed.

"Says the person that was just almost murdered by a sandwich."

"It was Oliver, in the park, with a sandwich," I joked, sending myself into another fit of laughter. My chest and face hurt so good.

The joke earned a laugh from him, the hand on my back coming to a stop. I felt the callouses on his palm through the thin fabric of my tank top. Goosebumps erupted across my back as my breath caught. I wished his fingers were just an inch higher so they would brush against my bare skin.

"You're just trying to distract me from the truth. Face it, I've figured out your secret." The smile on his face dropped away at the same time his hand did.

"I wish I had my own restaurant." I lifted my sandwich for another bite but changed my mind and laid it back in the container. I wiped my hands on my shorts and reached for the box of crayons in my bag instead.

Oliver accepted the box when I offered it to him but kept his attention focused on my eyes. "You should open one," he told me.

It's just a pipe dream. I wish you would let this go.

"I want to, one day. I'm just working on saving and perfecting recipes right now." I tucked my hair behind my ears while I kept my eyes focused on my half-finished food. I had been saying that for years. Probably would keep saying it for the rest of my life.

I knew that it wouldn't do well around here. Most small businesses in our area didn't last a year. If they were lucky, they might get five. It felt like the number of small businesses got smaller and smaller every year, the shutdowns due to the pandemic wiped out a large chunk of the remaining ones. The majority had moved to bigger areas nearby where they had a better chance of surviving rather than staying around here until they were forced to close.

Oliver plucked a crayon from the box and shifted his gaze to the coloring book spread between us. He offered the box back to me. I chose one and twisted my body so I could color with him. We were both right-handed, so position wasn't ideal. He shifted a little, so our knees were pressed together as we both faced slightly inward. I could feel the heat of his skin through his pants against my bare knees.

"What would your restaurant be?" he asked.

"I want it to be a safe space for everyone. People with allergies often get stuck being able to eat very little, sometimes nothing at all, when they go out with their families. Food is such a social thing so feeling left out like that can make the whole experience even more stressful than it already is. It would be top eight allergen free with easily modified options for people like me with allergies that don't fall on that list." I paused to see if he wanted me to stop talking, bracing for him to tell me it was a stupid idea. An impossible idea.

His eyes lifted to mine as he lifted the corner of his mouth and gave a little nod to encourage me to keep going.

My heart fluttered. "We would be completely transparent about all our ingredients, with everything easily accessible online and in person, as well as transparent about our cross-contamination pre-vention." I twisted the crayon in my fingers, digging my thumb nail into the edge of the wrapper. "I want to make it where people can request dine-in modifications online so when they come in, they can just tell us their name instead of having to go through the embarrassment of trying to make modifications in person if they want."

Oliver's brows pulled down as his eyes widened. "Why is it embarrassing? Isn't it just advocating for yourself?"

"Sometimes it can just feel like a lot and stressful, like you're just asking for attention."

He scowled a little but then let his face go blank. "Making sure things are safe isn't asking for attention." His words were soft and reassuring. I knew he meant well, but it felt like he didn't understand.

"I also want to offer cooking classes. It's easier to access information and recipes nowadays, but it can still be an overwhelming process. A lot of parents have zero experience ever dealing with allergies until their kids are diagnosed with them. So, on top of having to advocate for their kids, they are also having to navigate learning all this information they've never had to think about."

Oliver's hand moved to my thigh, resting there just for a moment before he moved it away. I wanted to catch his wrist and drag it back. "That sounds amazing, Emery. You should do it."

I chewed on my bottom lip. "Small businesses don't really work out around here," I said. It was easy to dream, to plan, to hope but I didn't know if I could handle putting in all the work only to have my dreams crushed by reality.

"So, what if you do it just for the heck of it? You could go into it expecting to have to shut down in x number of years if you wanted. Even if you're just open for a couple months, think about all the lives you could touch during that time. If you made a difference for one kid, one family wouldn't it be worth it?"

A lump formed in my throat. I chugged more Gatorade to try to wash the ache of incoming tears back down. "I guess you're right."

His hand was back on my thigh. This time he squeezed it once, twice, three times before going back to coloring. I let my hair fall back across my face to hide my small smile.

Remember this, I told myself. *When the voices in my head try to tell me the opposite, remember this.*

Chapter 15

Oliver

November Now

THE RINGS FELT HEAVY against my chest, the chain too tight around my throat, as I turned onto the road I've been avoiding for two years. The little restaurant Granny started almost fifty years ago was located in the historic downtown area of Mountain View just one street over from the shop. After Emery left us driving past it felt like another tear in my broken heart.

Taking over the shop after Granny and Pop passed already meant spending my days haunted by the memories of them etched in every inch of the place. I could only imagine how much worse the restaurant would be.

The building was barely visible in the low light of the streetlights. Emery's car idled in a parking spot right in front, exactly where we agreed to meet after work today. She looked up when I parked next to her. Her eyes met mine and the chain around my neck grew tighter. Every groove of the metal felt like it bit into my skin. My fingers clawed at it and the clasp slipped from my grasp each time I found it.

Over a year's worth of grief that I had fought so hard to ignore crashed over me. My lungs burned and my throat felt tight.

Granny stood in front of my truck, hands on her hips, and shook her head at me. She threw one hand up and her mouth moved with words I couldn't hear. Her short grey curls were pushed back out of her face with a thin headband and her apron covered in flour. This ghost of her looked more like she did when I was younger, happy and healthy with full cheeks.

"Oliver," she yelled but it was muffled and distant. Granny threw both hands up this time. Then she waved me towards her. "Oliver, Oliver, Oliver," she repeated. Each time she said my name it grew a little louder. She stepped off the sidewalk toward the driver's side of my truck.

I clenched my eyes closed hard enough it hurt. My fingers continued to claw at the chain but sweat slicked my skin so I couldn't grip it.

The door of my truck popped open. Hands covered mine on the chain. "Ollie, look at me. I'm right here, baby, look at me." The scent of vanilla surrounded me. A hand cupped my cheek, and her thumb swiped under my eye.

The burning in my chest intensified and my pulse thundered in my ears. Fuck, was I dying? What was this?

"Do you want this off? Here, move your hands for me." Her fingers pried my hands open. "Breathe for me, Ollie."

I sucked in a breath and focused on her soft touch on my neck. The sound of my heart quieted and I heard the tiny click of a clasp. My hands flew back to the chain and my eyes popped open. The bright light of the streetlight above us burned. "No," I croaked out. I hadn't taken the rings off since Pop's funeral. Now my unsteady hand pressed them against my skin while the chain dangled loosely. "I can't."

Emery pressed her forehead against mine. Dark streaks of mascara ran down her cheeks and her eyes were bloodshot. "I'll put it back on. Can you keep breathing for me?"

I sucked in another breath. My chest still burned, and I could still feel the chain pulled tight around my neck. "What's happening?" I asked. "Em, what's wrong with me?"

"You're having a panic attack. Just keep breathing. I've got you." She pressed one of my hands against her chest and sucked in a deep breath. I breathed with her, the burn lessening with each one. "You're safe, Ollie," she whispered.

"I saw Granny." Wetness coated my face. I blinked my eyes and felt fresh tears fall. It was just an empty building. I shouldn't be this upset over an empty building.

"We don't have to go inside tonight if you're not ready."

I moved my hand from her chest and wrapped it around her. She let me pull her as close as our position would allow. Her arms wrapped around me and she buried her face in my shoulder. All the time we were together before I was always so focused on making her feel safe I never stopped to notice how safe I felt in her arms.

"Can I get in your truck?" Emery asked a few minutes later.

I answered with a nod and loosened my grip on her. Her fingers slipped into the collar of my shirt and tugged the ends of the chain free. She redid the clasp and the last bit of tightness in my throat eased under the familiar weight of the metal around it. My body ached to reach for her when she slipped away.

Her arm brushed against mine and her hand closed around the key in the ignition. The engine rumbled to life. Emery held her hands in front of the vents. The warm air blew against my face, making me notice for the first time that my whole body was trembling. "I'm sorry," I whispered. My body slumped forward until my forehead rested against the steering wheel.

Emery's hand smoothed gentle circles on my back. "Is this the first time you've been here since...?" My silence must have been enough of a response. "You could have told me. We could have eased into it more." Her hand left my back.

"Em, please, I need..." How did I tell her that I needed her touch back? I didn't know how I made it this long without her touch and now I felt like I would fall apart even more if I didn't get it back.

I didn't hear her lift the center console to turn the front seats into a bench seat. She had me cradled against her before I realized what was happening. Time lost all meaning while she held me and told me she wasn't going anywhere.

Chapter 16

Emery

IT TURNS OUT DECIDING on the appearance of the interior was more difficult than I realized. We had paint samples in every shade of white imaginable. Swatches of wallpaper and flooring samples were scattered everywhere. The inspiration pictures I found online varied so much I had no idea what style I wanted anymore.

Decision paralysis was a beast. I had all the potential ideas of what I dreamed of over the years, but it felt wrong to change a place that had once belonged to Pop and Granny. Maybe we should just keep it the same as a memorial to them.

My brain felt hazy, like every thought stretched out so long the end of it slipped from my grasp before I could process it. It was like my brain was running on dial up and disconnecting before I could get completely there.

"It's too hard," I whined from my spot on the floor surrounded by the mess.

"What about this one?" Oliver pulled up another photo from the moodboard I shared with him and held up his phone. This one had a brick accent wall with white wood paneling covering the bottom third. The other walls were the same shade white as the paneling. He reached for the peel and stick brick tiles and held them up next to paint swatches we narrowed our selection down to.

All I could focus on were his hands and the expectant way he looked at me. Two weeks of working on sorting through my ideas together hadn't left any room for discussing whatever was between us. It had just been two weeks of almost touching and catching each other staring a little too long while we sat in his truck after work each night.

Two weeks of pretending like there wasn't a giant elephant in the room.

I fucking hated it.

Asking him to do this with me was a terrible idea. It actually might be one of the worst ideas I'd ever had. I didn't know it would hurt him so much to be back here. Last night was the first time he was able to make it through the front door.

"I think I need a break," I answered with a sigh. The paint colors had looked so starkly different in the store but now they were blending together into a giant blob.

He dropped the sheet of tile. "Okay, maybe we should work on the menu first. That might help you decide everything else, right?"

I cradled my head in my hands and sucked in a deep breath. In a flash Oliver was in front of me, one hand on my wrist and the other rubbed the back of my head. My body wanted to melt into his touch, but I didn't have that right anymore.

"Hey, hey, talk to me." His fingers stroked through the back of my hair. It was all so much, the smell of him and his touch paired with the heavy haze in my head. I should have been comforting him, not the other way around. "Are you feeling okay?" And, fuck, the gentle tone of his voice. He should be frustrated with me for dragging him into this with me and then refusing to make any decisions.

I tried to nod but only succeeded in pressing my hands too hard against my eyes. Oliver's callused fingers tugged my hands away so he could press one palm against my forehead. "I'm not sick," I mumbled.

His tired eyes pinned my gaze. It hurt my heart to see the worry lines on his forehead deepen and the lines around his mouth pull downward. I was supposed to be making him fall in love with me again. That wasn't going to happen if we went back down the path of him always needing to fix me.

"This is a lot. Let's take a break for dinner," he offered. He probably needed the break more than I did. Spending hours in here after struggling so hard to just walk through the door couldn't have been easy on him.

A groan tumbled from me. I lifted my face to the ceiling and rubbed my temples. Deep exhaustion settled in my bones like someone had zapped all my energy away with a snap of their fingers. Fuck, I needed to sleep for a week.

I tried to mentally catalogue how long it had been since my last period. I still wasn't regular, but the various medications and supplements I took helped me have cycles more often. It was easier to track my symptoms rather than try to count days. Trying to think of how I had felt the past few days was like wading through a fading dream.

This had to be my luteal phase starting. It always hit me like a brick wall. Another one of those fun PCOS things. The brain fog and endless exhaustion were such a constant part of life I had adapted to where I hardly noticed them as long as I was keeping my hormones balanced. The symptoms were always harder to ignore during this phase of my cycle, but the added stress I'd been under must have been making them even worse.

PCOS made my body more sensitive to stress hormones which in turn led to an increase in symptoms that only stressed me out more. It was an endless cycle.

I pushed myself into a standing position. Maybe I was putting too much thought into this. We could have just left the place as it was to start with. There was a good chance that this whole thing was going to fail anyways and investing this much energy into a place we would be closing in a few months felt like a waste. We weren't going to get anywhere with anything when my head felt like I was moving through goo.

"I'm going to go home." Home to where Matt and Riley were probably cuddled up being all cute. It would just be another painful reminder that I still didn't know what I was doing. "We're both exhausted and I think we've looked at that exact combination a hundred times now."

***

The Christmas garland draped over the tv greeted me as I opened the front door. I swear, I could feel steam shoot from my ears. My whole body burned. This was the first time I had seen the house in the light all week since I had been out late each night. My eyes skated over the tv stand noticing all the small fall décor items that had been swapped for Christmas.

I rubbed a hand over my face. "Riley," I yelled, "what the fuck is this?" I heard her and Matt giggle in the kitchen as I walked to the hallway to yank down the attic door. I climbed the ladder high enough to poke my head in and see that the boxes I had stacked next to the entrance were missing. I rolled my eyes, climbed down, and then went to Riley's room. The boxes of Christmas décor were stacked in the corner of her room, the one on top open.

These two idiots were going to drive me crazy. This is just what I needed when all I wanted to do was crawl into bed. I grabbed the top box, biting my tongue to hold back the laughter that was bubbling at my throat. This was such an annoying sister thing to do, the exact thing she would have done to me growing up. I swear sometimes she acted like she was the younger sister. I tried to muster up some of the frustration I had been feeling with myself earlier and redirect it toward Matt and Riley, knowing that they were looking to get a rise out of me. The idea that my sister had someone to be cute and annoying with made it hard to be mad at them.

I marched out of her room holding the mostly empty box and dropped it at their feet, trying my best to keep a scowl on my face. "It's not Thanksgiving yet. Put them back." I hoped they would think the shaking in my voice was from anger and not laughter. I spun on my feet, stomping toward my room and slamming the door closed behind me.

We were only a week away from Thanksgiving. In the grand scheme of things, it probably wasn't a big deal to start the Christmas decorations now. Riley was nice enough to let me make all the décor decisions for the house even though she still paid half the rent and got the smaller room.

"That was a little underwhelming," I heard Matt say in the kitchen.

I pressed my ear against the door trying to understand their quiet voices. I heard Riley tell him to take something back to her room. Footsteps started down the hallway. I pulled my door open to catch Matt as he reached my doorway. He raised an eyebrow as I stood there with my arms crossed.

"What?" he whispered.

"Are you encouraging my sister to cause trouble?"

He raised an eyebrow. "How do you know it wasn't all her idea?"

"I know it probably was, but you clearly encouraged it." I tapped my fingers against my arm. "Are you coming to Thanksgiving dinner?" I knew the answer would be no. Riley had been keeping their relationship quiet out of some weird fear that he was going to leave her. There was no way that was going to happen, Matt's feelings for her were written so clearly on his face all the time.

He shifted the box in his arms. "We haven't talked about it."

"You should talk about it."

"Trust me, Emery, I want to. She's still working through things, and I don't want to push her before she's ready. I told you that I'm in this for the long run. I'm not going to rush things and risk scaring her away."

I poked a finger out toward him. "You need to stop being so gentle with her. She's going to keep dragging this out until you push her. I love my sister, but she isn't the type to take any chances."

He lowered his voice, his tone turning tense as he spoke, "I love her too, and I know she isn't ready. I'm going to keep loving her gently the way she needs me to."

My heart soared seeing the look that flashed across his face. This man was down bad for her. He was also stupid and way too nice. "She doesn't need to be handled with kid gloves. She needs to know how completely obsessed with her you are." My voice shook as I tried to keep it low enough for Riley not to be able to hear from the kitchen.

I heard the rack in the oven rattle like a pan had been shoved in a little too hard and then the oven door slammed closed. I held my breath, my finger still waving at Matt, as the look on his face turned sheepish. We could both feel Riley's eyes on us but neither dared to look toward the kitchen. How much had she heard?

"Be nice," I heard her yell. My eyes snapped to where she stood in the doorway between the kitchen and living room, her eyes narrowed at us for a moment before she disappeared.

I turned my attention back to Matt. "Don't break her heart and don't let her get away."

"I'm not going to. How many times do I have to tell you that?" He looked down at the box in his arms. "I bought the ring. I've been carrying it around every day waiting for the moment she tells me what she wants. I'm going to marry your sister, and I'm going to wait as long as it takes to let her get there."

Tears stung my eyes. "You're good for her, Matt. You're going to fit in well with our family. I couldn't think of someone better to be her husband and my brother-in-law." I gave his shoulder a shove before backing into my room and closing the door again.

I leaned against the door and closed my eyes. *Please don't let my sister make the same mistakes I did.*

Chapter 17

Emery

September Then

O LIVER MET ME IN the parking lot as I opened my door. I swear this man had some sort of radar for whenever I was nearby. I didn't even have to tell him I was coming by. I could show up and he would be there by my car before I even had time to notice him noticing me. He opened the passenger side door and pulled out the tray of cupcakes. I had been bringing baked goods over twice a week now since Oliver told me they had all been asking for more since that first batch. It had turned into my favorite Tuesday and Thursday errand.

He lifted the lid to peek inside. "What flavor do we have this week?"

I pressed the lid closed before he could grab one. "Go wash your hands first."

"I'm going to. Just wanted to know what amazing treat awaited me."

I rolled my eyes as he flashed a crooked smile. "It's September first, so logically they are pumpkin spice flavored."

"September isn't even fall, Emery. Pumpkin spice isn't even that good."

I waited for him to wrinkle his nose or point out that it was still summer, the ninety-two-degree high for today being a great reminder of that. Fall was my favorite season and as far as I was concerned if all the big companies had started pushing their pumpkin spice flavored things already, starting a little early with my own was fair game. This year I didn't have anyone to spoil my fun, so I was going to celebrate as long as I wanted.

"Hell yeah, I love pumpkin spice."

I beamed at him. "Really?"

He sat the tray back on the passenger seat and leaned in the car more. The scent of grease and sweat mixed with the clean scent of his deodorant filled the car. I wanted to lean in and breath it in, not sure when the combination became one that caused heat to stir in my stomach. He narrowed his eyes at me as he studied my face. "What kind of response were you expecting?"

I pulled my eyes away from him and focused on grabbing my things. I lifted up my insulated cup and reached for my purse on the floorboard. Oliver's hand grabbed the bag and the other nudged my shoulder. My skin buzzed from his touch. "Emery," he prodded.

I huffed. "I'm just used to the opposite, okay? People tell me it's silly to celebrate fall this early." I held up my cup filled with a hot pumpkin spice latte, a recipe I had been working on for a while. I'd never been able to have the real thing, so it was my best attempt. "I'm drinking hot coffee while it's still so hot and humid outside I felt sticky just walking between my house and car."

He didn't laugh like I expected him to, didn't even flash a smile. His jaw flexed, and his mouth tensed into a straight line. "It's not silly to enjoy things, Emery. Don't ever let anyone tell you the opposite again." His eyes heated, flaring with something that looked like anger. My brain spun as I tried to make out his expression. Why would he be angry about that? He held my gaze awaiting an answer.

I swallowed. "It's not that serious, Oliver," I choked out.

His jaw flexed tighter, the muscles bulging in a way that looked painful. "It is, Emery," the way he said my name was filled with exasperation and something else I couldn't distinguish.

I yanked my purse from his hand, the heat of his eyes becoming too much. "People are allowed to have their own opinions."

"They are, but it doesn't mean they get to ruin your joy for something." He pulled the cup from my hand and took a drink; my mouth fell open in shock. I watched his throat work as he swooshed it around his mouth tasting it and then swallowing. He put it back in my hand and leaned back out of the car. "I think I'm going to have to help you with that one, something is missing." His face appeared in the open door again. His mouth lifted in a smile as he reached across and pushed up my chin to close my mouth. He was so flirty today and I wanted more of whatever this was. More of him touching me. "Come on, I want to stay out here and hang out with you, but everyone has been waiting for these. You've got us all wrapped around your finger waiting for our cupcake fix."

Everyone was already in the lobby waiting for us to walk in. Oliver sat the tray on the counter pointed at his brother, "I get first dibs," he warned as he walked over to the bathroom to wash hands.

Granny smiled at me as she walked around to wrap me in a hug. "Did Oliver talk to you about the anniversary party?" She squeezed me so hard my ribs hurt. I squeezed her back. I learned the second time I was here that if I didn't hug her hard enough, she would squeeze harder. She was strong, always catching me off guard when I remember she was in her seventies.

All my grandparents passed away before I was born or when I was too young to remember. Granny had been filling that void I didn't know there was since I met her. Whenever I came by, I usually spent the hours until I had to go back to work up front with her. Seeing Oliver was great, but the time with Granny was just as special to me.

"No, he didn't mention anything," I said as I glanced over at him walking out of the bathroom. He flashed a smile at me as he rubbed his hands together and went straight for the tray. "The one in the middle has the most frosting," I called to him.

"We're doing a small little thing here at the shop next month to celebrate fifty years of business. I was thinking about bringing in some treats to share with customers that day. Pop was planning to do some raffles to bring people in."

"That sounds like a lot of fun," I told her as I gave her another squeeze before breaking the hug.

Oliver joined us and passed her a cupcake. He bit into his and frosting smeared on the tip of his nose and upper lip. I reached forward to wipe it away without thinking, just as Granny did the same. She smiled softly at me as she shifted her hand to give him a smack on the arm. "You were supposed to tell her about the anniversary party."

The look on Oliver's face turned sheepish. "You should come. It would be a great opportunity for you to drum up some interest in your food."

"Are you inviting me or asking me to bring something?"

He shrugged as he took another bite of the cupcake. "Both," he said with his mouth full. Granny smacked his arm again.

"Dear, we would love to have you spend the day with us and if you want, you're welcome to bring something. I'll also be providing lunch for all the employees for the day."

Oliver's face dropped as he turned to Granny shaking his head. "I told you about her food allergies," he whispered. His eyes swept over my face studying my reaction. He still came over every night for dinner, never pushing again to bring something or do the cooking. After our picnic lunch in the park, he seemed to understand better how self-conscious I was about my allergies.

It was nice to have someone to keep me company and share food with again.

"Actually, what if I bring lunch for everyone? It would be nice to get everyone's opinion on some lunch recipes." I dropped my eyes to the floor. I could bring in a hearty fall soup and some crusty sourdough. Next month meant all the apple houses would be open so I could do some apple-based desserts.

A hand patted my back. I looked up to see Oliver standing beside me smiling. "I can see the wheels turning in your head. Are you already planning out what you're bringing?"

I blushed and nodded. He laughed and looked at Granny. "What do you think?"

She patted both our shoulders. "I think it would be nice to not be the one doing all the cooking."

Oliver's arm slid around my shoulders, pulling me against him. He whispered a thank you into my ear and then held me there until someone started calling his name.

Chapter 18

Oliver

November Now

Ava

> brie said you're sick. let me know when you make it back home safe.

> do i need to bring you anything?

Oliver

> Calm down Mom I'm home it's just a little fever i'll be fine tmorrow

> what's your temp?

> idk

> Going to take a nap is that okay mom?

> you're such a big baby when you're sick

> emery will be over there soon. don't be an asshole to her.

T HE DOOR TO MY apartment creaked open. I groaned and pulled the throw blanket over my head. "No, I'm fine," I grunted and my throat burned from speaking. My pajamas felt like they were clinging to my clammy skin. I hadn't been back home for very long.

Aubrey had taken one look at me when she got to work this morning and practically forced me out the door. She claimed I looked like walking death. Wade and Drew had been quick to back her up. No one listened to me when I said that I was fine. I didn't get sick.

The couch cushions shifted under the weight of someone sitting down next to me. They peeled the blanket back from my face and pressed a soft hand against my forehead. The faint smell of vanilla filled my stuffy nose. I opened my eyes and was greeted by an angel.

Emery smiled down at me but it didn't reach her eyes. Her hair was pinned half up with one of those claw clip things but a few stray strands fell across her cheek. I reached up and smoothed the strands away. She was fucking pretty. "You look like shit," she declared. "When was the last time you took medicine?" She leaned forward and started pulling things from a canvas grocery bag on the floor by her feet.

My laugh turned into a cough. Every muscle in my body protested when I tried to cover my face. Emery dropped a hand to my back and rubbed soothing circles until the coughing fit passed. "I'm fine," I managed to say at last.

"You're sick."

"I don't get sick. I just need to rest and I'll be back to normal tomorrow."

She shook her head and tsked. The beeping of a thermometer felt like a knife driving into my aching skull. "Open up," she encouraged before slipping the thermometer into my mouth. "Looks like killing yourself at work is finally coming back to bite you." Cute little frown lines formed between her eyes watching the numbers go up.

I reached up and smoothed a thumb over the lines. She shouldn't be here. I was going to get her sick and I never wanted her to feel this bad. It felt like I had been ran over by a bus and then it backed up to ran me over again to make sure the job was done. I couldn't even remember the last time I was ever this sick.

"Your fever is way too high. Have you taken anything?" she asked again.

I tried to sit up but my vision tilted. Emery's hands pressed me back down onto the couch. "No. I was just going to let it run its course."

A bottle of cold and flu medicine appeared in her hand from that magical bag. She held it and packet of pills in front of my face. "Which one?"

The sight of the giant cold pills made the razor blades in my throat dig in harder. I pointed to the bottle of liquid. My head swam when I sat up enough to tip the little cup of medicine into my mouth.

Emery stood from the couch. "No," I pleaded.

She stepped close enough to bend over and press a kiss against my forehead. The brush of her lips against my skin filled my whole body with warm and butterflies. "I'm going to go warm up your soup and I'll be right back." Her thumb smoothed over my cheek making my eyes flutter closed.

"I want to take a nap," I mumbled. Soft lips pressed against my forehead again. "Don't want to get you sick."

***

My head rested on the softest pillow in the world. I snuggled in closer to it and pulled the blanket tighter around myself. In the background there were faint hums and blasts that sounded familiar. I lifted one arm over my head to block out the noise and pull the pillow even closer. A surprised squeal made my eyes snap open.

The pillow was Emery's stomach. My arm was stretched over her torso with my hand firmly squeezing one of her full tits. She looked down at me with wides eyes.

I scrambled off her, freshing pounding starting in my head and my muscles screaming. My arms shook under me from bracing myself over top of her. A louder blast sounded from the tv. I turned my attention to it to discover my favorite show playing. "I'm sorry...I..I" I stammered searching for anything to say.

"You get a pass because you're sick," she reassured me.

I shook my head. I couldn't believe I would just grab her without permission like that, sick or not.

Her hands fisted the blanket wrapped around my shoulders and pulled me back to laying against her. Once I was settled against her she dragged her fingertips through my hair. The movements soothed me until my eyes started to feel heavy again.

"You're a terrible patient by the way," she whispered. "But you still deserve to have someone take care of you."

My head felt heavy and foggy trying to make sense of her words. I couldn't remember anything other than her showing up this morning. Once glance at the window told me it was after dark now. An entire day together that I couldn't remember because of my stupid sick brain. "I'm sorry," I said again.

She shushed me and continued to play with my hair. "Go back to sleep, baby. Let your body have a break, okay?"

The scene on the tv reminded me of something I had been meaning to tell her. Over the past two years I'd been doing a terrible job of doing things that I enjoyed, but I had started fan fiction again. When the nights were long and sleep hard to come by while I struggled to lock away my emotions, fan fiction had become comforting escape.

"I started writing again," I told her. My throat burned and made my speech break. I kept my eyes on the tv, afraid to see her reaction even though she'd never given me a reason to be.

"Can I read it sometime?"

I tried my best to fight the sleep clouding my mind and focused on how right it felt to be with her like this. The familiar comfort of my favorite show in the background, her body under mine. The sex with her was always great but there was something extra special about the intimacy of just cuddling on the couch. Just like the intimacy of being in the kitchen together, cooking and cleaning while we talked about everything under the sun. I could listen to her talk for an eternity and still want more.

"I missed this," I muttered under my breath.

Emery's fingers still in my hair for a moment. The weight of sleep started to pull me under again and I struggled against it. Just a few more minutes. I need just a little longer here with her. I committed the feeling of how her chest rose and fell under me with each breath she took. The softness of her body against mine. The concern on her face that told me she still loved me. My eyelids grew heavier with every blink until I could force them open again.

"I missed this too," she whispered as I let myself fall back into the blackness of sleep.

Chapter 19

Oliver

December Now

MATT SWUNG THE DOOR of his car open once I confirmed he was pulled on the rack correctly. "So why does Shelby keep telling me Emery has been coming by the shop a lot lately?" he asked.

I motioned for him to get out. "Twice is not a lot."

He smirked as he squinted at me. "She's not been at home much lately. Any idea why that is?" He climbed out and slammed the door behind him. He knew all about all the times that Emery had been by late at night to check on me when the others told her I was working too late. He had sent her at least once himself.

I had no idea if Emery had told her sister about the restaurant. She said they were best friends, but to me it seemed like Riley was with Matt and didn't know anything that was happening in her sister's life.

I crossed my arms and shrugged. "Probably has something to do with you and Riley always being up each other's ass." The two of them were worse than teenagers. They couldn't be in the same room without touching and couldn't go twenty-four hours without seeing each other.

He sat in my rolling chair and propped his feet up on my tool cart. "You sound jealous." I smacked his feet until he put them back on the ground.

"Emery and I aren't back together. And Shelby wasn't supposed to say anything about her coming by here." I walked around the rack making sure his car was secure.

"Oh, there's something going on between them," Drew yelled from under the car he was working on. "You should have heard them arguing in his office a couple of weeks ago."

I smacked my head against the side of Matt's car. "Why are all of you people so fucking nosy?"

"Look, I'm sure Emery is a lot of work, but I think you should give things another chance."

I glared at Matt as I hit the button to lift his car up. "That's not up to me. You know she's the one that ended things." Emery wasn't a lot of work, and I hated that he would say something like that. She was brash and that was one of my favorite things about her even though others had made her feel like she had to shrink that part of herself.

The door to the lobby swung open and Aubrey came out carrying a ticket. "You've got an oil change and rotate specifically requesting you. I told her that you would be a few minutes." She held the ticket out to me with a raised eyebrow and tossed her long red braid over her shoulder. I snatched it from her hand looking at the name.

"Are you kidding me right now?" I mumbled the letters of her name blurred together and my heart thudded. Just what I needed.

The door swung open again. This time Emery stepped out into the shop wearing something that was either a long sweater or a very short dress over a pair of opaque tights. Her eyes widened when she saw Matt. Matt made a motion like he was zipping up his mouth. Aubrey and Drew laughed. I looked in the window to the lobby hoping to wave down Wade for back up, but he was busy arguing with Shelby.

Emery's mouth moved like she was trying to speak but the words wouldn't come. She gestured with her thumb over her shoulder. "I'm just going to come back later," she croaked out. I wanted to run to her and pull her into my office again. Kiss her. Fuck her. Fight with her. Whatever she would give me.

The two weeks of helping her with the restaurant had been excruciating. It had been taking everything in me to keep my hands to myself. To wait for her to bring us up.

We hadn't been back since the day she'd left without telling me what was wrong. She brushed me off again that night when my worry had gotten the better of me and I texted her. That had been the week before Thanksgiving and now here we were in the middle of December. Other than her coming over to take care of me while I was sick we hadn't talked any during that time. Part of me was convinced I dreamed her being there taking care of me. I'd spent the last two weeks trying to figure out how we went from her caring for me to no contact.

Then it hit me that Matt had said she hadn't been home much. Was she working on the restaurant by herself? Did I do something to make her decide she didn't want my help after all?

My hand went to the chain under my shirt, running over the ridges of my grandparents' wedding rings, remembering how Pop had made me promise to fight for Emery. I pushed past Aubrey and headed straight for Emery. I grabbed her hand and pulled her to my office, not caring how rough I was being.

I slammed the door and twisted the lock, then grabbed her hips to press her against it. A shocked gasp escaped her mouth. "What are you doing?" she asked.

What was I doing? I didn't know. All I knew was the waiting was killing me. My heart felt so raw from all the grief being at the restaurant brought to the surface and it wrecked my ability to regulate any of my other emotions. All the time we were spending together only reminded me of how much I couldn't control myself around her. I was done trying to ignore it.

"I don't know." I squeezed her hips, resisting the urge to push the sweater up. "I need to kiss you. Just one more time. Can I?" If she was working on the restaurant without me, that meant my opportunity to win her back was slipping away. Dammit, I should have made a move sooner. I'd been too focused on taking things slow, so I didn't scare her off that I'd probably missed my only chance. She gulped as she nodded, her pupils blew out and her hips pressed back against me.

Our mouths collided like an explosion, our teeth and tongues fighting for control. Her hands dug into my back, and I could feel her nails through the fabric of my shirt. Her lipstick smeared between us. She bit my lip hard enough I tasted blood. I groaned. She was so feisty, so angry, as she took what she needed from me. I bunched her sweater in my hands, fighting my need to take this further. Her hands found my shoulders and pushed me away.

We stood there, both panting, and stared at each other. She looked so pretty like this, chest heaving as she pressed back into the door, red lipstick smeared everywhere. "Fuck. Why do you have to be so good at that?" She pressed the heels of her hands into her eyes.

I lifted the right side of my mouth in a smile, the way I knew used to drive her crazy. I didn't hide how I adjusted myself in my pants.

She dropped her hands to the hem of her sweater and tugged it down as far as she could. "I knew you would like this one."

I groaned and looked at the ceiling. "Are you trying to kill me? I haven't heard from you in weeks, Em."

She feigned innocence. "My car needed an oil change. You do a better job than the other places." She twisted the hem of her sweater. "And I was going to tell you that I'm coming over on Wednesday." Her hands covered her face as she pressed her head back into the door. "Oh my god, Matt is here. Aubrey could have warned me. He's going to tell Riley."

I wrapped my hands around her wrists and pulled her hands away from her face. "He's not going to tell her."

"Oliver, they know what we're doing in here. Hell, they probably think we're doing more! You don't know what your face looked like when you stalked your way over to me."

I pinned her back against the door, running my thumb over her bottom lip and smearing her lipstick even more. I hoped my mouth looked as messy as hers. "What did my face look like?"

"Like you were going to fuck my brains out." She brushed her thumb against my bottom lip. "We look like that's what happened."

I opened the cabinet on the wall next to us and pulled out a roll of paper towels. "I guess you better clean up your mouth if you don't want them to know."

She shoved the roll away and then shoved my shoulders until I released her. She squatted down to retrieve the job ticket with her keys. "I told you I don't like being told what to do."

Emery turned toward the door. The lock clicked free when she twisted the knob.

"Are you working on the restaurant without me?" I blurted.

Her shoulders stiffened. "Just working on ideas. Don't worry, I won't do any actual work without you."

I rubbed a hand over my beard and resisted the urge to pull her back to me. "Okay, yeah, good. I'll see you on Wednesday."

Just like that she stomped out of my office and then strutted out of the shop, that sweater threatening to show her ass with every step she took.

I tore off a paper towel and cleaned her lipstick from my mouth. Wade had already started on Matt's car by the time I rejoined them. Everyone else stood around with their eyes wide.

"Don't tell Riley," I barked at Matt.

He held his hands up and mimed zipping his mouth again.

Aubrey tapped her foot and crossed her arms. "Do you really think this is a good idea, Oliver? None of us want to see you get hurt like last time." I rolled my eyes at her, knowing that Ava would be blowing up my phone soon.

"I'm not letting her get away this time," I said.

Aubrey glared at me as Drew moved to stand beside her. He held out his hand and tapped his palm. She pulled a folded bill from her pocket and slapped it into her hand. Matt laughed so hard he wheezed. I kicked the leg of his chair, sending him rolling backwards. He jumped up and walked out the side door of the shop.

Chapter 20

Emery

December Now

I PULLED THE SMALL makeup pouch I kept for emergencies out of my bag. "Shit," I said when I looked in the mirror. Lipstick was smeared around my mouth and chin. My mascara had smudged under my eyes. I pulled a makeup removing wipe from the pack and started rubbing away the red around my mouth.

The passenger side door opened, and Matt dropped into the seat. The tube of concealer I dotted over my clean skin slipped from my hand. I glared into the mirror and used my ring finger to blend it. "What are you doing?"

He folded his hands in his lap. "Things were getting heated in there. I thought I would come hang out with my sister-in-law instead."

"I'm not your sister-in-law yet."

He drummed his fingers against his leg. "Not yet, but you will be." He sat in silence while I used the makeup wipe to clean off my finger.

I wadded the wipe up and shoved it into the bag I kept tucked in my door for trash. I sat back in my seat and dug the heels of my hands into my eyes. My body felt like a mix of contradicting emotions, and I could feel a good cry coming. "You can leave now," I told him.

"I wasn't around for the first time you and Oliver were together, and he hasn't been forthcoming with the details." He drummed his fingers again and rested his head back to stare at the roof of my car. "Were things always this tense between you two?"

A laugh sputtered out of me, the kind that made my whole body shake and my chest ache. It felt like crying in the form of laughter. "We weren't together. We were friends with benefits. Things were, well not like this."

"No, according to him you were together."

"He got confused, that was the problem."

We sat in silence for a few minutes until I saw Matt shift out of the corner of my eye. I turned toward him, resting my cheek against the head rest. Those kind blue eyes of his stared into mine. "Do you think I'm confused for falling in love with your sister?" He pushed his glasses up with one finger.

I faced the roof again. "It's not the same situation and you know it."

"It is the same situation. Riley and Oliver haven't told me your story, but I've figured out enough on my own to know you've been hurt in the past and you're scared to let someone get close again." He gripped the door handle. "Stop dragging my best friend around. You're both adults, and you're going to do whatever you want to, but make sure there's no room for 'confusion' this time." He got out of the car and slammed the door behind him. Matt walked halfway back to the shop but then turned around and motioned with two fingers toward his eyes, then pointed toward me.

I pressed my head back against the head rest and half laughed, half cried to myself. What the hell just happened?

I think Matt just turned all the shit I give him back on me.

Chapter 21

Oliver

September Then

I COULDN'T TAKE MY eyes off Emery relaxing on her couch. The tight short dress she wore today rode up her thighs enough that I could see she wasn't wearing shorts under it like she normally did. An oversized cardigan slouched off one shoulder showing skin covered in tattoos that drove me crazy. Agreeing to just be friends while she worked out what she wanted had been such a terrible idea.

I had been up front about my attraction to her from the beginning and she didn't try very hard to hide she felt the same way about me. A sharp prick against my fingertip pulled my attention back to the dishes I was supposed to be washing. Blood beaded at the end of my middle finger from a small knife nick.

"What do you want to watch tonight?" Emery asked from the couch. She asked me that every night and I always let her pick. I spent more time watching her reactions than to whatever played on the tv anyways.

"We could watch the next episode of *Gilmore Girls* if you want." I tore a paper towel from the roll on the counter and applied pressure to the cut.

"Come on, Ollie, we've watched what I wanted to every night. What's your favorite show?" She twisted around to face me, the dress riding up even more.

I sucked in a breath and looked away from the soft thighs I was dying to get my hands on. From here I couldn't make out the details of the ink that covered them, but I didn't have the self-control needed to get a closer look.

Just friends.

Her eyes fixed on the paper towel I clutched against my finger. The name of my favorite show faded from my brain watching her pull her dress down while walking toward me. This was my favorite show. She pulled open a small drawer and dug around until she pulled a band aid free.

The first touch of her hand on mine took my breath away. "It's already stopped bleeding," I tried to say.

"Just to be safe," she replied. She smoothed the band aid around my finger and then lifted it to her mouth. Her lips ghosted over the bandage in a gentle kiss that felt far less innocent than it was.

I shifted my stance and tried to keep my breath steady. My favorite show. I still hadn't answered her. I tried to redirect my thoughts to anything other than the woman in front of me. "*Andromeda Portal,*" I whispered. It was my secret guilty pleasure show. "I was obsessed with it as a teenager."

"Hmm, you don't strike me as a sci-fi nerd. How obsessed? Are we talking about writing fan fiction and going to cons level of obsessed?"

"Yes. And posters in my room." Maybe if she knew how much of a secret nerd I was we could put a stop to this tension between us.

She cocked a brow at me. "Do you still write fan fiction?" Her hand still gripped mine and I could feel her touch everywhere. Since the day she walked into the shop she had completely captivated my attention. I hadn't even opened any of the dating apps on my phone. Two months was a long dry spell for me, and it was starting to get to me.

My face heated and I cleared my throat. "No, I stopped after my mom caught me." It hadn't been anything super graphic like some fan fiction out there. The 200 thousand word fic was mostly a self-insert slow burn. The main actor had been my first celebrity crush and my bi-awakening.

My mom just happened to walk into my room the day that I finally wrote a kissing scene. She called it gay porn and grounded me for a month. She also banned me from ever watching the show again. I went along with it silently, never telling anyone, because she promised not to tell my dad if didn't make a big deal about it.

After that I would watch the show at Matt's house but it always felt a little tainted by the bitter memory.

"Well, that's disappointing. I love reading fan fic."

"Emery, are you secretly a nerd?"

She held up her fingers in a slightly parted pinch. "A tiny bit." Her hand released mine and she leaned against the counter. "Will you tell me about it while we watch?"

"Only if you promise not to judge me." I turned my attention back to the remaining dishes in the sink. "And not tell anyone."

Emery pressed a hand over her heart. "I promise. Your secrets are safe with me."

I kept my gaze turned to the sink while I told her everything. I started with the background information about the show and eased into details about my fic. The next thing I knew I was coming out about my bisexuality, something I hadn't really done despite claiming the label for so long. No one I was close to knew. After the incident with my mom I had been too scared to tell anyone.

Even after my sister came out as a lesbian and my cousin Wade as pan, I still kept my secret. I was always the problem child in the family. Adding being queer on top of that felt like it would make me too much of a disappointment.

My relationship with my parents was already strained enough without giving them one more reason to look down on me.

I'd grown so used to keeping the secret I hadn't even told my best friend even though I knew he would accept me no matter what. He thought my parents didn't want me watching the show or going to cons because it was science fiction and they were too religious to be okay with that. Letting it out felt like a weight lifting from my shoulders. Relief settled over me and I braved a look in Emery's direction. She smiled softly at me and opened her arms wide. I let her pull me into a hug, her soft embrace feeling like the safest place I'd ever been.

"Thank you for trusting me," she said. My heart swelled in my chest.

"Thank you for letting me talk about it," I told her. I squeezed my arms around her tighter, not ready to let her go just yet.

Chapter 22

Emery

December Now

R ILEY ADDED THE ANOTHER freshly wrapped present to the growing pile next to her. She stretched her arms out behind her and leaned back, letting out a long groan. "I think we're getting too old to keep doing this on the floor," she complained.

My own shoulders and back ached from the prolonged about of time in the floor wrapping Christmas presents for our family. My sister and I didn't do anything half ass, including spoiling our family. She even had a sizable pile of gifts just for Matt. She presented each one to me beaming and blushing before wrapping them. Love looked good on Riley.

I couldn't help but wonder if I had the same look on my face when I thought about Oliver. My lips and body still buzzed from the memory of him pressing me against the door yesterday. Maybe it was time for us to stop trying to deny the chemistry that still existed between us and just fuck already. A memory of his head between my thighs and all the things his mouth made me feel flashed across my mind.

"So, is Matt coming to Christmas with you?"

Riley rolled her eyes the way she did every time I tried to push the subject of her keeping Matt a secret. The two of them were perfect for each other. It had been obvious since the moment I caught them at the festival during their first date over the summer and helped keep our family distracted while they escaped that they were a soulmates. Even before that while they were just messaging on the dating app I forced her to sign up for, I knew that he was the one for her. I'd never seen anyone make her look so love sick.

Something gnawed at the pit of my stomach. Guilt, maybe? Here I was always trying to push my sister out of her comfort zone and stop lying to herself about her relationship with Matt while I was doing the exact same thing with Oliver.

I wanted things to go back to how they were between us before everything fell apart. Hell, I wanted things to be better than they were then. I wanted him to fall in love with me and let myself fall for him. Yet, the fear of history repeating itself still haunted me. What if we tried for real this time and he realized that I wasn't really worth it? Or if the other shoe dropped and I broke his heart all over again.

I never wanted to hurt him like that again.

In front of me Riley twisted tape around her fingers. Her wild curls fell across her face but couldn't hide the uncertainty on her face. "I think I love him, Em."

The wrapping paper in my handle crinkled and tore. My heart pounded against my chest. I had been waiting on her to make that confession for six months but the fear that twisted her mouth made it all feel wrong. "He's good to you, right? Like I know he is when I'm around, but he's not different when it's just the two of you?" I prodded. Matt was the sweetest man ever. Even the way Oliver talked about him convinced me that he was a literal angel. But no one ever caught on to how Levi was behind closed door and I would go to the ends of the Earth to make sure my sister never ended up in the same situation.

Riley shook her head with enough force to make her curls whip around. "No, he's perfect." She sighed and the blush on her cheeks deepened. "I didn't know someone could be so perfect for me. But what if I'm not enough for him? What happens when he finally wakes up realizes I'm just a waste of his time?"

I wadded up the torn wrapping paper and threw it towards her. It bounced off her forehead and her eyes widened. "Stop being mean to my sister. Don't forget, you're also the sweetest person ever. You're just as perfect for him. Everytime I think that man couldn't be more disgustingly in love with you he proves me wrong."

As if the universe was trying to prove a point Riley's phone lit up on the floor next to her with an incoming call from Matt. She bit her bottom lip and flicked her eyes up to me as if asking for permission. "I'll make it quick. I know we promised no phones."

I waved my hand at her and she raced down the hall to her room. The two of them were inseparable and I knew it must be driving her crazy not having him here tonight. I pulled out my own phone and pulled up my text thread with Oliver. My nails clicked against the back of the case while I tried to think of something to say to him. We used to text all the time but since he came back into my life we hadn't really been able to get that part of our relationship back. I desperately wanted his flirt messages blowing up my phone again.

Emery

I can't stop thinking about tomorrow.

Oliver

> Are you going to drool over my forearms the whole time?

> Might change it up an drool over your hands instead.

> Are you flirting with me right now?

> You pushed me up against a door and kissed me breathless yesterday.

> I knew you loved that.

> And I'd do it again. All you have to do is ask. Along with all those other things you love.

I clenched my thighs together. How was it this fucking easy to slip back into texting each other things like that? We shouldn't be doing this.

Riley cleared her throat drawing my attention away from my phone. I dropped it face down on the floor like it burned my palm. "Who are you texting?" she asked with a cocked brow.

I shook my head and struggled to stop the images swirling around in my mind. "Nobody. You never answered my question about Matt," I reminded her.

We glared at each other, caught in a standoff of who would break first. We both looked away at the same time. Riley reached for the next unwrapped item in our pile. It was a lego set for our nephew Aaron that I had spent hours searching online for. Silence settled heavy around both of us. It had been a long time since the two of us had kept secrets from each other. Normally we were the type of best friends that called each other just to update each other on the minute details of our day just because we had to share everything.

I couldn't tell her about Oliver yet, not when there was a chance she would say something to Matt about it. The last thing I needed was for Oliver to find out about my lingering feelings through a secondhand source. "Remember how I used to talk about opening a resturant?" I asked breaking the silence.

Riley's mouth stretched into a wide smile. "Are you going to do it for real?"

I shrugged my shoulders as if I hadn't been spending every night for the past month sitting in my car outside the restaurant poring over my notebooks containing years of ideas trying to condense them into something made sense. "Maybe. Nothing is set in stone yet, but I'm working on it."

My sister launched herself over the supplies between us and tackled me to the floor. My back hit the hard surface with enough force to knock the breath out of me. "Oh my god, I'm so proud of you. It's going to be amazing. Can I help? I can't believe you're finally doing it!"

I beamed and wrapped my arms around her. There were still so many secrets between us but it was a relief to have any this tiny truth out in the open. I still felt so uncertain about making my dream come true. Now I had the support of my sister and Oliver. Somehow just having the two of them cheering me on made the impending chance of failure feel just a little smaller.

Chapter 23

Emery

September Then

> I want to cook for you. Come over to my apartment tonight.

> I don't know.

> You can watch so you know everything is safe if it'll make you feel better.

> My kitchen is completely free of all your allergens.

> Has been for weeks.

> Why?

> I got rid of everything you're allergic to the night you told me.

> Had to make sure my apartment is safe for you.

> Why?

> Because you're my friend.

> Why do you want to cook for me?

> Because I want to. I don't think I need more of a reason than that.

> Sounds suspicious.

> Woman please. Just come over tonight.

> Apartment 2F. I won't even make you do the dishes.

I SHIFTED MY WEIGHT from one foot to the other while I waited for Oliver to open his door.

If something goes wrong, we can just go to my apartment.

The ingredients for what I had planned to cook tonight were ready to go in my fridge, all I had to do was pull them out. It wasn't that big of a deal. If I walked in and saw any red flags I could leave. I shifted my weight again, closed my eyes, and started to count to ten.

The door popped open. Oliver's hand wrapped around my wrist and pulled me in. I opened my eyes as the door closed behind me. He squeezed my wrist. "I know you're nervous, but I promise I did so much research and have scrubbed this entire apartment multiple times this week to make sure it would be safe."

"You didn't have to do that," I said..

He shook his head and pulled his brows together. "I did. You deserve to be treated to dinner too. I wasn't kidding when I said I got rid of everything that you're allergic to that first night."

My heart squeezed and my stomach flipped. Just friends. That's all we could be right now. "Oliver, we're just friends."

He pointed to his nose. "I told you that I'll do anything I need to for my friends." He lifted the right side of his mouth in a slight smile as he released my wrist. "I haven't even started cooking yet. If I do anything that might hurt you, I need you to tell me. I want you to know that you're safe and allowed to ask for whatever you need."

I followed him to his kitchen. His apartment was identical to mine. Small, with an open room that acted as the kitchen, dining, and living rooms. On the wall to the right of the front doors there were doors for the bathroom and bedroom. The flooring changed from LVT to tile to mark the transition between "rooms". He pulled a chair from his small table and spun it around. "Chair or counter?" he asked.

He didn't have much furniture. The living room consisted of just a couch, coffee table, and a small tv stand with narrow shelves on either side of the tv. One side held a gaming console and several game cases. The other was filled with mismatched picture frames. I pulled my attention from where I had focused on the photos sitting on the shelves next to his tv. "What?"

"Do you want to sit in a chair to watch or on the counter?"

"I can just stand. It'll be easier." I smoothed my hands over the tight mini skirt I wore. It hit mid thigh and was too short to wear any shorts under. I'd been getting braver with the things I wore around him, almost like I was testing just how committed he was to keeping things strictly platonic between us.

He marched over to where I stood and wrapped his hands around my wrists, his thumbs rubbing in circles against my skin. "It's already bad enough that you have to supervise. You're at least going to sit down and relax." He tugged me over to the chair and pressed my shoulders until I sat down.

"It's really fine, Oliver. I'd rather be cooking than watching."

He patted the top of my head, making my face heat. I grabbed his wrist and pulled his hand away. He bent down to look me in the eyes. "I know you would, but you deserve to be spoiled too."

Fuck, he was so close. I could feel the heat radiating off his body. My fingers tightened around his wrist. "We're just friends," I said slowly, stressing each word as I studied his eyes.

"You keep saying that, Em. I'm starting to think that you're trying to convince yourself, not me."

I swallowed and unfolded my fingers from around his wrist. "You keep acting like it's something more."

His mouth turned down as his jaw flexed. "Sometimes you make me think that you're not used to people being nice to you." He bent over more, getting close enough that he braced his hands on the back of the chair. The clean scent of his body wash wrapped around me. "Why do you think I think we're more than friends?"

My mouth went dry. I moved my tongue around trying to work up saliva. "You're really close for someone that is just a friend." The heat of having him this close brought me back to the moment in my kitchen two nights ago.

I'd kissed his finger after he cut it and the gesture flooded me with so much need I hadn't been able to let go of his hand. The way heat flared in his eyes only made it worse.

When I tried to change the subject, he trusted me with his biggest secret. The hug we shared after had been the best hug of my life. Once he was gone for the night the ghost of his arms around me lingered and I craved his touch again.

We weren't just friends. Friends didn't flirt with each other as much as we did. Friends didn't find excuses to stretch dinner plans late into the night watching one more episode after another so we could avoid the goodbye just a little longer.

"You're letting me awfully close for someone that only wants to keep me as a friend," Oliver pointed out. Fuck, he was so close I could feel his breath on my face.

"I'm not ready for a relationship."

One of his hands moved from the back of the chair to tuck my hair behind my ear. "But you want something more than friendship."

I swallowed again and nodded.

His eyelids were heavy as he let his focus dip down to my mouth and then back up to my eyes. The hand in my hair moved down to my neck, resting against the side as his thumb stroked my jaw. "Tell me what you need."

I pressed my back against the chair. "I feel like we're supposed to be something more."

"Me too."

"I don't know what I need right now, just that I'm not in a place for a relationship."

He nodded slowly, his eyes hypnotizing me as they bounced between my mouth and eyes. His pupils were blown out as his eyes caught mine once again. "Figure out what works for you and let me know." He started to straighten up, his fingers brushing over my neck as he pulled his hand away.

My eyes fixed on his mouth as he moved, want gnawed at my stomach in a way I hadn't felt since before my ex left me. The hair above his upper lip curled down over it. I wanted to know what it would feel like rubbing against my mouth. My hands shot up on their own and bracketed his face, pulling him back to me. "Can I figure it out later? Right now, I really just need you to kiss me."

His mouth lifted in that crooked smile as he slid his hand back to my neck. "Just this one time." His tongue flicked out and over his lips. Electricity shot through me watching it. "I'm going to kiss you once and then I'm going to cook you dinner. Nothing else until you can tell me what you want."

I nodded my agreement and tried to lean in to close the distance. His hand on my neck held me still. "Ollie, please, kiss me," I begged.

"Yes, baby," he said as he brought our mouths together.

Holy. Fuck. His hand stayed on my neck, that thumb brushing over my jaw. He kissed me slowly at first and his beard scratched ever so slightly against my skin. I opened my mouth and tilted my head up begging for more. He teased my lips with his teeth and tongue as I pressed our mouths together harder.

The way he called me baby echoed in my head. No one had ever called me that. I didn't even know it was something I wanted until the word left his mouth.

My hands slid from his face down to his shoulders as I pulled him closer, sliding my tongue against his. My skin danced with electricity. I pushed him back so I could stand and pull him against me. His hand that had been braced against the chair went to my waist, teasing the top of my skirt and holding me steady.

He pulled his mouth from mine and rested our foreheads together.

"Oliver," I pleaded.

He stroked my cheek. "That's it, baby, that's all you get right now."

"Keep calling me that," I breathed. "I like the way you sound when you call me baby." My face heated as the words left my mouth, so I buried it in the space between his neck and shoulder.

His arms pulled me tight against him in an embrace. "Noted," he said with a small laugh. I shifted my face so one eye was uncovered to look up at him. He smiled at me softly.

My next thought hit me like a train, reminding me that aside from telling him to kiss me we hadn't talked about anything else. *I threw out everything you're allergic to.* He didn't say he stopped eating it.

"Ollie, any chance you've eaten anything that I'm allergic to recently?"

He pulled back, lifting my face with his forefinger and thumb so my eyes met his. "I told you I threw everything out."

"But have you eaten it recently, like at work or anything?"

A blush climbed up his neck and he cleared his throat. "I did some research about allergies and," he paused to clear his throat again. "And I read about people with severe allergies having reactions after kissing someone that ate what they're allergic to. I've been avoiding eating it all together." His thumb brushed over my bottom lip, pressing and then dragging it downward making my head spin.

I grinned and pushed his shoulder, the arm around my waist tightening to keep us pressed together. "Been planning on kissing me?"

"Just wanted to be prepared for if the opportunity presented itself." His eyes dipped to my mouth as his thumb pressed into my lip again,

"If you keep doing that, we're not stopping with just the one kiss," I said, exaggerating the movements of my mouth until the tip of his thumb slid against the inside of my lip.

He closed his eyes and leaned his forehead against mine again, his hand moved around to tangle in the back of my hair. I could feel him growing hard between us, the want in me growing stronger. His fingers in my hair tugged as he lifted to press a kiss to my forehead, the subtle movement making the sweet gesture feel charged.

He pulled away and pressed me back down into the chair. "Sit here and talk to me while I cook," he said, tugging at my hair again until I looked up at his face instead of at the bulge pressed against his pants.

I raised an eyebrow at him. "I told you I don't like being told what to do."

He huffed. "I told you that sometimes you're just going to have to get used to it." He smoothed his finger over my raised eyebrow until I relaxed it. "Let me take care of you, baby, please."

I bit my tongue to hold in the argument forming in my head. "What are you cooking?" I asked instead.

He picked up a binder from the counter and flipped through the pages, the paper protectors crinkling as he did. He held it out to me showing me a printed-out recipe. "This is option one," he flipped the page, "and this is option two."

I took the binder from him and flipped through the other pages. My eyes caught on phrases like dairy free and nightshade free. There were some recipes that called for avocado, and he had crossed it out and written in substitutions. One called for ghee, but he had already crossed it out, writing in coconut oil or vegan butter without avocado oil. My hands started to shake. "What is all this?" I whispered as I rustled the pages back and forth.

"I told you I did some research."

"Oliver Thomas Franklin, this is not just doing some research."

He squatted down in front of me, his face red as he laughed. "Did you just pick a random middle name to full name me with?"

I poked a finger against the binder in my lap. "This is serious," I tried to steady my voice, but it shook with panic anyways. I pressed my tongue against the roof of my mouth and took a deep breath.

"My middle name is James, by the way. If you're going to full name me, at least use the right one." He pried my fingers from the binder and turned the pages back to the options he had presented me with. "One or two?" he asked.

"Oliver!" I scolded him.

He let out an exasperated huff. "Emery."

"Why do you have a book of safe recipes?"

"Because I wanted to. Do you have any more redundant questions or are you going to make a decision?"

I crossed my arms and shifted back against the chair. The binder started to slide from my lap. Oliver caught it and pushed it back up, flipping the page back and forth again. I rolled my eyes.

He stood up and took the binder with him back to the counter. "That's fine, I'll pick. I'm thinking this lemon chicken with orzo sounds pretty good."

I snorted. "I'm surprised someone whose favorite sandwich involves bologna knows what orzo is."

He spun around to face me, crossing his arms over this chest. His jaw flexed as one side of his mouth lifted in a cocky grin. "Oh, she's got an attitude now. For your information, I've cooked with it before."

"I've had an attitude this whole time," I muttered. I narrowed my eyes in a glare hoping he couldn't see how much I wanted to pin him against the counter and kiss that crooked mouth. Or for him to pin me against the counter.

He tapped the fingers of his left hand against his right bicep before dropping his arms. "I like it." He lifted a finger and gestured to a coloring book on the counter. "I got you that, if you want to color while I cook."

***

Oliver stood and picked up our empty plates. I stood with him, trying to pull them from his hands. "You cooked, I do the dishes," I told him.

He stacked the plates together, so he had a hand free to push me back down into my chair. "I told you that I'm not making you do the dishes."

"There aren't even that many," I complained. "You washed half of them while you were cooking." It was hot and sort of irritating how smoothly he had moved around the kitchen as he cooked. This was a man that cooked on the regular, not someone that relied solely on fast food or frozen meals like most single men I had met did.

He researched recipes and put together an entire binder of options.

He cleaned as he cooked. I didn't even do that.

He didn't even ask for help as he had cooked. He just let me color while he worked and we chatted about our day.

"And now I'm going to wash the rest of them."

I rolled my eyes but stayed in the chair. As much as I wanted to fight until he let me do something other than insist on taking care of me, I wanted to get him out of this kitchen and onto the couch for other activities more. I tapped my foot impatiently against the floor.

"You alright over there?" he asked as he placed a plate in the drying rack.

"Just waiting on you." I stood from the chair and moved to look at the photos on his tv stand. Most were of him with his grandparents and siblings at various ages. There was one of him holding a pair of drum sticks with one hand and his other arm around a taller blonde boy that was all long limbs, big teeth covered by a mouthful of braces, and big ears holding a saxophone. Next to that was a picture of the two of them at high school graduation.

I felt Oliver move behind me. He wrapped his arms around my waist to pull me against him as he rested his chin on my shoulder. "I'm going to assume this is Matt," I said pointing at the photos.

"Do you understand now why I had to take a trombone to the face for him?" His breath tickled my ear. I leaned back into him.

"I understand what you mean by as awkward as it gets."

He brushed his lips over my neck. "As much as I want to talk to you about my family, there are other things I would rather talk about right now." His callused fingers scraped against the waistband of my skirt and the fabric of the shirt tucked into it.

"Like the fact that you've been keeping it a secret that you can cook?" I teased, trying to cover how my breath caught with every brush of his fingers.

The pressure of him against my back pulled away and his hands spun me by my hips to face him. My hands went to his wrists and then slid up to those forearms that had been driving me crazy since that first day. "I spent a lot of time at Granny and Pop's house growing up. She insisted that all of us know how to cook well enough to get by as adults." His eyes dropped to my hands on his arms. "Compared to you I'm –"

"Watching you cook was kind of hot," I interrupted him. I pushed my hands up his arms, squeezing my way up to his biceps until my fingers dipped under the sleeves of his shirt. That earned me a smile and his eyes on my lips. I leaned forward to catch his mouth with mine, but he leaned away. "I want to kiss you again," I pouted.

"Not until we talk."

His hands moved to my wrists and pulled my hands from his arms. "Talking is overrated, I'd rather make out with you instead," I complained as he led me to the couch. He sat down and then pulled me down onto his lap. I wiggled against him until his hands moved back to my hips to hold me still.

"Tell me what you want this to be."

"I don't know." I bit the inside of my mouth. His face tensed as I wiggled against him again, his eyes staring into mine prodding for something more. "I'm not in a place for a relationship right now, so we can't go there." My hands dropped to my lap, and I rubbed the edge of my skirt between my thumb and forefinger. "I wouldn't mind exploring physical things with you."

One of his hands moved to mine, settling over the hand worrying with the edge of my skirt. His thumb stroked over the back of my hand, an electric shock shooting up my arm straight to my heart. "Are we talking about a friends with benefits situation?" He paused for me to nod. "Tell me what that looks like for you."

"Two friends that also happen to enjoy each other's bodies," I answered. I flipped my hand over and tangled my fingers with his. "I think that's pretty straight forward."

He tucked my hair behind my ear. "What are the rules?"

I rolled my eyes and let out an awkward laugh. "Why do we need rules?"

"It's always good to have rules, baby. We're not doing this without clear boundaries."

I turned around until I straddled him. The new position made my shirt ride up my thighs. The hand that I held moved to rest on my thigh and that distracting thumb started brushing over the butterfly tattoo that took up the majority of the skin there. "No sleepovers. No dates or labels. We're just hanging out and making each other feel good. This stays between us, so no PDA."

His eyes held mine. "Sounds good to me. Just so we're clear, I'm not much of a relationship guy so you're not saying anything I'm not used to." His statement felt jarring after spending so much time together. The Oliver I've gotten to know would make such a perfect boyfriend.

Ava's comment at the salon that day resurfaces in my memory. Even then it didn't fit with the impression I had of him.

"Do you have any rules?" I asked.

"You're in charge here. I want clear communication about anything you like or don't like."

I leaned in closer to him as I covered his hand with mine, dragging it further up my thigh. "What if I don't want to be in charge? What if I want you to just have your way with me?" I dropped my eyes to his mouth to see his tongue dart out over his lips.

"Then you tell me that." One of his hands snaked into the back of my hair, fingers tangling with the strands and pulling. "What about protection?"

"Condoms are a must. My body hates birth control so I'm not on it anymore." I paused and locked my eyes with his. "I'm allergic to latex so we have to use the latex free kind."

His fist left my hair and moved to smooth the tense muscles in my jaw. "Okay, that's fine. Do you have any at your apartment?"

I shook my head. Oliver would be the first person I'd been with since my breakup, and before that my ex and I hadn't been using any protection for a long time. Memories of negative pregnancy tests flashed across my mind. Then the positive that made me feel like for once something in my life was going right.

Until it ended in an ultrasound room, my doctor delivering the news with a business like demeanor as if my whole world wasn't collapsing. The final straw in an already unstable relationship. I had the ring, the happily ever after, and it all crumbled away.

"You're broken. Why would I want to stay with someone like you?"

"Baby, hey, where'd you go?" Oliver's hand cupped my jaw and his brows knitted together.

"I'll have to get some," I answered. He didn't need to know all my baggage, all the ways I failed before.

"I can, if you want. It's not that late, I can run to the pharmacy."

A snort laugh escaped from me, surprising us both. "No, I'll get some tomorrow."

"Okay. Anything else I need to know?"

I shifted backwards, leaning away from him and dropping my hands in front of me, tugging at the hem of my skirt. Blush heated my skin as I tried to find the words. I've always taken a long time to finish with my previous partners, sometimes even by myself. I struggled to get wet enough, something I had learned was part of the hormone imbalance from my PCOS and I always felt self-conscious about it. With enough patience and extra lube, sex could be a great experience for me, but asking for it became harder and harder with every partner that acted like it was a chore. Or they acted insulted that I wasn't soaking wet for them.

Oliver lifted my chin and stroked his fingers against my skin while he waited for me to bring my eyes back to his. "What are you not telling me?"

Tell him, Emery. If he isn't okay with it, that's your sign to run right now.

"I usually need lube, and it can take me a while to...get there."

The corner of his mouth lifted, and his eyes softened. "Okay, that's no big deal. I'm not kidding, Emery, anything you need you tell me. Need me to go slower, tell me. Need me to go faster, tell me. Need a break, tell me. Need me to use a vibrator, tell me."

I choked on my spit, his hand moving to rub my back while I struggled to pull myself together. "You would do that?" I finally managed.

"Anything to take care of you, baby, but you have to tell me what you need."

I leaned forward, bracketing his face between my hands so he couldn't move away this time, and kissed the corner of that crooked smile. The hand on my back dropped back to my thigh. I shifted against him and dropped my hands from his face so he could take over.

"Where's the boundary tonight?" he asked against my mouth.

"Let's just go with the flow. I want you in control."

The hand on my thigh shifted up and around until he cupped my ass under my skirt. He gave it a hard squeeze drawing a gasp from me as our mouths moved against each other. "All these short skirts and dresses you wear have been driving me crazy." His other hand fisted my hair and pulled my head back as he pulled his mouth from mine to move to my neck. "Do you have any idea what your ass looks like, baby? I haven't been able to stop thinking about how it would feel in my hands."

I pressed my ass against the hand cupping it until he squeezed harder. "I guess it is a pretty good ass." It was a great ass, I knew that. It had always been a part of my body I had been proud of.

He laughed against my neck as he pulled my hair harder. He nipped my skin and traced his tongue over it. "So confident, that's my girl." His teeth dragged over my skin until he was pulling the V-neck of my shirt to the side. "These tattoos have been driving me crazy too." His teeth and tongue ran over the flowers and vines on my collarbones until a whimper slipped from me. "I haven't been able to stop thinking about tasting them."

I moved my hips against him and leaned forward trying to get his mouth back to mine. His hands held me steady, a gentle pressure against my ass and scalp, as he moved lower and traced the top of my breast with his lips. I caught the side of his face with one hand, sliding my nails against his beard. "There are more," I whispered.

His eyes lifted to mine. "More tattoos?"

I tried to nod, forgetting about the hand in my hair. "Yes."

He loosened his hand in my hair. "Am I being too rough?"

I shook my head. "I think I like it." I scraped my nails along his arm.

"Tell me if you change your mind." His hand dropped from my hair to my neck, pressing just slightly. "Do you want to show me your other tattoos?"

I pressed against his lap letting my skirt bunch up more between us. "I think I'll just let you find them."

Oliver lifted his hips and flipped me onto the cushions on my back in one smooth motion. He untucked my shirt and pushed it up over my stomach. I watched as his brows knitted as he looked at the snakes winding over the top of my soft stomach and around my ribs. He pushed my shirt up higher, unveiling the medusa nestled at the bottom of my sternum under the swell of my breasts. I held my breath as I watched his eyes soften. He dragged his fingers over the black lines leaving a trail of goosebumps over my skin.

"Ollie, please say something," my voice shook. Did he know what it meant? It was my newest tattoo, one that had taken three sessions to complete because of the emotions it stirred each time.

He covered my body with his and brought our mouths together again. "So beautiful." His mouth was soft against mine, gentle, a stark contrast to his earlier touches.

I slipped my hands under his shirt and scraped my nails over his lower back. "There are more." I shifted under him, lifting my hips to grind against him.

His hand flexed against my ribs, the rough scrape of his callouses making goosebumps sprout across my skin. The growing pressure between my legs made me think maybe it wouldn't take me that long this time. I'd never been more turned on in my life. Suddenly it felt like the past two months had just been one long game of foreplay. He shifted over top of me again, one of his legs pushing between mine until his knee pressed in just the right spot. "Is that okay?"

It was very okay. I lifted my hips grinding myself against his knee, the layers of fabric between us giving me just enough friction to ease the needy ache.

Both his hands moved under my skirt and gripped my hips, urging me to move faster against him. My breathing quickened and small moans tumbled out of me. Oliver stared down at me with heavy lidded eyes. "Talk to me, baby."

My fingers skated over the bulge of his stomach under the hem of his shirt and the coarse hair there tickled my skin. "Touch me," I choked out.

His lips found mine again at the same time that he dragged a finger between my legs over top of my panties. He groaned into my mouth and then pulled back. Oliver lifted his hand to his mouth and slipped two fingers inside. Heat flared through me watching his tongue swirl around his fingers.

"What are you doing?"

His fingers left his mouth with a pop. Arousal coated the inside of my thighs. Wetness soaked through my underwear. "Getting them wet for you." His mouth lifted in a smirk and his knee pressed against me again. "Feels like you didn't need any help with that."

This time his hand slipped under my panties and found my clit with ease. He drew lazy circles around it and kissed me at the same pace. Time lost all meaning while pleasure slowly built inside me. Oliver murmured encouragement against my lips and told me how good I felt. My fingers dug into his back when he pushed one finger inside me and hooked it. He stroked the spot I'd only been able to hit with my favorite toy and his thumb continued to circle my clit.

"Don't stop," I pleaded with a gasp. My hips rocked against his hand and he matched the rhythm I set. I couldn't believe I was going to come this fast from just his fingers. Even my favorite toy took longer.

My impending orgasm built until I hovered on the edge ready to fall. I clenched around him and rocked harder chasing the friction to send me over.

The pressure inside me dissipated, the edge disappearing. I let out a frustrated groan and move my hips faster trying to get it back. Muttered pleads with my body to let me have this slipped from my lips. Oliver's hand stilled and he pressed the other against my hip to still my movements.

"It's okay. There's no rush, Em."

"But I was right there. It felt so good." I tried to buck my hips against his hand.

His mouth moved to my neck, biting and sucking hard enough I knew there would be a mark left behind. He tortured me with slow bites over my neck and chest, finger still inside me but not moving. The anticipation from his thumb hovering over my clit had pleasure building inside me.

"What are you doing to me?" I asked in a breathy whisper.

Oliver pressed another bite into the soft swell of one breast. I'd never let anyone mark me like this. The thought of stopping him faded when his thumb pressed against me. A second finger pushed inside me. His tongue flicked against one nipple and his hand finally left my hip allowing me to move against him.

I tried to clear my head and focus on how good his fingers felt, to push away the nagging thought that I should have finished by now. Each time the edge fading away Oliver whispered encouragement in my ear, shushing me every time I told him we could stop if he wanted. He pressed one hand across my pelvis, applying pressure that intesified every movement of his fingers inside of me.

My orgasm tore through me at last without warning. The waves of pleasure washed over me so long I thought there may have been a second one blending with the first. A small rush of liquid coated his hand and my inner thighs.

Did I just? No, I couldn't have. Even on my own I'd only managed to make myself squirt a handful of times. It took my favorite toy, a lot of patience, and being in just the right window of my cycle.

"That's it, fuck that's so hot." Oliver's face pressed against my chest as he stroked me through the aftershocks.

When my breathing slowed, I pushed one hand toward the button on his pants. "Can I touch you?" I asked.

He mumbled something I couldn't understand and pulled my hand away. A few more minutes passed before he pushed off the couch and I caught a glimpse of the wet spot on the front of his jeans.

"Did you –?" I cut off my question because I knew the answer from the sheepish smile on his face. My core clenched with fresh arousal.

Oliver walked into his room and returned in a fresh pair of sweatpants. He carried a second pair folded in his hands. He rubbed the back of his head and pink washed over his cheeks as he presented the pants to me. "You don't have to, but I thought it might be more comfortable."

More comfortable than the wet panties that were sticking to me. The thought of wearing his clothes filled me with an unexpected thrill. I'll never be the girl that got to be cute wearing a man's oversized clothes after sex. Or wear my partner's clothes at all because they were always too small. Oliver and I were close in size so I knew the pants would fit. I accepted them and slipped into the bathroom to change.

Oliver waited on the couch and his eyes widened watching me walk back to him. I smoothed my hands over the fabric that fit snuggly against my hips and thighs. His eyes followed the movement, and his mouth parted, tongue flicking out over his bottom lip.

He pulled me down onto the couch against him. The way his fingers trailed over me had me thinking he might be trying to start something again. He cleared his throat and wrapped his arm around me. "Do you want to watch the next episode of *Andromeda Portal*?"

I settled against him. "Sounds great."

Chapter 24

Oliver

December Now

EMERY'S EYES HELD MINE as I pressed the heel of my palm into the dough, kneading it with more force than necessary. Her eyes flicked down to watch the way my forearms and fingers flexed while I worked. She was practically drooling. "Tell me why you're really here, Emery." After spending weeks pretending like there was nothing between us only to share that heated kiss in my office, I was going crazy with how much I wanted her. I really would have fucked her against that door if she had asked.

Emery shifted in the chair. "I promised to teach you how to make the pumpkin cinnamon rolls."

I rolled my lips between my teeth and pushed into the dough again. "No, that's an excuse and we both know it. Tell me why you keep coming up with excuses to see me." Press, stretch, fold. My hands kept working. She kept staring.

"We're friends again," she told me.

"Are we friends? You said you wanted to work on the restaurant together and then went almost a month without talking to me. Then you showed up at the shop like you didn't completely ghost me."

The muscles in my jaw worked along with my hands as I continued to knead the dough. Thoughts of my hands on her and all her tiny reactions filled my head. I folded the dough and placed it in the bowl to rise. Emery's eyes tracked every motion of me dusting my hands off on my apron. I started toward the chair where she sat.

"Don't forget about those flirty little text messages you sent me out of the blue last night." I positioned myself in front of the chair and bent down until our faces were level. "Tell me what you want," I demanded.

"I will when you tell me what you want," she demanded back. "I don't want to hear that you'll be whatever I need you to be."

I moved closer, close enough to make her press back into the chair. "You keep saying that you're mad I showed back up in your life, but I don't believe you."

She swallowed and fixed her eyes to mine.

I leaned close and braced my hands against the back of the chair. "Everything you've done the past few weeks has made it very clear that you're happy I'm back. You said yourself you're mad I'm not mad at you. You're the one that keeps showing up and driving me crazy. Admit that you missed me."

She broke eye contact. "Why are you still so nice to me? We were amazing together and I threw it all away because I was too broken for it. I can't figure out why you don't hate me."

My hand tangled with the back of her hair and tugged until she tilted her face up to me. Her pupils dilated and she licked her lips showing me she still liked that move. "I told you then, and I'm going to tell you now, I could never hate you, Emery. I don't know why I have to keep repeating that." My other hand moved to her neck and wrapped around the side as my thumb stroked up and down. I could remind her what else I told her that day before she walked out my door, but now didn't seem like the time to bring up those emotions.

"I missed you," she whispered. Fuck, that was the best thing she'd ever said to me.

Relief flooded my body. "I missed you too, baby." My hand moved up until my thumb could touch her bottom lip.

"I still don't know if I'm ready to be what you need."

"Tell me what you think I need." I tightened the hand in her hair to keep her face tilted up. Her hands lifted from her lap to the apron ties around my waist and pulled them free.

"Someone that trusts you."

I leaned back and pulled the knot around my neck free, sending the apron fluttering to our feet. "What else?"

"Honesty," she said quietly. I don't know where the fuck she ever got the idea that she wasn't being honest with me. The word felt like a low blow knowing I was the one that kept lying in this relationship.

My eyes roamed over her body as I hooked my fingers into the belt loops of her skirt. *Please, God, let me touch her just one more time.* I shook my head, the movement so subtle she almost didn't catch it. "Right now, I just need you."

"What does that mean?" She let me pull her out of the chair bringing our bodies as close as possible without touching. Consent. I needed her full consent and then I could devour her.

"I need you to let me kiss you again." My hands gripped her hips but didn't move lower. "I need to touch you."

"What about the other stuff?" She gripped my hands with hers and pinned them in place.

"We were pretty damn good at the friends with benefits part before. What if we did it again?" I wanted her to disagree. For her to tell me no, that we were both more to each other this time. If she gave me the chance I would do everything I could to love her the right way, no more lies.

"Are you going to fall in love with me again?"

I never stopped loving her. I told her I never would. Was it a lie to agree since it wouldn't change what already was? Emery guided my hands slowly backwards, down over her ass, and to the hem of her skirt.

"Are you going to fall in love with me?" I repeated her question back to her. My heart swelled at the possibility that she might say yes.

Emery bit her tongue. I knew that meant she had never stopped either. We were a mess, the two of us caught in this web of our own making. If we could just be honest with each other, we could avoid so much potential heartbreak. But this beautiful woman could break my heart as many times as she wanted, and I would hand the pieces right back to her because I was a masochist. In lieu of answering my question, she opted to move my hands under the hem of her skirt to rest against the tights covering her upper thighs.

I kissed a trail over her jaw and back toward her ear, my beard scrapping over her soft skin. Her silence was enough to let me know that maybe things would work out in our favor this time. I would keep pretending as long as she needed if it meant she would be mine in the end.

"Baby, remember the rules. You're in charge here, always will be. Tell me what you want." My words were low in her ear as I held my hands still where she placed them.

"I want you," she breathed.

My hands slid up her thighs so slowly I thought I was going to lose my mind in anticipation. The scratch of my callouses against her tights was a familiar noise that I hadn't realized I missed. I closed his hands over the globes of her ass and pulled her toward me until our bodies collided together. Every movement was achingly slow, giving her chance after chance to change her mind.

"Tell me what you want me to do." I traced her neck with my breath. "Tell me what you need."

"Fuck me like I never stopped being yours." She pulled my head up and kissed me as hard as she could. It was messy, all heat and clashing teeth, the way our mouths rediscovered each other. Our kiss at the shop had been years of pent-up anger, but this was all the pent-up longing. My hands squeezed her ass so hard that I knew I would leave hand shaped bruises. "Still an ass man," she said against my mouth.

"You have the kind of ass that turns every man into an ass man." She knew that. That was why she wore all those tight short dresses and skirts that showed off the curves of her hips and ass. It was an amazing ass. I sucked her bottom lip into my mouth and scraped my teeth across it drawing a whimpered moan from her. It had been too fucking long since I'd heard that noise.

Then I was pushing her backwards. We fumbled our way to the couch. I turned us so I could sit and pull her onto my lap. My mouth broke from her and moved to her neck, biting and sucking my way down. Her hands pushed at the hem of my shirt, desperately trying to pull it free. She leaned back to drag it over my head. I growled as she forced my hands away so she could yank my shirt over them. I seized the opportunity to pull her cardigan free from her and threw it somewhere.

My hands moved back to hold her in place so I could run my mouth over the tattoos covering her shoulders and chest. "There are new ones," I said against her skin. There was barely any skin not covered in ink now. I couldn't help but wonder who got to see all the new marks before me. Who got to taste them.

"There are a lot of new ones," she told me. She scraped her short nails over the rings on the silver chain around my neck and down over my chest. Her eyes locked on lines of ink under my dark chest hair. "You got a tattoo," she gasped. Her eyes caught on a splash of color and her gaze tracked to the watercolor swirls on my right shoulder and upper bicep. "You got two tattoos."

"There are a few of them now." My hand fisted her hair again and pulled her mouth back to mine. My other hand rocked her hips against me. "We'll do a tattoo tour later when I can focus." She would be the first and only person to get a tattoo tour from me. The first to touch and taste them.

There hadn't been anyone since her and I never wanted there to be. One taste of her and I knew no one else would ever come close.

She groaned. "If you're the least bit naked I'm not going to be able to focus."

"Same." I couldn't even focus now with her on my lap. I needed to get the rest of these clothes off her.

Then we were all tongues and teeth and hands and friction against each other. It was rough, like our bodies were angry at us for keeping them apart for so long. The way she touched me was so familiar I could have sworn we had just done this yesterday.

A phone ring broke through our haze. It was the same generic ringtone the phone came with that I never got around to changing. I wasn't at the damn shop. Why was someone calling me? My family really needed to back off. I anchored her to my lap with one hand while I lifted my hips to pull my phone from my back pocket. My mouth stayed on hers as I held it behind her head to look at the screen.

Matt. Why was he calling me right now? He was with Riley tonight. I showed the screen to Emery and her eyes widened.

"Hey, man, what's up?" I tried to clear my throat and slow my breathing.

"Hey, something happened. Um, Riley and I sort of got in a fight and I don't know what to do. I think I fucked it all up. Can I come over and talk?"

"You're on your way now?" I raised my brows at the stunned Emery on my lap. "Actually, I'll come over to your place instead."

"Shit," Emery muttered over and over. She scrambled off my lap and tried to straighten her clothes. "What's wrong? Is my sister okay?" She looked around frantically for her things.

I grabbed her hands. "Matt and your sister had a fight. He wants to talk about it."

She nodded her head and started looking for her cardigan. She found her phone in the kitchen. Tears filled her eyes while she studied the screen and then frantically typed. I gently pulled it from her hands and looked over the messages that filled the screen from Matt.

Matt

> I'm leaving for the night. Your sister is really upset, but she asked me not to stay. I don't know where you are, just that you need to come home and take care of her.

> Make sure she knows I'm not going anywhere. I'm going to give her some space until she is ready to talk to me, but I'm not going anywhere.

Emery

> Is this about Christmas?

> I shouldn't have pushed you to push her.

> I can't believe I'm such a screw up that I ruined my sister's relationship too.

> You Harrison women really need to stop saying stuff like that about yourselves.

> She's going to be mad at you too. Please don't let her push you away.

She bit her lip and started looking for her purse. It took a moment for me to shake away my shock at reading their messages. They were all probably overreacting, but right now all I could think about was getting her calmed down. My arms wrapped around Emery bringing her to a stop and I pulled her against me. She folded into me, bending down until her head was tucked against my chest. "It's going to be okay," I said into the top of her head in a tone that I hoped was calm and comforting.

"The fight was my fault. Oliver, why do I keep ruining everything I touch?" she asked through gritted teeth.

"You don't ruin everything. You just make it a little more challenging." I smoothed my hands through her hair and peppered kisses over the top of her head. "It's just a fight. We're going to talk to them and let them cool off. Then they're going to work everything out." I moved my hands to the sides of her head and tilted her face up. "It's going to be okay." I covered her mouth with mine in a slow kiss. I didn't want to let her go when she was this upset. But I knew she needed to get home to her sister, and I needed to deal with Matt. All I wanted to do was take care of her.

"I need to get home to my sister."

"Be careful, okay? Let me know when you get home."

"We're just friends with benefits," she reminded me. Right, we were sticking to that lie still.

I pressed my forehead against hers. "Friends with benefits doesn't mean I can't care if you get home safely, that comes with the friends part. Now go home. Rain check on the benefits?"

She nodded and pulled her cardigan up on her shoulder covering up more of that glorious skin I should be exploring right now. "Rain check on the benefits and the tattoo tour."

Chapter 25

Emery

September Then

I DROPPED THE LAST biscuit on top of the chicken pot pie as my phone buzzed on the counter. I transferred the skillet to the oven and wiped my hands on my apron.

Oliver

On my way up

Emery

Door is unlocked.

I grabbed a tea towel, wiped up the flour from the counter, and shook it off into the trash can. I moved to the sink and started washing the collection of dishes. I kept my focus on the mixing bowl in my hand as I heard the door open, not ready to see his reaction to the dress I wore.

The black bodycon dress hit right at my ankles, the fabric hugged my shape in all the right places, and the thin straps put the tattoos on my collarbones and chest on display. I'd had it for a while, always waiting for the perfect time to wear it. It was a little much for dinner and chill in my apartment, but I was sick of opening my closet wondering when the right time would be. I knew Oliver would love the way it hugged my ass.

One hand came around from behind me and took the sponge from my hand, the other squeezed my ass right before he pressed his body against mine. I leaned back against him, pressing against the growing erection that I could feel clearly through his sweatpants. His hand released me and came around to take the mixing bowl from my hand. He started washing it as he pressed us together.

"That's my job, baby," he whispered into my ear.

"I can clean up while the food is finishing up in the oven."

"I know you can, but you're not going to." He pressed me harder against the edge of the sink while he fished out the next dish to wash. "We had an agreement."

I wiggled against him until his breath caught, my heart raced at the sound. "I told you I don't like being told what to do."

"You keep saying that, but I'm not sure you mean it, at least not all of the time." He kept me pinned until the dishes were done. "What are you wearing?" he asked as he dried his hands.

I wiggled until he backed off enough to let me turn around and I pulled off my apron. "Just a little something I needed your opinion on."

He backed off more so he could rake his eyes over me, the way his eyes darkened sent waves of satisfaction and want through me. "That's one way to ask me to tell you how sexy you are." He pulled me against him and smoothed his hands over my hips and around to cup my ass. "It doesn't feel like you're wearing anything under this."

"I guess you'll have to check and see." I looked over to the oven timer, sighing when I saw that it only had fifteen minutes left.

"Maybe I will." He moved a hand up to hook a finger under one strap, pulling it down over my arm. He dipped his face down to trail bites over my tattoos, following the light marks he left yesterday.

"The food will be done soon," I told him as I threaded my fingers through his hair.

"That's fine. Just having a little appetizer while we wait." He pulled the other strap down, walking me backwards right next to the oven until the counter dug into my lower back. He paused and swept his gaze over my chest. "Are the marks okay? I should have asked."

"Yeah, it's okay." I had spent too long admiring them in the mirror this morning when I noticed, remembering the way he had looked at me. No one had ever made me feel as wanted as he did. "Maybe just try to keep them below my neck." I didn't add that it would be easier to cover them up that way. I already had to worry about keeping my tattoos covered up at work and didn't want to add love bites to that.

He brought his face back up to mine and tucked my hair back, his eyes bouncing between my eyes and mouth.

"Why'd you stop?"

He grinned just before he brought his mouth to mine, kissing me until we were both breathless. "I've been thinking about fucking you all day," he said as he pulled away.

"Me too."

"So, we're really doing this?" One of his hands twisted in a strap making me wish he would just pull it the rest of the way down already.

I caught his mouth again, kissing him hungrily. Every move grew in intensity as we pressed against each other and let our hands roam. My face burned from the rough scratch of his beard against my skin. I wanted that feeling over my entire body. The ding of the oven timer made me jump.

Oliver's hands rubbed my back, but he kept kissing me. I started to pull away. He kissed me harder and then broke away just enough to say, "it's okay, I'll get it." He stayed pressed against me, moving just his upper body to press the button to stop the timer and reached for an oven mitt. He leaned over to the side and pulled the skillet from the oven and rested it on the stove top.

I pushed up the hem of his shirt. "I'm not very hungry right now."

"Okay. What do you have in mind?"

I tugged his shirt up more, urging him to lift his arms. "I want this off." He lifted his arms so I could drag it over his head. I raked my hands over his chest taking in the feel of his hair against my fingers, then down his thick midsection. I loved how strong and sturdy he felt under my hands. My fingers hooked into the waistband of his sweatpants. "These too."

His hands wrapped around mine and spun me to walk me toward the couch. "I want this dress off more." He backed me up until the couch hit the back of my legs but kept me standing. He hooked his fingers in the straps again and raised his eyebrows as if asking for permission.

"I don't know if that's fair, because then I'll be naked, and you'll still be half dressed."

He groaned, "you're going to kill me woman." He tugged his sweatpants down but left his boxer briefs on. His hands were back on the dress, tugging it down slowly, his eyes following along to drink in every bit of skin he uncovered. When the dress was around my ankles, he pushed me to lay down.

My relationship with my body has been up and down through-out my entire life. Most days I felt confident, I loved every curve. But other days I caught myself wishing for things to be smaller. Through my childhood I had been thin, but as I became a teenager my body quickly changed into something I didn't recognize, gaining weight at a rapid pace. I had done all the crash diets, putting my body through the constant stress of losing and gaining weight back. It wasn't until my twenties that I started to accept that this is what my body was now, and she deserved to be loved in her plus size glory. It never stopped others from trying to tell me that my size was something that needed to be fixed.

Oliver's warm brown eyes took me in as his rough fingers traced every flaw, every curve, every tattoo. It was clear how much he loved my body. "I know you already know how beautiful you are, baby, but wow." He tugged me off the couch toward the bedroom.

I giggled as he shoved me onto the bed. His mouth started at my collarbones against and traced new paths down to my breasts, stopping to tease each nipple, and then trailing down to the tattoo below them. His hands pinned my hips against the mattress, his short nails digging in, as he started on the vines that covered my stomach and trailed down over the curves of my hips.

He skipped over where I wanted him and moved to the butterfly on my thigh. I bucked my hips against his hands. He flicked his eyes up to meet mine as he moved to nip at my inner thigh. I let my legs fall open more hoping he would get the hint. After the things his fingers made me feel last night I was desperate to know what his mouth could do.

He moved to my other thigh and started working on the patch-work of tattoos there. I tried to lift my hips again, earning a cocky grin from him. "Need something, baby? I'm kind of busy right now."

I dropped my head back against the mattress. "You're such a tease."

His response was to press his nose just above my clit sending a bolt of want through me. His tongue ran over me so achingly slow I groaned in frustration. He shifted back to bite my inner thigh again.

"Oliver," I scolded in a whisper.

"Emery."

I lifted my head to see him looking up at me. I reached down to thread my fingers through the top of his hair. It was getting long again, and I couldn't decide if I like it this way or freshly cut better. "I need more, please. You're driving me crazy."

His tongue flicked over my center again just as slowly. I pressed his head down pleading with him again. His tongue swirled around my clit causing me to drop my head back against the mattress. He moved my legs over his shoulders as he settled into a slow rhythm that made my body buzz and ache. I closed my eyes and tried to lose myself in the moment. Just when I thought I was going to lose my mind from how slowly the pleasure built in me he started to speed up and slid two fingers into me. He pressed his fingers up hitting the same spot he did last night as he sucked my clit drawing louder moans from me.

I tightened my grip in his hair as he drove me higher and higher, until I was right on the edge but couldn't fall. Thoughts of how long I was taking started to creep in.

"Oliver?"

His mouth broke away from me, but his fingers kept working. "Tell me what's wrong. What do you need?"

"You don't have to," my words were cut off as he pressed harder inside me drawing whimpers out. "I'm sorry I'm taking so long," I managed in a breathy whisper.

He stopped moving. I opened my eyes, looking down to see a puzzled look on his face. His swollen lips and beard shined from my arousal that coated them, the sight sent a bolt of need to my core. I wasn't as wet as I had been last night despite thinking about this all day. I didn't think I'd even been wet enough to wet his beard like that. "You're not taking too long. Can I keep going?" His thumb stroked my clit and lowered his mouth back to hover over me. "You make such sexy noises while I take care of you. I could stay down here forever listening to you." His tongue flicked over me quickly. "Does it feel good?"

I nodded and let out a sigh when he brushed over my clit again.

"Just focus on that for me. You don't have to come, okay? Just enjoy how good it feels."

I moaned out okay as his mouth covered me again, sucking and licking until I was back on the edge. I focused on how he looked between my legs, the way he devoured me and pumped his fingers inside me. My thighs tightened around his head as I tumbled over the edge, coming so hard I screamed. He kept going until I was so sensitive I had to tug him away by his hair.

He looked so damn proud of himself. I covered my face and laughed as he climbed back over me. He nudged my hands away from my face. "What's so funny?"

"I don't think I've ever screamed like that. I can't believe I did that."

He pinned my hands onto the mattress to keep me from covering my face again. The sight of him over me, cocky grin spread over his face, his beard soaked from me sent more jolts of need through me. He lowered his face until his lips brushed against my ear. "I want to make you scream like that every time." Then he tried to inch back down my body. "I wasn't done down there."

I wiggled one hand free from his grip and slid it between us. He stilled over top of me and his eyes followed my hand. My fingers were clumsy, my whole body still felt boneless from my orgasm, as I pushed them under the waistband of his underwear and stroked him. "Are you going to fuck me or not?" I teased.

"I'm going to fuck with you my mouth one more time first."

I shook my head and stroked my hand over him again. "Need you inside me right now." The idea of his mouth on me again was appealing, but I could never come twice back-to-back like that. We would be here forever while he tried and eventually he would get frustrated with me.

He pulled my hand free and pinned it back above my head with the other one. "Be good and keep them there," he ordered. He released his grip on me so he could push his underwear off and grabbed a condom from the box I had left on the bedside table. He rolled it on, then reached for the bottle of lube. He coated the condom with it and then his fingers worked to coat my entrance. My hands lifted to his shoulders as he touched me.

"What did I say?" he growled as he pulled my hands back above my head.

I started to roll my eyes, but he pushed into me at the same time. The stretch of him filling me pulled a gasp from me. He held both my wrists with one hand as he dropped the other to circle my clit as he moved inside me.

"I can't come this soon again," I choked out, the sensation too much. He stopped moving. "I need more time between, right now I'm too sensitive. Just focus on you for now."

His eyes softened with concern. "Are you sure? Do we need to take a break?"

I shook my head and pressed my hips up toward him. "You already took care of me. Right now, I want to feel you come inside me."

His movements started up slowly, his eyes held mine like he kept waiting for me to change my mind. I scraped my nails against the hand pining me and dragged my teeth over his throat. He picked up speed when I begged him to. His hand tightened around my wrists, and he came with a growl in my ear. He released my wrists and braced himself on his elbows over me while he caught his breath. I ran my nails over his back and caught his mouth with mine for a slow kiss.

"Let's get cleaned up and go eat," I said after he pulled out of me.

"Fine, but we're doing that again after." He dragged a hand down my body until he cupped between my legs. "We're not done until you come on my cock."

My face heated.

"Be a good girl and put that dress back on for me. Maybe I'll bend you over the counter later and push it up your hips..." he let the sentence trail off. My fresh arousal coated his hand. "I promise I'll bend you over the counter later," he corrected himself.

The pressure building inside me already was intense. I was always a one orgasm and done kind of woman. Two in one night was so rare I couldn't even remember when the last time was that it happened.

"And if I can't come again?"

His breath blew hot against my ear. "I'm a stubborn man, Em, and I like a challenge."

The promise in his words made me melt into the bed. The pulse between my thighs and the way he smirked down at me told me he was going to get his way tonight.

"Come one baby, let's get you put back together so I can take you apart again later."

Chapter 26

Oliver

December Now

Emery

Riley is on to us. You left a hickey last night.

Oliver

I thought you liked when I did that.

I do.

Well Matt figured it out too.

I know. You should be proud of him. He threatened me the day he was at the shop.

I'll talk to him. He doesn't need to be threatening you.

> No, don't! I'm sort of proud of him for it. I've been threatening him for months.

> He's worried I'm going to break your heart.

> Well history does tend to repeat itself.

> No falling in love with me again. You promised.

> Baby, I think we both made that promise knowing we're not going to keep it.

I flipped my phone over with a groan. If only she would stop lying to herself so I could stop lying too. She had been right about everything I needed, but more than anything I needed her, even if it meant giving up everything else.

Matt, Drew, and Wade all raised their brows at me. Matt said Riley had asked for space today, and the man was so clingy he didn't know how to give it to her. He had shown up to the shop after school all bent out of shape over it asking for backup, hanging out until we closed for the day, and then begging for a guys' night. Drew and Wade had volunteered their apartment.

I caught the controller that was thrown toward my face. On screen a message popped up saying someone had invited Drew to join their party. He cleared the notification, blushing as he reached for his phone. He smiled as he typed out a message.

Wade rolled his eyes as he peeked over Drew's shoulder.

"Hey, Drew, who are you texting," I asked.

He blushed again and shoved his phone in between the couch cushions. "No one."

"Her name is Chloe," Wade answered at the same time. Drew glared at him and flipped him off with both hands. Wade returned the gestures with a laugh.

Matt pulled his phone out of his pocket for the hundredth time in the last ten minutes to check for notifications. I snatched it from his hands and then shoved Drew aside so I could retrieve his phone. I held out my hand to Wade.

"What? I'm the only one here without girl troubles."

Drew chuckled. "Wade, we're not stupid. We see how you are with Shelby."

Matt perked up. "What about you and my sister?"

"Nothing, she hates me," Wade mumbled. He dropped his head, and his hair fell in a curtain over his face. He held his phone out to me. "Clark and I just broke up last week, can you cool it on the Shelby stuff?" Wade grumbled crossing his arms over his chest and slumping back against the couch.

I didn't know who Clark was or that Wade had been in a relationship. My head really had been up my ass the past few months.

I dropped all our phones onto the kitchen counter and joined them all on the couch. I glared at Matt. "Are you not going to threaten him not to hurt your sister?"

Matt shrugged as he tapped his fingers on his legs. "You know she can handle herself." He looked down at his feet and mumbled, "she was one of my biggest bullies growing up."

"Matt, everyone was your bully growing up," Wade stated. "And Shelby was everyone's bully growing up."

"I can handle myself too, but that didn't stop you from saying something to Emery," I pointed out. I was still pissed at him for what he said the other day. She wasn't too much to handle. In fact, she was exactly the perfect amount for me. I didn't give a damn if she was going to hurt me again. I wasn't going to miss this chance.

Matt's face turned red. Drew kicked his foot and gave him a nod of approval. A smile cracked through the stern expression I was trying to hold. Matt let out a breath of relief. "I was just trying to watch your back like you always watch mine." It was hard to stay mad at him when he looked so nervous.

I laughed as I clapped him on the shoulder hard enough to make him wince. "How about we don't try to shake up this friendship dynamic, okay? Plus, Emery could eat you alive."

A phone buzzed on the counter. All our heads swiveled to see which one lit up. Drew jumped up once he saw it was his. I stuck out my arm to push him back down on the couch.

"No one checks their phones for one hour," I ordered. I glared at Drew until he picked up his controller and started Mario Kart. I shifted my glare to Matt. "You wanted a guys' night, so that's what we're doing. The first one to check their phone is buying dinner."

This time a phone dinged, I knew it was mine. I was the only one that didn't keep my phone on vibrate. My eyes stayed fixed on the three of them, but Wade held up his finger. It started ringing then, the volume still on full blast so I could hear it in the shop. "What?" I spat at him. I was keyed up from thinking about Emery all night and all day. Now thanks to Matt I didn't know when I was going to get to see her again. She was finally letting me back in and he just had to pick now to start cockblocking me. Three pairs of eyes widened at me.

"That one was yours," Wade said. "You might want to answer, it could be Ava." His assumption made sense considering that Ava was the only person that regularly called me and was not in this room, at least as far as he knew.

I swallowed hard and grinded my teeth together. This was so fucking stupid. I covered my ears as I tried to drown out the ringing.

"It's still ringing," Drew added. "Really should check, if it's Ava she is going to kill us for not answering."

"I can see it from here, man, I think it's Emery," Wade said with a grin.

I groaned and jumped up, spinning back to face them all. "Fine, figure out what I'm ordering for dinner." There was no way I was ignoring a call from Emery, not when calls from her historically meant something was wrong. I could ignore Ava and deal with the aftermath, but not Emery.

"Hi, baby," I whispered when I answered.

"Why are you whispering?" she whispered back. Relief flooded through me at the sound of her normal teasing tone.

"Matt requested a guys' night."

She sighed. "Sooo, I guess that answers my question."

I smiled, leaning over the counter with my back to the eyes watching me. "Baby, you say the word right now and I'll leave. I've been thinking about you all day."

She laughed -- the loud unguarded laugh I only ever heard her use around me. I had missed that sound. "I've been thinking about you too, but I'm not going to ask you to leave. Riley is a mess, so I can only imagine Matt is even worse." She paused for a moment, her soft breathing filling the line. She sighed. "I should go be with my sister. She's babysitting our nephew tonight."

I rubbed the back of my neck, knowing she was making the right choice but dying for her to say fuck it. I wanted to hear her ask me to choose her right now; to let me prove I would always choose her anytime.

"Okay, yeah, we should probably focus on them tonight. I'm enforcing a no phone rule, but I'll text you later."

"If there's a no phone rule, why are you on the phone with me?" The way she asked the question told me she already knew the answer.

"Because I'll always answer when you call, baby, you know that. I'll answer every single time even if it means I'm buying dinner for these idiots now."

She laughed hard enough that a snort echoed over the line. I could picture her face all scrunched up, one hand over her mouth trying to hold in the sound, and her chest shaking. I missed her so much.

Chapter 27

Emery

December Now

Riley is staying the night with Matt.

Come over

I'm going to have so many dishes for you to wash.

Oliver

That's an interesting euphemism. I think I'm going to need a little help on that one.

Get your mind out of the gutter, I meant that literally.

From what I remember you don't need help knowing what to do. *winking emoji*

Waiting for Oliver to come over was nerve-wracking. I destroyed my closest trying to choose what to wear, following up by destroying Riley's looking for my black dress. I couldn't remember ever being this nervous waiting for him before.

Maybe it was because the stakes were higher this time. He suggest we just go back to the friends with benefits arrangement and I said yes because I would take whatever I could get from him. Sure, I told him not to fall in love with me this time even though I desperatley wanting him to. It was so easy to fall back into our old pattern.

The black dress wasn't anywhere in the house. I hadn't seen it since the day I made her wear it. I pulled on the sweater dress that I wore to the shop the other day, remembering the hungry look in Oliver's eyes, and opted for nothing underneath.

A car door slammed outside. I peeked through the blinds covering my bedroom window to make sure Riley hadn't decided to come home for something. Oliver still drove the same Chevy truck he did two years ago.

I sprinted to the front door, flipped the lock, and opened it just as he raised a hand to knock. His mouth lifted in a smile as his eyes raked over me. I fisted his jacket and pulled him inside. He kicked the door shut behind him and I pulled down the zipper of his jacket. "Not wasting any time?" he asked with a chuckle. He pushed the beanie off his head and let me push the jacket off his shoulders. He was still in his work uniform, but his hands and arms were spotless with the skin red like he had scrubbed them raw before leaving work.

"You didn't go home first?" My heart raced. He always went home to take a quick shower before coming over. "You always did before." This time was different. I could feel it deep inside me that we both were more invested this time. Please, please, please, let him break his promise to me. If this man fell in love with me again I would do whatever it took to make sure I don't break his heart.

In the meantime, I'll just keep pretending and breaking my own heart in the process.

He caught my hands as I went for his buttons. "I needed to see you." He pulled me toward him, one hand going to my neck to position me where he wanted while he kissed me. "I haven't stopped thinking about you since Monday, and getting interrupted Wednesday just made things worse. I've been going crazy." He pressed my hand against the front of his pants, pressing his hips forward to rub his growing erection against my palm. "I've been walking around half hard all week thinking about kissing you against the door of my office. Replaying having you on my lap and your hands on my skin."

I tried to move my hand to stroke him, but he held it still. The pressure of his fingers around my wrist reminded me of something. "I have a present for you," I told him.

He kissed his way up my jaw to my ear. "Later," he said, dragging his lips over my ear. "Do you know how much torture it's been going two years without touching you? I still think about how you feel, how you sound." His voice was husky in my ear, the sound making the pulsing need between my legs grow more insistent. I was already so wet. He pressed harder against my hand as he dropped his mouth to the spot between my shoulder and neck. He dragged his teeth over my skin. "Tell me you've missed me."

I moaned as he bit and sucked, trailing over my shoulder and then down my chest like he used to. "I've missed you so much." I squeezed him lightly. "Tell me you've missed me."

"Every day, baby, every day." He brought my hands to the buttons of his uniform shirt. I worked quickly, shoving the shirt off his shoulders roughly. I yanked his undershirt over his head, one of his hands grabbing the back of the neck to help. I ran my hands over his chest, scrapping my nails down as I moved toward his belt. "Where's your room?" he asked.

I turned us around so I could back him toward my room, tossing his belt over my shoulder as we went. He spun us until I slammed against the wall of the hallway, his mouth back on mine. He sucked my bottom lip between his teeth and bit. He moaned into my mouth as I slid my hand into his pants. He was so hard and hot in my hand. He reached for my hand and pulled it out of his pants. "Where is that lipstick you were wearing Monday?"

"In my room."

"Put it on."

I raised an eyebrow at him. "Excuse me?"

"Please. You look so sexy when I make a mess of you." I rolled my eyes, feigning an attitude, remembering how he had looked with my lipstick smeared on his lips. *Mine, he had looked like mine.* It had been hot.

I let him push me into my room, snatching the lipstick off my vanity. I handed it to him and puckered my lips. "Make me look pretty," I said, batting my eyelashes.

"You're already so pretty, baby." He popped off the lid, tossing it onto my vanity, and then wrapped his fist in my hair, tugging the way I liked. His touch was delicate as he applied the lipstick to my mouth, contrasting against the rough tug of his hand in my hair. My heart fluttered. He slid the hand from my hair to recap the lipstick.

I dipped my face to his neck and pressed my lips against his skin, leaving a perfect lipstick mark. I worked my way down, leaving a trail of red lips all the way down his torso to the waist band of his pants. His hand was in my hair, urging me back up. I pushed his pants down as he kissed me, this time his mouth was languid against mine, the desperation gone. The back of my knees hit my bed, and he pushed me down.

He stared down at me. I reached up for him. "What are you doing?" I asked.

"Trying to decide how I want you first."

I sat up on the bed and wrapped my arms around his neck. "Don't think. We can get creative later. I need you." He let me pull him over top of me on the bed. The sight of him over me, covered in lipstick, made me ache. *Mine.* I pressed my thighs together, the pressure between them too much. His hand pushed up the hem of my sweater and he trailed his fingers lightly over my skin.

"Open your legs for me, baby. Let me take care of you."

I locked my eyes with him and I spread for him. He smirked as his fingers circled my clit, drawing a moan from me. He went straight to touching me exactly how he knew I liked. My thighs were shaking from how close I already was just from the memory of how he used to touch me. His fingers pulled away and his eyes stayed glued to my face when he sucked his fingers in his mouth.

"Fuck, I missed that taste," he groaned. Then he leaned close to me and trailed his nose over my jaw. "Tell me how you want to come," he whispered in my ear.

My hands went to push his underwear over his hips and he slowed his touches. "Need you in me. I want to come on your cock."

He pulled away and kicked off his underwear, reaching for my nightstand. His eyebrows raised when he opened the drawer and held up the pair of padded handcuffs.

"I told you I had a present for you," I explained with a wiggle of my eyebrows.

He mumbled something that sounded like later and he tossed the handcuffs on top of my nightstand. Condoms spilled onto the floor when he pulled one out, Oliver dropped his head and swore. I muffled a laugh as I watched him fumble with the packet.

He rolled the condom on and hovered over me again. He coated himself in lube even though I was sure I was wet enough we didn't need it this time. "I'm going to try my best to make sure you go first, but I'm not going to last long, baby." His fingers dug into my hips as he pushed into me, one hand drifting back to my clit once he was fully seated. "You feel so good. So perfect," he groaned.

The way he touched me, the way he looked at me, told me we were already headed down the path to repeat our past. I didn't care. The way our bodies responded to each other, the way we felt together, made it hard to think about the disaster we were tumbling toward.

I didn't last long, my orgasm crashing through me hard and fast. I dug my nails into his back as I clenched around him. His voice was low in my ear as he whispered but I couldn't understand a word he said. I was so lost in the waves rushing through my body I didn't even realize when he came.

His mouth covered mine again. I couldn't help the way my arms tightened around him, needing him even closer. Oliver's hips started to lift away from me to pull out.

"Not yet," I begged while I looped my legs around his waist. It had been too long since I felt him like this. With my head cleared from the lust filled haze all I could think about was how I didn't know if I would ever get to feel him like this again. We'd been separated before. There was no way to know if it might happen again. I needed just a little longer with him here against me, inside me.

Oliver brushed my hair back from my face and kissed my forehead. "It's okay, I'm here, baby. I'm not letting go." He knew. He saw right through me just like he always did. But I also saw right through him. And I knew those words weren't just for me.

Eventually I loosened my full body choke hold on him and let him lift off me. He tugged me off the bed in a swift motion that kept us close. "Come on, let's take a shower. We're getting lipstick everywhere."

I chuckled. "I thought you wanted to make a mess."

He pressed a kiss to my forehead. "Now I get clean you up."

Chapter 28

Emery

October Then

OLIVER DIDN'T MEET ME at my car as soon as I pulled in. I slowly unbuckled my seatbelt as I glanced toward the shop, spotting him in front an open bay door hugging a thin redhead. I snapped my gaze away when Oliver's eyes found mine over her shoulder.

My head spun and my chest tightened, my pounding heart and lungs fighting for space. My fingers ran over the zipper of my jacket as I started to count in my head.

One.

It's probably no big deal. He can hug whoever he wants.

Two.

He's not mine, he can do whatever he wants.

Three.

We're just friends with benefits. We never said anything about not seeing anyone else.

"I can look at whoever I want to, Emery. Stop getting so jealous. You have my ring on your finger. Why don't you trust me?"

Four.

Don't freak out.

Five.

Just ask him.

He was up front with me that he didn't do relationships. Even Ava mentioned how much of a flirt he was.

Out of the corner of my eye the passenger side door opened. I could barely hear Oliver's voice over my own thoughts. "Hey, baby, are you okay?"

He moved the tray of cookies to the dash and dropped into the passenger seat. His hand on my arm made my face heat. "Emery, hey, what's wrong?" His hand moved to my face, cupping my cheek and urging me to look at him.

"Who was that?" I croaked out. I turned to him and confusion washed over his face. "I know we didn't say anything about only hooking up with each other, and I know I don't have any right to be jealous..." My words came out in a rush before trailing off as his face became more confused. "She's really pretty so...like I understand if..."

His thumb stroked my face as he shifted closer to me in the seat. "Are you jealous right now?"

My face was heated with anger and embarrassment. I dropped my eyes and reached behind me for the door handle. Oliver's other hand moved to my neck, pulling me forward. Our mouths were only inches apart, his lips starting to lift in a small smile. I could smell her perfume, something earthy and fresh, mixed with the smell of him.

"Baby, look at me," he pleaded. I let my eyes rise up to meet his. Shock shot through me as I focused on his face, seeing his brows pinched with concern. The smile on his mouth was gone, replaced with a frown as the muscles of his jaw worked. Worry lines creased his forehead. "That was Ava's wife," he explained in a soft tone.

Relief flooded me, followed closely by embarrassment as my stomach dropped. My chest tightened more, my mouth struggling to say something, anything. My brain felt empty.

"She's going to start working up front to help Granny and stopped by today to get some paperwork taken care of." He stroked my neck and moved the hand on my cheek to my hair, brushing it back away from my face as he twisted his fingers in the strands. "I'm not seeing anyone else."

I dropped my gaze again, waiting for my brain to catch up. My stomach twisted, disgust with myself boiling in the pit of it. I let my eyes meet his again, sucking a breath as I tried to make my voice sound convincing. "I mean, you can if you want. We never said we wouldn't."

His lips twitched in the ghost of a smile as his tongue flicked out over them. His eyes dropped to my mouth. I sucked in a breath, waiting for him to agree that we could still see other people. For him to tell me that I had no right to be jealous. "I don't want to," he said instead.

His mouth covered mine. His lips were rough against mine, his hand in my hair twisting in a light pull. The hand on my neck tightened, pressing down with the smallest pressure, as he pulled me into him. I couldn't get enough of the rough, possessive way he always handled me.

Alarm bells rang in my head reminding me of our no PDA rule. We were in the parking lot of his work; his whole family was right there able to see us. I pushed the thoughts out of my head.

Fuck it, I thought to myself as I cupped the back of his head and pressed his mouth tighter against mine. He sucked my bottom lip between his teeth and scraped lightly, pulling a moan from me. He broke the kiss, resting his forehead against mine.

"I'm sorry we never discussed it. I promise, baby, I haven't thought about anyone else since I first saw you." He lifted his face away from mine so he could press a kiss against my forehead. "I would have been jealous if I pulled up somewhere and saw you hugging another guy."

I pulled away from him so I could cover my face with my hands. My face still blazed from embarrassment. My brain felt sluggish processing all his words. *He hadn't thought about anyone else. He would be jealous.*

"Ollie, we're just friends with benefits. You're allowed to be interested in other people. I told you I wasn't looking for a relationship right now and you said that you're not a relationship guy." I didn't believe the words coming out of my own mouth and knew they probably didn't sound convincing to him either. "I know you're used having the freedom to hook up with anyone you want."

I liked that he hadn't thought about anyone else, that he didn't want to.

I shook the thoughts out of my head, knowing that train was headed somewhere I wasn't ready for. Oliver's fingers smoothed over my wrists. "I'm so embarrassed," I said. I pressed my palms tighter over my eyes.

He tugged my hands away from my face, holding them in the air on either side of my head. His mouth lifted in that fucking crooked smile I couldn't get enough of. "Don't be. I'm sure from your point of view it looked pretty bad." He leaned in closer, the trace of her perfume hitting me again. "Please don't be embarrassed. I want to know if I do anything to upset you."

I chewed my lip as I tried to focus. His hands squeezed around mine as he pulled me back to him. "Is it weird that it still bothers me that you smell like her? I know it wasn't anything, but—" He cut me off with another rough kiss before pushing me back into my seat, leaning over me to grab my seatbelt. He buckled it and then reached for his own seatbelt.

"We can fix that." He reached over to turn the keys in the ignition.

"What are we doing?" I asked.

"I'm taking an early lunch and we're going home." He twirled a strand of my hair around his fingers. "I'm going to remind you whose I am until I only smell like you." He leaned closer, brushing his lips against my ear. "I don't care how many times it takes or how long," his whispered words sent shivers through my body. Oliver's left hand moved to my thigh, his fingertips digging in, so his short nails scraped against my tights as he pushed up my skirt. "Better start driving before you get too distracted."

I snorted and rested my head against the steering wheel. His fingers twisted in my skirt. "We're not going home for a quickie in the middle of your workday just because I got a little jealous over something stupid."

"It's not that far away, but if you're feeling that impatient, I guess we can find somewhere secluded close by."

"Oliver James Franklin, you need to get back to work!" I chided with a giggle.

He blew out an amused huff and moved his hand between my thighs, cupping and pressing the heel of his palm against my center. "I've been working six days a week for a year straight, baby. If I want to take a break in the middle of the day I can." He stuck out his bottom lip in a pout. "I can't believe you're going to make me beg."

I clenched my thighs around his hand to stop his movements teasing me through the fabric of my tights and underwear. "I don't want to get you in trouble."

"I'm practically the boss, this place is going to be mine soon. Pop is always telling me I need to get out and have fun while I still can."

I pretended to think about what he was saying, even though I had to hear both Pop and Granny tell him at least once a week that he really didn't have to work so much, that he needed to have more fun. The man practically lived at the shop, working Monday through Saturday ten or eleven hours a day to make up for Pop not being able to do as much as he used to. They kept threatening they were going to retire, and he was going to miss his chance to live life outside of work. I bit my lip and narrowed my eyes at him. "Fine, but not because I was all stupid and jealous. I can't say no to you." I reached for his hand between my legs and moved it over to his own lap. "No distracting me while I'm driving, you know the rules."

"You can say no if you want to."

I twisted forward in my seat and shifted the car into reverse. Before I backed out of the spot I glanced at him. His intense eyes studied my face. For the first time I noticed how tired he looked. Maybe I should try to talk him into taking the rest of the day off. "Nope, I'm not going to pass up an opportunity to have that talented mouth of yours on me."

"Mhm, I like the sound of that," he agreed. His hand squeezed my thigh and shifted in his seat until his mouth hovered next to my ear. "In case it wasn't already clear, if anyone could turn me into a relationship guy it's you."

Chapter 29

Oliver

December Now

Wet curls hung around Emery's flushed face. A droplet of water fell from her eyelash and trailed down her face. The faint freckles over her cheeks captured my attention. I brushed my thumb over one cheek tracing a path over her freckles.

Emery sucked in a breath and her eyes fluttered closed. Her hands lifted to my waist pulling me closer. I pressed her against the shower wall and rested one arm above her head. "Why are you looking at me like that?" she asked.

My thumb traced over her nose following the path to the other side of her face. "I didn't know you had freckles." All the times I saw her naked before I never saw her without makeup. The closest I'd come to seeing her with less than flawless makeup was when I smudged her lipstick in my office. She'd never been this vulnerable with me. Her jaw and forehead were marked with faded acne scars.

I couldn't remember a time when she had ever looked more beautiful to me.

Emery's eyes opened and her jaw clenched. Her hands fell away from me. She twisted her fingers together in the small space between us.

"What's wrong?"

"I haven't...I forgot..." she bit her bottom lip, cutting off her words. Her chest expanded in a deep breath, and she let out a ragged exhale. "I didn't even realize how long it's been since anyone has seen me without makeup."

Her words felt like she handed me a piece of herself. The easy way she trusted me again made me feel like the past two years apart were just a terrible nightmare I finally woken up from. Like she had never left.

She tilted her face down, breaking eye contact. "Will you tell me what you're thinking?"

I cursed myself for ever agreeing to the lie that we wouldn't fall in love with each other this time. A million years ago I thought I wasn't a relationship guy but then she came into my life and turned my world upside down. The moment Emery Harrison smiled at me everyone else ceased to exist. Every time she trusted me with another part of her it became a little harder to keep pretending.

"That I should have brought a condom in here," I said instead. It wasn't a lie. I wanted to spin her around and fuck her against the shower wall, to watch the water trail over her bare face while she looked at me over her shoulder knowing that no one else got to have her like this. My hands skated down her body and I lowered myself to my knees in front of her.

She was like putty in my hands when I lifted one leg and draped it across my shoulder.

"Ollie," she gasped before I touched her.

My gaze zeroed in her swollen pink pussy. Above me she pressed her back against the shower wall and one hand tangled in my hair. "Did this pussy miss my mouth, baby?"

She exhaled roughly. Her hand urged my face towards where she wanted me.

I flattened my tongue and licked her in a slow swipe. "Do I need to remind you who takes care of you?" I swiped my tongue over her again before she could answer. "I've missed the way you scream my name while you soak my beard."

Garbled pleas tumbled out of her.

"Don't come, okay, baby? I want to drown between your thighs. I want to stay down here forever listening to those needy little noises you make."

Her hand fisted in my hair and pushed my face against her. "Feels so good," she whispered when my tongue circled her clit. Her leg was already tightening around me. She'd never been this responsive before.

I slid two finger inside her and hooked them until I found the spot that always made her fall apart. My other hand pressed against her pelvis. It didn't matter how much time had passed since the last time I had my mouth on her, I remembered every detail about how she needed to be touched. I didn't know how much time she would give me this time. All I knew what that I wouldn't waste a single minute of it.

Maybe, just maybe, she would realize that it was always meant to be us in the end.

***

Emery stood in her room wrapped in a towel digging through her dresser drawers. "I don't know if I have anything that will fit you," she said blushing. When she texted me to come over, I hadn't been able to think clearly about stopping by my apartment to grab a change of clothes. All I knew was that I had to get to her before she could change her mind. I knew everything she had would be a little big on me, and while it didn't bother me, I knew it would bother her. We were close enough in size that it wouldn't be dramatically oversized, not that I would care if it was. As confident as she was with her body, she sometimes would get upset about not being able to steal my clothes and have them be oversized on her.

Younger me had been self-conscious about my height and weight, always looked over by girls because of it. It didn't matter to me now; Emery never made me feel like there was anything wrong with me being the same height as her, and I loved her curvy body.

I dropped the towel from around my waist and reached for my boxer briefs on the floor. "That's fine, I can just wear these."

Emery's breath hitched as she watched me, her eyes roaming over me. "Can't let you do that; I won't be able to focus on anything else."

I dropped my underwear back on the floor. "Okay, naked it is." Her pupils dilated and her tongue flicked over her lips. The towel around her started to slip, reminding me of the promise she made on Wednesday. "Are you going to give me that tattoo tour you promised?" I asked. In the shower I had been so distracted by her face I didn't even think about all her new tattoos.

She stepped closer to me and traced her fingers over the splash of color on my shoulder and upper bicep. "You first." Her eyebrows knitted as she traced her fingers over the colors. "Why does this look so familiar?"

I laughed. "The night with the body paint," I offered as a reminder. The memory of her spread out on the drop cloth naked in
front of me while I colored in her tattoos filled my mind. The way
she had sat up, dipped her fingers in the paint, and started swirling
them over my skin. *You need a tattoo so I can color it in too.* I took a
picture of her artwork on my skin before I washed it away, and had
it tattooed on me planning to surprise her. Everything fell apart the
next day before I could show her.

Her mouth formed a soft O, her eyes widening to tell me the
same memory was flashing through her head. "How long has it been
there?" she asked.

I shook my head. "I don't think you want to know the answer
to that."

She dropped her eyes and fingers to the Roman numerals over
my heart. "And these?"

I placed my hand over hers and pressed her palm against my skin.
It felt so right to have her hands on me again. Things had to work
out between us this time. If not, I might just die from not having
her skin against mine ever again. "Granny's and Pop's birthdays," I
answered.

Her lips trembled as she stared at the ink. "I should have been
there. I don't think I'll ever be able to forgive myself for it," she
whispered.

I caught her chin with my thumb and forefinger, lifted her
face up to meet mine. "Don't do that to yourself, baby. Don't
make yourself carry that weight." Her eyes shimmered with tears.
I couldn't tell her that I was already carrying the weight for both of
us, that I knew I could have tried harder to find her. I knew where
she worked, her favorite grocery store, and her favorite tattoo artist.
I could have made the effort, but I had been so scared. I thought I

was helping her by keeping the pain of them being gone away from her.

"I miss them so much," she said in a shaky voice.

I smoothed my hand through her wet hair, my fingers catching on knots from how I had mussed it up. It wasn't this curly before. I loved all the different styles she experimented with before but this one was my favorite. "Me too, baby."

I held her against me until her shoulders stopped shaking and her breathing normalized. Once I was sure that the threat of her crying had passed, I pulled back enough to see her. My fingers hooked on the top of her towel. "Are you going to show me yours?"

Her mouth twisted into a devious grin as she untucked the corner of the towel, letting it slip down to just above her nipples. "You said you had a few." Her eyes went to the three stick figures on my left calf.

"Ava, Drew, and I got that one together."

She smiled and dropped her towel, pointing to two flowers intertwined on her ribs below the snakes of her medusa tattoo. "Riley and I have a matching one too."

We let our eyes roam over each other, pointing to each new tattoo as we did, exchanging explanations. She laughed at the one on my inner bicep that said "Mr. Hero" that came from a promise to Drew. Tears filled her eyes when I explained the forest of trees on my thigh, the words overcome and resilient twisting together in the trunk of each tree.

She pointed to the patchwork of food that now stretched down her left leg to her ankle, naming each one. The skin was so crowded the lines had started to overlap. Her left thigh now had smaller silhouettes of butterflies surrounding the large one, the butterflies turning into flowers as they moved down her leg until it became overlapping flowers, vines, and butterflies all the way to her ankle.

The flowers and vines that covered her hips now sprouted up until they twisted together with the snakes of the medusa tattoo, bees and dragonflies flew across the small patches of empty skin on the swell of her stomach. She twisted so I could see the tiger stripes that cover the stretch marks on the backs of her thighs and ran over her ass. Every line of ink over her body told a story, the story of the growth she had been through without me.

God, she was so fucking gorgeous. Her struggles, her imperfections, and her wins all inked on to her skin for the world to see.

I dug my hands into the backs of her thighs, lifting until her legs wrapped around my waist and her arms went around my neck. She didn't protest that she was too heavy for me to lift like she used to. Instead, she crashed her mouth into mine and let me carry her back to her bed. I took my time learning every new line with my fingers and mouth as she did the same to me. Every new tattoo, every new scar on my hands and arms, every new fine line on my face. She memorized every one of them while I memorized every part of her.

Chapter 30

Oliver

October Then

Emery pulled into the parking lot with her head on a swivel and her teeth sank into her bottom lip. I flagged her down and wrapped up my conversation with a customer, passing him his keys. Emery came to a stop next to me and rolled down her window. I rested one arm against her car to lean into the window.

Her wide eyes stopped scanning over our surroundings one more time and finally settled on me. "Hi," she breathed out shyly. One of her hands dropped from the steering wheel and rested over her stomach. The tight denim mini skirt she wore rode up on her thighs barely covering anything. Her brown striped sweater was cropped revealing the way the top of her stomach rolled over the top of the skirt while she sat. I couldn't wait to get my hands on all that skin later.

"Hi, baby," I answered. My mouth itched to lean in and kiss her, to smear the dark plum lipstick she wore today. I shouldn't have agreed to the no PDA part of our arrangement.

"It's a lot more crowded than I expected." Her eyes roamed over the parking lot again. "I don't see any open parking spaces."

"Pull up to the front door. We'll get everything unloaded and then I'll run your car across the street to the coffee shop." I reached in and nudged her arm away from her stomach. Another car pulled in behind her and honked their horn. I leaned back to glare at them. My eyes caught on a familiar face that made red hot anger rear in my chest.

Emery glanced in the rearview mirror at the driver. I patted her car door and stepped back to give her room to move. The driver in the car behind her pulled up next to me. I crossed my arms over my chest as he rolled his window down.

"What do you want?" I asked him. My heart thudded against my rib cage.

My dad furrowed his brow. Looking at him was like looking at myself in twenty years, like looking at photos of Pop from when I was a baby. He wore a Mountain View Baptist Church t-shirt and the sight of it made my blood boil. "I'm here to celebrate with the family." His face softened.

"I don't think that's a good idea." I couldn't believe I used to look up to this man, used to defend him despite everything. It took years to admit to myself how traumatic my childhood had been because of him. Once I did, I couldn't look at him without feeling every ounce of anger I bottled up as a child.

"I won't stay long, son. I just want to pop in and say hi to everyone."

My shoulders creeped up toward my ears. I forced myself to relax them. I couldn't stop him from joining in today's celebration. He was still part of the family no matter how much I hated it. My molars clenched together painfully. "Stay in the lobby," I gritted out.

I sprinted over to where Emery and Pop were pulling things out of her car. One of my arms looped around her, steering her toward the door. "Who was that?" she asked.

"No one. Why don't you go to the break room? We'll meet you in there with everything." I looked back over my shoulder toward Pop. He nodded to let me know that he understood. I pulled open the front door and pushed Emery through.

"Does Granny need help with anything?" Her eyes raked over the packed lobby. Ava helped Granny at the counter with raffle entries. My aunt Jenn worked on setting up a table on the opposite side to distribute refreshments.

In the breakroom I lifted the crockpot she carried from her arms and placed it on the counter. Her arms wrapped around me when I crowded her against the wall furthest from the door where no one would see us. I dropped my face to the space between her shoulder and neck inhaling her vanilla perfume. Her hands rubbed circles against my back. "Are you okay?" she whispered.

"Better now that you're here," I answered. I pressed a chaste kiss against her neck. "Will you do me a favor? Stay in here for a little while."

She pressed one hand against my face and pushed it up to make me look at her. Something flashed behind her eyes that I'd never seen before. The corners of her mouth pulled down in a frown.

"Hey, everything is okay." I leaned into her hand that cupped my face. "Just someone I don't want to talk to."

"Oh." Her frown deepened and her forehead wrinkled. My heart raced waiting for her to ask for more of an explanation.

I pressed a kiss against her forehead. "Yeah. I'll explain another time, I promise. Just for now, please stay in here." Up until that moment, I hadn't stopped to think about all the secrets we both kept hidden. One day I would tell her, but I needed her to just know the parts of my family I was proud of for a little longer.

Voices broke through the heavy silence that blanketed us. Emery's eyes held mine for one more second before she pushed me away. She reached for the crockpot and plugged it up. Pop and Drew entered carrying oversized tote bags with straps that strained under the weight of whatever she had stuffed in them.

Emery blushed when Pop sat his bag down with an oof. "I may have gone a little overboard," she said.

I pulled her against my side, and she relaxed into my embrace. She let me press a kiss against the side of her head. Pop gave me a knowing look. Drew looked away pretending not to notice. He pulled his phone out of his pocket and stared at the screen while he walked out into the shop.

"I'll leave you to it," Pop said. "Let us know when lunch is ready."

Once we were alone again Emery caught my mouth with hers. This kiss was quick but her mouth against mine still made my head spin. "I'll take care of this. Get back to work." She pushed gently against my shoulders.

I let my eyes linger on her for a moment. Forget friends with benefits or whatever else she wanted to call this. I was fully captivated by this woman. The goofy grin on my face dropped away the moment my eye settled on my dad standing next to my toolbox.

"Pop said you're going to be taking over the shop soon," he said.

My hands formed fists at my sides and I shoved them into my pockets. "Yeah, I love this place and you know he wanted to keep it in the family."

Years ago, the plan was for my dad to take over the shop. Granny and Pop would have been able to retire on time if he hadn't up and changed his mind without warning. It was before things started to go downhill and my childish brain always associated the choice with the beginning of things going wrong.

If he had stayed here instead of trying to find himself, maybe I would have had a shot at a normal childhood.

"You should come by the house soon. Your mom and I have missed you. Maybe you could go to church with us on Sunday? Ava keeps saying she will but then something always comes up."

I couldn't stop my eyes from rolling. Of course, Ava would be too scared to come out and tell my parents there was no way she would step foot anywhere near the place that turned against her when she came out at seventeen. Despite everything, my sister still cared more about keeping the peace when it came to my parents.

"How's work?" I asked to change the subject. After leaving the shop he floated around a few different jobs before landing on the county road crew. Before his drinking got bad, he talked about going to seminary school. Even after he got better, he would bring it up sometimes. People loved his testimony. It was him having a lesbian daughter, not his own actions, that destroyed that dream. The church almost forced him out of his position as a deacon for it and made him step down from being the youth group leader for a few years.

"Hey, dad," Drew interrupted.

My dad turned his full attention toward my brother. I took the distraction as an opportunity and went back to the lobby. I needed to be as far away from the woman I had hidden in the breakroom before I accidentally led him to her.

Chapter 31

Emery

December Now

I WOKE UP WITH one leg thrown over Oliver's hip, my face pressed against his chest. His arms were wrapped tight around me, and his face buried in my hair. I tried to shift onto my side but his body followed mine. Oh fuck, his hard length pressed between my legs hitting the perfect spot. He groaned into my hair.

A smile bloomed over my face as his heart started to race against my face. I had almost made him go home last night, but after his very convincing argument of exhausting us both with round four at 2a.m. I allowed him to stay. I didn't even know I could come that many times in one day. One of his hands drifted to my ass, squeezing hard and pressing me tighter against him.

My whole body felt blissfully sore.

"Remind me why we never did sleepovers before." I pressed my lips against his chest

"Why are you asking me? That was your idea." The arm under me started to flex and he groaned. I tried to sit up to let him free his arm, but he pressed me back down. "No, it doesn't need the blood flow, not as much as I need you here." His voice was even deeper than normal, raspy from sleep.

I giggled against his chest and tightened my leg around his waist. His skin was warm against mine felt like heaven. I couldn't remember ever waking up wrapped around someone like this, not even with Levi.

"Are you trying to start something again?" He bucked his hips against me, the press of him making my sore pussy clench.

I loosened my leg. "So sore," I mumbled against his chest.

"Do I need to kiss it and make it better?" I looked up to see him waggling his brows, his eyes heavy with sleep. Shit, I could get used to this view. I reached a hand up to stroke his face. My arm scratched against the stubble on my chin, reminding me why I never liked sleepovers. I tried to push myself out of the bed to take care of it before he could notice.

His arms tightened around me.

"Ollie, I need to brush my teeth and pee," I whined.

"I don't care if you have morning breath," he mumbled, his eyes slipping closed. "I've never woken up with someone before. Are you really not going to let me enjoy my first time?"

"At least let me go pee," I counter offered.

He opened one eye. "Fine but come straight back." His arms loosened around me. I wiggled out of bed, turning back to see he was already back asleep.

I took care of my business in the bathroom, wrapped myself in a robe, and tip-toed to the kitchen. The place was still a disaster where we cooked dinner last night and skipped cleaning up. We had been so distracted by each other we had barely been able to cook and eat. I disinfected the counter, my face heated as I remembered how he had sat me on it, spread my legs, and told me he was still hungry for dessert. He had always had a dirty mouth, but last night he had stepped up his game like he had been saving all these things up during the time we were apart.

I pulled out a mixing bowl and then turned to the pantry to grab the dry ingredients I needed. Strong arms wrapped around me from behind. "I thought I told you to come right back," he said into my ear.

I let Oliver pull me back against him. "I'm going to make breakfast." I felt his stomach growl against my back.

He planted a kiss behind my ear. "Fine, I guess we need our energy." He spun me around in his arms to kiss my mouth.

"Don't you have to work today?" I had almost forgotten that the shop was open on Saturdays, and Oliver never took a Saturday off. It was their busiest day. He would make sure one of the guys had the day off if things were looking slow before he would take it.

"Everyone keeps nagging me to take time off, so I did."

I felt like I had been zapped in my chest. We were already back to him doing things for me. His arms tightened around me.

"Don't go there, Emery. Taking the day off to spend with you is all for me."

We worked in tandem; I made the pancakes while he fried bacon. He tried not to flinch when the grease popped at him, making a joke under his breath about being naked.

We ate standing up at the kitchen counter. Oliver pointed out that I still hadn't finished teaching him how to make the pumpkin cinnamon rolls. I pulled out my recipe notebook and we got to work on the dough.

"I probably need to run home and get some clothes," he said as he covered the mixing bowl so the dough could rise.

I shuffled things around in the pantry looking for powdered sugar. "I need to go to the store. We don't have everything we need."

"Alright, let's swing by my apartment and then we can go to the grocery store."

I gave him a pair of sweatpants and a hoodie to wear, trying to ignore how they were just a little too big on him, so he wouldn't have to put his work uniform back on. "Pack some clothes to keep here."

He gave me that crooked smile. "Are you saying you intend for me to be sleeping here again?"

I shrugged my shoulders and gave him a deadpan expression, "if you're lucky."

***

Oliver's phone rang as we loaded the groceries into my car. His eyes went wide, and he showed me the screen. Matt again. I was really starting to second guess if I liked him or not. Oliver pressed the phone against his ear. I leaned closer so I could hear.

"Hey, man, what's up?" Oliver answered.

"Nothing much, just wanted to see what you're up to today. I was thinking we could hang out later," Matt said in a shaky voice.

"You aren't spending the day with Riley today?" Oliver's face twisted with confusion.

"Yeah, I'm at her house right now, but I thought we could do something later. It's been a while since we hung out." I could hear muffled giggles in the background. Oliver's truck was still in the driveway and the kitchen was still a mess. If they were there, they already knew what was going on.

"I just saw you Wednesday night and Thursday," Oliver said.

"Hey, Oliver, do you know where my sister is?" Riley's voice interrupted whatever Matt was going to say. Yeah, we were busted. I grabbed OIiver's wrist and pulled his phone to me, making static noises with my mouth before pressing to end the call.

Oliver's face was still twisted with confusion. "They know," I explained.

He rolled his lips between his teeth and nodded. "Soo, what now?" He knocked his knuckles against the trunk of my car. "Is it really a bad thing if they know?"

"Oh my god, yes, it's a bad thing. Riley is probably getting her hopes up right now that this is more than what it is."

"So, tell her what it is."

I narrowed my eyes at him. "You mean how you told your family the truth about what we were? Because I seem to remember them thinking I was your girlfriend." Anger flashed through me as I remembered the day I met his mom. He had been so against me meeting his parents that I had never told him, scared I would stir up something between them.

"I never told them you were my girlfriend." His jaw tensed. He swung the passenger side of the car open, knocking his knuckles against the door frame.

I cross my arms. "You just never corrected them. Is that why Ava told me she was so excited to have me as a sister-in-law?"

He slumped into the passenger seat. "Can we talk about this when we get home? No arguments in the car, remember?"

I took a deep breath and nodded. Once I was in the driver's seat, I cranked up the radio until I couldn't hear my thoughts. We belted along with it the whole way home.

Chapter 32

Oliver

November Then

M Y PHONE VIBRATED IN my pocket as I passed the ticket for the car I had just finished to Granny. I pulled it out, surprised to see Emery's name on the screen calling me. In the time that we have been friends, and the month or so since we started sleeping together, she never called me. She was strictly text messages only. Our only phone had been when I called her that first day.

"What's wrong, baby?" I asked in a lowered voice as I marched outside.

Her laugh was shaky, the one she used when she was trying to hide the fact that she was upset. "How do you know something is wrong?"

I lifted my hat off my head and started to run my hand through my hair, forgetting that Ava had cut it too short again, not even leaving me enough to be able to style. I had been too focused on Emery in the chair next to me with her hair freshly dyed blue-black and cut in a long pixie to notice what Ava was doing to me. "You've never called me before," I explained.

She went silent.

"Em, please tell me what's wrong."

"My car broke down," she said in a quiet voice. I ran back inside to get my keys before I fully processed her words. "I was driving, and it just died. I called a tow truck, but they said it'll be an hour before anyone can get here."

I grabbed a jump box and headed outside to my truck. "Pop, I'm taking the trailer," I called without looking to see if he was even nearby. "I'm on my way, baby," I said to Emery.

I kept her on the line while I drove to her, thankful that our apartment building was so close to the shop. She apologized over and over as she recounted what had happened. She was on her way over to the shop when her car started slowly losing power before shutting off completely. She had been coming down a hill when it shut off and had coasted into the parking lot of a gas station.

She jumped out of her car as I backed the trailer up, pulling the sleeves of her cropped sweater over her hands. She bit the inside of her cheek, her eyes wide with worry. "I'm sorry. I could have waited for the tow truck. I just didn't want you to be worried about me not showing up at the shop," she said quickly as I walked up. She caught her bottom lip between her teeth, pressing down hard enough I worried she might hurt herself.

I wrapped my arms around her and pulled her against me. "I told you to stop apologizing. It's not a big deal. I'm going to get your car loaded up and then we're going to go to the shop." I slid a hand down to her ass and gave it a squeeze. "Everything is going to be okay." I caught her mouth with mine, swiping my tongue over the lip trapped between her teeth until she opened her mouth to me.

She stiffened my arms. "Ollie, I've never hauled a trailer before."

My brow furrowed. She lifted both her hands to cover her face as she took a deep breath. "It's okay, you don't have to. I'm driving," I tried to reassure her.

She shook her head so hard it had to hurt. "No, you can't. I told you I always have to drive." She sniffled behind her hands. I tugged at her wrists until she lowered her hands enough so that I could see her eyes.

"What are you not telling me?" I dug through my memories of all the little details she had let slip over the past three months. She told me she didn't drive because she wasn't a passenger princess, but that was all she would tell me. I knew there was more to her past than she had let on, that most of it had to do with her ex, but all she ever gave me was that he was an asshole.

He was an asshole that didn't think she should open a restaurant. An asshole that didn't like that she was close to her sister. There were a lot he didn't like thats, or he wouldn't let her do thats she would occasionally let slip. He made her always feel like she needed to apologize. Even without her saying it outright I was becoming increasingly more suspicious that he had been abusive. I didn't know if I would be crossing a line if I asked.

I clenched my teeth as I pulled her hands lower to completely uncover her face. Her eyes and nose were red, her bottom lip swollen with an indent from her teeth. "Was it something he did?" I asked.

Her eyes widened and she swallowed hard. "What are you talking about?"

"Your ex. Did he do something to make you feel unsafe in a car?"

Her eyes filled with unshed tears as she shook her head and tried to pull her hands away from me. I let go. "I don't want to talk about him," she whispered.

I pulled her into another hug, rubbing my hand in a small circle on her back. "Okay, I'm sorry, I didn't mean to upset you." I kissed the top of her head. "Let me get your car loaded up. Then you're going to tell me what you need to feel safe enough to let me drive you to the shop. We're only five minutes away. Can you trust me that long?"

She buried her face in my shoulder and nodded. "I'll try."

***

Emery twisted the sleeves of her sweater around her hands when I climbed in my truck. She had a coloring book open on her lap, a box of crayons laying on the seat next to her. The sound of my door closing made her look up. Her eyes were still red, but I didn't see any tears. I reached over and stroked my fingers through the longer pieces of hair framing her face, leaning over the center console as close as possible.

"I'm sorry," she whispered.

God, I hated hearing her say those words so much. I hated seeing my firecracker of a woman reverting to this broken state. It always happened at what felt like the most random times. One second, she would be her beautiful bright self, and then the next something would trigger her, making her revert to making herself small. I wanted to find the asshole that did this to her.

"Baby, there's nothing to be sorry about. I'm pretty sure the alternator went out. I already called the part store, and the delivery driver will have it at the shop soon."

"But you had to leave work to come get me and now you're probably going to stop whatever you were doing to fix my car."

"You're damn right I am." I smiled at her as I dropped my hand to stroke my thumb over her swollen lip. "That's what friends are for."

She blushed and swiped the side of her hand under her eye. "Don't talk to me while you drive," she mumbled.

"Okay. Anything else?"

"I need the radio blasting."

I fought back a chuckle, not wanting her to think I wasn't taking her seriously. I knew that already; she always had the radio blasting. The sound of her music let us all know when she pulled into the shop.

She twisted her sweater again. "Levi was really mean," she finally said.

I lifted the center console up so I could pull her closer to me. I stroked my hand over her jaw and down her neck, then back up as I waited to see if she would say anything else.

"He always wanted to pick fights while he was driving, and when I would ask him to stop, he would get reckless." She kept her eyes on her lap as she spoke.

I pulled her face up to look at me. "We're going to make time for you to get comfortable driving my truck and hauling the trailer, okay? You never have to let me drive again."

She nodded, the corners of her mouth lifting in the smallest smile. "Thanks, I...that sounds good." She buckled her seatbelt, signaling the end of the conversation.

I started the truck, turning up the volume on the radio until she gave me a slight nod. I reached over to squeeze her thigh, then pulled my hand back to give her space. Her hand shot out to catch mine, folding her leg up in the seat so her thigh was exposed to me, and the coloring book was balanced on her calf. She placed my hand on her thigh, lifting her mouth in another small smile. Her eyes stayed fixed on the open page of her book, but I didn't need to see her full face to know how big of a step this was for her.

My heart swelled as I let myself study her profile for another moment. This woman was going to kill me. I would hand her my heart on a silver platter with no regrets and watch her butcher it if it made her happy.

Chapter 33

November Then

I PACED AROUND MY apartment waiting for Oliver to come over. The place was spotless, probably the cleanest it'd been since I moved in. Dinner was done and already on the table. The dishes were all washed and put away. After we ate, I would swipe the dishes from the table before he could protest.

Guilt chewed at my stomach. I shouldn't have called him today. Things would have been better if I'd just waited until the tow truck dropped my car at the shop. Oliver already had enough on his plate at work; he didn't need me to call and pull him away.

"I have things to do at work, Emery. You can't just expect me to drop everything because you need my help."

"You're so fucking helpless all the time. You wouldn't be able to do anything without me."

I felt so stupid. I hated being a damsel in distress and I knew that Oliver was the type to swoop in to save me if I ever needed him. He acted like it didn't bother him, but I knew it was just a matter of time. One day he would get sick of it.

My fingers twisted the sleeves of my sweatshirt. I should change into something cuter. Or something sexy. Aside from the dress I wore for him the night of our first time I hadn't worn anything sexy for him. He might like that. There was new lingerie sitting untouched in my dresser that I bought myself after the break-up.

"Emery, what's wrong?"

Oliver's hands gripped the tops of my arms. The contact made me jump. His eyes widened and his hands fell away from me. My arms wrapped around me in a hug on instinct and my eyes dropped to the floor.

"Hey, hey, it's okay. Baby, tell me what's wrong." His hands hovered in the air around me. He tilted his head down, forcing my eyes to meet his. "Did your car give you any more problems?"

The long pieces at the front of my hair slapped against my face when I shook my head with a hard jerk. My face felt wet. I lifted a shaky hand to swipe at the tears on my cheeks.

Oliver settled his hands on my upper arms again. This time he rubbed up and down. I tried to relax into his touch. My brain filled with images of him saying the hurtful words Levi used to say. I folded in on myself more.

"You didn't have to save me earlier. I'm not helpless. I could have handled it on my own."

"I just wanted to help, Em. You know I would do the same thing for any of my friends." His voice was so damn calm. Why was he so calm? He was supposed to be mad at me for interrupting his workday.

"You didn't have to leave work for me. I had it figured out. You had more important things to take care of." I studied his face for tense edges to give away his frustration, his anger. All I could find was wide eyed concern.

"Like what?"

"Like paying customers." I struggled to stop my voice from rising. My muscles tensed, and my heart thudded against my chest.

He didn't even let me pay for the labor of him changing out the part or hauling my car. After a lot of back and forth he finally let me pay for the part at cost for the shop.

Oliver's fingers dug into my arms. Something flared in his eyes. "I want you to listen to me very carefully, Em. Nothing is more important to me than taking care of the people I care about. It's a very exclusive group, and you're part of it. Understand?" He paused until I nodded. "We're not having this conversation ever again. You needed help and I helped you." He had never been this stern with me. His tone only made my guilt heavier.

"At least let me thank you."

"You did that already, baby. You thanked me about a hundred times while I worked on your car." One of his hands released my shoulder and moved to my chin. He lifted my face and flashed the crooked smile that made desire coil low in me.

I dropped to my knees in front of him. We'd done a lot of things since we starting having sex, but he stopped me every time I tried to get my mouth on him. His hands gripped me again before I could hook my fingers in his waistband hauling me back to my feet.

"No, hell no. The first time you suck my cock isn't going to be because you think you owe me something."

I pushed out my bottom lip in a pout. "You never let me."

He pressed a callused thumb against my lip and tugged it down before pressing it back up. "I would rather have my mouth on you." His thumb stopped me from pushing my lip out again.

I opened my mouth to speak, and his thumb pressed inside. I sucked him in and swirled my tongue around him. He let out a low groan. His thumb popped out of my mouth and his hands gripped the back of my thighs.

"Ollie, no," I tried to protest when he hoisted my legs up around his waist. My arms wrapped around his neck holding on tight. He covered the distance to my bedroom in no time.

My back hit the mattress knocking the air out of me.

"You really want to thank me for today?" he growled. His fingers gripped the waistband of my leggings.

I whimpered in response.

"Thank me by not trying to pick a fight with me over this again." He yanked my leggings free. Oliver was always demanding and dominant when it came to sex. This felt like something different, something more intense. His heated gaze raked over me. Then he pulled me up and yanked my sweatshirt over my head. He pressed me back down against the sheets. "Thank me by letting me take care of you. But don't you ever try to thank me by getting on your knees again."

"I want to take care of you too." My breath came out in pants even though he hadn't touched me yet. I clenched my thighs together, needing pressure. Anticipation raced through me.

"If you really want to then I'll let you do whatever you want later. But I refuse to let you touch me for any other reason. Tell me you understand." The mattress dipped under his weight, and he caged me in. "Use your words and tell me you understand."

"I understand," I answered him.

His mouth captured mine in a demanding kiss that made me clench my thighs tighter. My chest heaved with my rapid breaths. The fabric of his clothes brushed against my hot skin. I clenched the hem of his shirt in my hands and tugged it up. Oliver growled against my mouth and pressed my hands back against the bed.

"Clothes off," I demanded.

He broke away from me leaving me gasping. The mattress shifted again as he stood from the bed. Cold silicone bounced on the bed next to me. I turned my head to see Oliver pulling my vibrators out of my nightstand. He dropped them one at a time onto the mattress. The variety of different types were another part of my post break-up shopping spree. Levi used to give me shit for the one that I owned while we were together. I got back at him in my mind by buying one for every need I might have.

Oliver caged me in once again. His beard rubbed against the side of my face and his breath was warm against my ear. "Which one is your favorite?"

"What?" My brain must be fried from the stress of the day. He couldn't be asking what I thought he was. I blinked up at him.

"I think about using these on you every time I open that drawer for a condom. Which one is your favorite?"

"Ollie, you don't have to. Maybe we should just stop and eat dinner."

The heat in his eyes dimmed. He cupped my cheek with one hand pulled back enough that I could see his full face now. "Is that what you really want? I'm not lying when I say that I really want to watch you come on one of these toys."

"You're not doing it just because I tried to give you an apology blowjob?" I asked.

"Nah, this was my plan already for tonight. The apology blowjob pissed me off a little, but I still really want to make you come." He moved off me and settled between my legs on his knees.

I turned on my side to look down at the collection of toys. My favorite was the u-shaped one that stimulated my clit with suction and my g-spot with vibrations. It was the only one that guaranteed a fast and explosive orgasm every time. I wasn't lying when I told him that sometimes orgasms were hard for me even during solo time. My eyes caught on the small palm sized one with suction for my clit. "Am I allowed to ask for you inside me while we use a toy?" I asked him.

His eyes darkened. "This is about you right now. Remember, I'm going to let you take care of me later. Then after that we'll try one of these out while I fuck you."

"Why can't it be about both of us?"

"Emery, be good and show me which one is your favorite."

I sighed and reached for the u-shaped one. Oliver growled against my neck. His sweatpants tented and his hands forced my legs further apart. One finger drew slow circles around my swollen clit while I struggled to explain to him how the toy worked.

He reached for the nightstand one last time to retrieve the bottle of lube. He squirted the liquid on his fingers and warmed it up before spreading over me. One finger sank into me. "Does showing me your toy turn you on?" he rasped. "God, Em, do you hear how wet you are?" He pumped into me filling the room with the sound of my arousal and lube mixing together.

The first time he used lube and acted like it was all from me, ignoring the fact that I was struggling to get wet had been a little mortifying but I warmed up to it quickly. I didn't know why I found it so hot, only that I did.

"Does seeing my toy turn you on?" I teased him between the breathless gasps he pulled from me.

His finger pulled out and then his hand wrapped the red silicone in my hand. His eyes held mine while he lifted it to his mouth. Heat coursed through me and my empty pussy clenched around nothing watching him pressing the vibrating end into his mouth.

"Are you being a good boy and getting it wet for me?"

His cock twitched in response. He released the toy with a wet pop. "Fuck, no one's ever called me that before. I think I like it."

He reached for my hand and wrapped it around the toy. Then he guided my hand and the toy between my legs. His face followed the movement until he was close enough that I could feel his warm breath against me. The tip of the toy pressed against my entrance. "Do you start with the vibrations on your g-spot or do you focus on your needy clit first?" He pressed against my hand until I pushed the toy inside me.

"Vibrations first," I moaned. It wasn't on yet but my whole body buzzed from the anticipation. This was my favorite part, getting myself worked up before I turned it on. "Then the suction when I get close."

"Do you want me to turn it on?"

When I nodded, he pressed the buttons the way I showed him until the toy came to life on the lowest vibration setting. My hand gripped his wrist and my whole body went taunt. It all felt so much more intense with him here.

"Relax for me, baby. You look so sexy right now." His lips brushed the inside of my thigh. "That's my girl," he praised me when I relaxed. "Fuck, I could lay here and watch you enjoy yourself forever."

Every nerve in my body felt like a live wire. Heat swelled inside me, and I felt like I was racing toward the edge. I could come like this without the suction on. "Ollie, I'm so close. I need you." My hand cupped the side of his face. "Please, I need you up here."

Oliver moved up the bed until he was next to me. I shuddered as he pushed me onto my side and curled around me. His fingers tangled in my hair, and he pulled my head to the side to give him access to my neck.

"You going to come for me already, baby? You're so fucking perfect. Look at you taking what you need from that toy like such a good girl for me."

My hips bucked when he turned on the suction. His hand tensed around my hip holding me in place. Behind me his own hips ground against my ass. "That's it. That's my girl," he whispered in my ear.

White hot pleasure flooded through me in waves and I pulsed around the toy. Oliver's teeth sank into my shoulder, and I felt him buck against me while I rode the waves of my orgasm.

The stimulation turned painful against my sensitive clit. I scrambled to pull the toy out of me. Whimpers flowed out of me. My hands shook around the freed toy as I pressed the buttons to turn it off.

"Feel better now?" Oliver asked me.

I felt completely boneless, more satiated than I'd ever been from an orgasm. "Best orgasm of my life," I muttered deliriously.

"Me too."

I furrowed my brows and turned to look at him over my shoulder. "What?"

Oliver chuckled. "You kept grinding that sexy ass against me and you looked so fucking hot. You screamed my name even when it was the toy making you come."

I rolled over to face him, my eyes catching on the wet spot on the front of his grey sweatpants. "You came in your pants again?" No one had ever come just from seeing my pleasure, but Oliver had done it twice now.

"Like a damn teenager," he confirmed. "I lied, that was for me too."

My mouth spread into a wide smile. I made him lose control like that. Sure, it wasn't in the way that I really, really wanted to, but I still had. That was the hottest sex of my life, and he hadn't even been inside me.

I reached behind me for the other toy I considered suggesting to him. I held it up between us. "I can't wait to use this one with you." The thought of it already had my body buzzing for round two.

Chapter 34

Oliver

December Now

"Em, can we please talk about earlier," I asked, sitting down in the floor next to her. I dried my hands off on a dishtowel and tossed it onto the coffee table. She twirled her colored pencil in her fingers. We had come back to her house and picked right back up with baking the pumpkin rolls. She kept acting like nothing had happened, while also closing me out.

It was after dinner now, the argument eating away at me in the back of my mind. This was bigger than Riley and Matt knowing there was something between us. She clearly brought up something from our past that bothered her.

We had a lot of things from the past that we never worked through. Things we kept pushing to the side because if we were just friends with benefits they didn't matter. No wonder things had been so explosive in the end. In hindsight it was easy to see all the little moments where we had both mis-stepped, the little things that built and built until they boiled over.

"I don't want to fight," she said keeping her head down.

"It doesn't have to be a fight, baby. Just talk to me."

She sighed and dropped the pencil in her hand, lifting her head enough in my direction so that I could see her eyes peeking through her hair. I pushed her hair back.

"I know it doesn't have to be a fight; I just don't know how to have a healthy conversation about it." The way her eyes sparkled told me how proud of herself she was for admitting that instead of clamming up further. I was proud of her. "It doesn't matter how much I try to work on it in therapy, I always get freaked out in the moment."

We could do this. While she had been working on herself, I had been doing the same. I kept my promise to Drew and called my therapist the next morning. I knew I should have kept going years ago to work through all my childhood trauma but never found the time to put in the work. That day had been the eye opener I needed. I wanted to get better for her.

Healthy communication had been one of the big things I asked my therapist to help me with. Emery deserved someone that could be open with her, not someone that communicated the way my parents do.

"Okay, let's figure it out together." I took her hands in mine and encouraged her to turn toward me. We adjusted our positions until my legs bracketed hers. "Three rules: no yelling, be honest, and if it gets too heated we separate and come back when we've calmed down."

"There's something I never told you," she said after she nodded her agreement to my rules. I let her pause and work through her thoughts. The urge to ask questions instead of waiting boiled inside me. "That day I watched the front while Granny was at the bank, your mom came into the shop." She paused again, her eyes moving rapidly as she watched my face for the smallest signs of anger. "She called me your girlfriend."

The heavy weight of the anger I always carried toward my parents filled my chest. All that work to keep her protected from them and my mom still ruined it. "I'm sorry, Em, I never told her that. You know I don't really talk to my parents."

She chewed the inside of her cheek. "Yeah, I figured that out later, but she had to have heard it from someone. All I did was tell her my name and she knew who I was. The only people that knew about us were your family, so I thought you told them that I was your girlfriend. And then one day Ava made the comment about me being her sister-in-law one day." Her forehead wrinkled and her eyes dropped toward our hands.

"I never told anyone that you were my girlfriend, but I never corrected anyone. You're right, I did let them believe whatever they wanted to."

"Because that was what you wanted?"

I squeezed her hands. "Yes, because that's what I wanted."

She looked up at me. "Why didn't you tell me what you wanted? Why did you let me drag you into just being friends with benefits?"

I tugged her hands until she climbed onto my lap. I cradled her face in my hands. "Because you were the best thing that ever happened to me, and I was going to do anything you needed me to in order to keep you in my life."

Her eyes brightened. I held my breath waiting for her to panic, for fear to flash across her face. "What about now?" she asked, her voice timid.

"Well, baby, not much has changed."

There it was - panic and fear washed over her face. Her eyes dropped away from mine. "I don't know what to do," her voice broke, and she sucked in a breath, blinking rapidly. "I want so much with you, Oliver, I always have. I'm just so broken, I don't know what to do. I lied before. I don't want us to just be friends with benefits this time."

She slumped against me as her shoulders shook. I held her tight, rubbing my hands up and down her back. "It's okay, baby, you don't have to have all the answers. I lied too. I know you're scared, I am too. But if you'll trust me I promise I'll do everything I can to prove to what you mean to me. You never have to have the answers. We can stay right here, okay? Just stay right here with me, no labels, just figuring it out and enjoying each other."

She sniffled and laughed against my neck. "I do really enjoy you." I brushed my thumb against the side of her face to catch her tears. "We actually kind of suck at the friends with benefits thing," she said with another laugh.

"Oh, for sure. Fucking you is great, but neither one of us is good at keeping feelings out of the picture." I looked down at her the best I could. "To be fair, being with you is unlike anything else I've ever experienced."

"Ditto." She sat back, her eyes meeting mine again. "Hey, I never asked. When is your birthday?"

It was my turn to laugh. "That's random," I said. She glared at me and then rolled her eyes. "January twenty-fifth." She smiled, her eyes getting the far-off look that always told me she was planning something. I tickled her side. "Are you going to tell me when yours is?"

"November third," she tossed out. She started to stand up, but I pulled her back down.

"We've been together for two of your birthdays and you didn't say a word?"

She shrugged my hands off. "It's not a big deal. I usually make my own cake anyways." I let her stand up this time, quickly following and cradling her thick thighs in my hands encouraging her to wrap them around my waist. She let me lift her up.

"It is a big deal. I can make you a cake. In case you've forgotten, I'm a decent cook. I can't believe you would deprive me of an opportunity to spoil you."

"I don't like being spoiled, you know that." She frowned as she dropped her forehead against mine. I tilted my head up to press a kiss on her lips.

"Even if I'm spoiling you for selfish reasons?"

"I don't think that's a thing." She squirmed in my arms, so I lowered her back to the floor. She moved back to her spot in front of the coffee table and picked up a colored pencil. She held it out to me. "Color with me like we used to and catch me up on the time I missed? I feel like we still haven't taken the time to talk and catch up."

I wrapped my fingers around her wrist, bringing her hand to my face to press a soft kiss to the back of her hand before taking the pencil from her. "Are we still a secret?" I asked her.

She threw her head back and let out a laugh that filled the quiet house. Each time she started to say something a snort would escape and she would slap both hands over her face. The sound made my shoulders feel lighter. Warmth spread through my chest. I missed that sound so fucking much.

The dark dam inside me that had built up over the past two years burst wide open. This was my Emery. This time she really was mine, no flimsy excuses to hide what we were doing. I had a real chance with her.

"Are you going to tell me what's so funny?" I asked through my own laughter.

Emery's cheeks were rosy. The light behind her eyes glowed. "Ollie, it's it obvious? We never were a secret, even when we thought we were." She pointed a finger at my face. "And it's all your fault."

"How is it my fault? You're the one that used to spend all your free time at the shop."

"That look on your face." She swatted away the hand I had trailing up the inside of her thigh. "You can get laid later." Emery shifted away from me and tapped her hand against the open coloring book on the table.

A few minutes passed with the only sound the scratch of our pencils over the paper. Out of the corner of my eye I watched Emery bite her bottom lip and tuck her hair behind her ear. The red on her cheeks deepened. "After Christmas," she whispered. "You can tell people I'm your girlfriend after Christmas."

I fumbled the pencil in my hand drawing a long red line across the page. "Why after Christmas?" My voice came out broken and louder than I intended. I cleared my throat as my face turned red.

"I think Matt has something planned for Christmas and I don't want to take attention away from them."

"How do you know more about what my best friend has planned than I do?"

"I've been shameless meddling in their relationship for months now." Emery shrugged her shoulders at me and her mouth curved into a mischievous grin. "I know things."

The word girlfriend echoed in my brain. I'd never had one of those before. My heart pounded painfully against my chest. I felt like a nervous teenager again. I've always been the person that people want to hook up with, but never the person they wanted a relationship with.

I was fine with that. A person with a childhood like mine didn't even know how to have a relationship. I was doing everything a favor by letting them place me in the one-night stand box.

Emery said she was my girlfriend. It was the best fucking thing I'd ever heard. We both still had so much work to do, but there was no one I'd rather have by my side for it.

"So, you're my girlfriend, huh?" I said with as much nonchalance as I could muster. "Like, officially this time?"

"If we're doing this, we're doing it right this time." She looked up at me through her lashes. Her hair fell forward hiding her face again.

My elbow bumped against the coffee table in my rush to get closer to her.. In a flash I pulled her up from the floor and pushed her onto the couch. I dropped to the floor in front of her barely noticing the flash of pain in my knees. My fingers clutched the waistband of her sweatpants. "Lift your hips, baby."

"Ollie, what are you doing?" Emery's hand cradled my cheek.

I pressed into her palm letting myself get lost in those soft eyes and radiant smile. She wore sweatpants and the old hoodie I gave her. Her face was completely bare of makeup. God, she looked so beautiful right now and she was all mine.

"I need you. Please, I'm begging, Em. I need to be a good boyfriend and eat my girlfriend's pussy."

A pretty pink blush covered her neck and chest. I loved making her react like that.

I loved her.

I couldn't for the time to come when I would get to tell her again how much I loved her.

Emery held my eyes with hers for a long agonizing minute before she finally lifted her hips. She let out a surprised yelp and held onto my shoulders when I yanked her pants off. Her legs spread open without any encouragement giving me plenty of room to play.

Chapter 35

Oliver

Thanksgiving Then

Granny smacked my hand away from the plate of steaming rolls. "Not until everyone gets here," she said, waving the spatula she held in my face.

"Come on, I'm starving. The only people missing are mom and dad," I argued. She smacked my hand with the spatula.

"I don't understand why you keep inviting them," Ava said from where she stood cutting the turkey. Ava alternated between hating our parents and defending them at speeds I couldn't comprehend. To their faces or to people we weren't close with she would never admit the ways our parents hurt her. But around Granny and me she was less guarded.

Granny waved the spatula at Ava. "Because he's my son, and they're your parents. Don't you think it's time for the two of you to forgive them?"

Ava reached for a serving spoon on the counter and waved it back. "I'm not forgiving someone for ruining my childhood. This family works better without them." If only it were all in the past like Granny thought. Mom and Dad still actively ruined our lives, just not in the ways that they could when we were kids. One of these days this pot was going to boil over and we were all in for quite the show.

I rubbed a hand over my face, then snatched the spoon and spatula out of their hands. "Okay, nope, we're not doing this today." I glared at my sister. "Think about Drew."

Aunt Jenn laughed as she pulled a pan out of the oven. She dropped her oven mitts down on the stove top and turned around to face us all. "She's right, Mom, things always get so tense when David is around. Twenty years later and we're all still tiptoeing around him." She swung her head between Ava and me. "And the two of you need to stop acting like your brother doesn't know about it. He was young, not stupid."

It's not that we thought Drew didn't know. It's that he was at the prime age for those to be all his core memories about our parents. At least Ava and I still had some good memories from the time before. We just tried to downplay how bad it was around him because he didn't need to carry the pain the way we did.

Granny snatched her spatula back and pointed it at each of us. "I get two days out of the year to have you all together, don't ruin it." She pushed past my aunt and started transferring the fried okra from the skillet on the stove to a serving bowl. "Is Emery coming, Oliver? We made everything safe for her in case."

Granny was a prickly woman set in her ways, but when it came to making sure everyone was included, she always went all out. The moment I explained Emery's allergies she had started changing the way she cooked to accommodate but never got offended when Emery wouldn't eat anything she made.

My heart felt heavy as I shook my head. My family had assumed that we were a couple, and I had never corrected them. Emery was the only one under the impression that whatever was between us with a friends with benefits situation. "No, she's spending the day with her family."

The garage door opened, my mom coming into the kitchen followed by my dad. I dropped my eyes to the floor. Every time I saw him it got harder. The older I got the more I noticed how much I looked like him. The thought always sent me spiraling back through all my fears growing up.

It wasn't always bad, but isn't that how it always goes? Before shit hit the fan, before his drinking got bad, he was my honest to God hero. He was this godly man that everyone looked up to. Hell, even after he was still that man because we all covered it up. People always like to say that in small towns everyone knows everyone's business. The truth was that in small towns it was easy to cover up the town's favorite youth leader being the town alcoholic, even after he was arrested. Even after the plea deal and rehab.

Then once he started opening up about his struggles for the sake of sharing his testimony people loved him even more.

Everyone knew him as the nicest guy. I knew him as the angry drunk.

I spent years feeling guilty about the anger I harbored for him. That was my dad. He was my hero. He wasn't a bad guy, he just had his demons to deal with.

Every time I looked in the mirror and saw his face staring back at me, I felt the need to work harder, to be better than him. I would be the man everyone thought he was. I would be the man I needed when I was a kid.

You're not him, I constantly remind myself.

My mom's soft arms wrapped around me. "It's so good to see you again, son," she said. Her voice was higher than normal, as tense as the fake smile on her face. They must have been arguing on the way here.

"Hi, mom," I mumbled.

She ruffled my hair and then turned to Ava. Ava forced her own smile as they talked. Dad appeared in front of me next. I turned my back to him, shuffling the rolls on the tray until they were lined up perfectly, then knocked my knuckles against the counter.

"Hi, son," he said behind me. I tensed my jaw. "Pop said you have a girlfriend now. Is that who you were hiding from me at the shop? Do we get to meet her today?" His voice was gentle and cautious. I could hear the hurt he tried to cover. I knew it wasn't fair that I was keeping my parents so far away, that they both claimed they were trying to be better now. It just all felt too late, like they should have done the work before they fucked the three of us up, not after.

Reality always seemed to contradict that they were doing better. I shoved down the urge to check if he smelled like alcohol or if Mom had any suspicious bruises.

I shook my head. "No, she's with her family." I couldn't bring myself to deny that she was my girlfriend. I swallowed the retort about how he had no business meeting her that tried to climb up my throat.

Calm down, Oliver, he doesn't get to make you mad.

"You look more like Pop every day," he said patting my shoulder.

More like Pop, not like him. My shoulders relaxed as I let my mind reframe the perspective. Sure, my dad looked just like Pop so looking like one meant looking like the other, but there was something about looking like Pop that filled me with pride. Pop was a good man. He worked hard and gave his family everything. Everything I had learned about being a good man, I learned from him. He taught me how to work, he taught me how to take care of my people, he taught me to be kind, he taught me how to love.

"Thanks, dad," I said quietly. His hand lifted from my shoulder, and I heard him shuffle away.

Ava's arm swung over my shoulders, and she bumped her hip against mine. She rested her head against my arm as she gave me a squeeze. "We can do this, baby brother," she said.

Emery

> I should have come to your family dinner instead.

Oliver

What's wrong?

> They won't stop asking about Levi,

My family won't stop asking about you.

I could leave right now and come crash your dinner. That'll really give them all something to talk about.

> Nah, I should come there.

My dad is here. I don't think that's a good idea.

> Why? I want to meet your dad.

> And your mom.

> No. You really don't want to.

Ollie, why won't you talk about them? Or let me meet them?

> I'll tell you one day

Text me when you get home. I'm coming over

> I miss you.

***

I stood up from my place on the couch and moved toward the coat rack. "I think I'm going to head out," I announced.

"Hold on, dear," Granny said. She turned toward Pop and gave him a soft smile as she squeezed his knee. They had a silent conversation with their eyes. Seeing them like that always filled me longing to have that one day, but today it just made my stomach twist with the need to get to Emery.

"We need to have a family meeting about the restaurant."

Aunt Jenn leaned back against the chair she sat in. "I told you I'm not going back."

"David and I don't want it either," my mom stated.

All eyes went to Wade. He held up his hands and shook his head. "Hell no."

"Granny and I have someone in mind but wanted to get every-one's agreement before we tell her," Pop said with his eyes fixed on me. I felt all the other heads in the room turn toward me. "She's not part of the family yet, but we know it's just a matter of time."

My head spun. I really needed to correct him, but I couldn't. It was what I wanted, to have her be mine. I'd wait my whole life if I had to. My brain snapped back to the day that her car broke down and I left work to rescue her. Such a simple situation had thrown her into a full-on freak out. If she couldn't handle having me help her in that situation, how would she react to us giving her a restaurant?

I cleared my throat. "Pop, I don't think she'll take it."

"I know she's a little hardheaded, but I'm sure we can find a way to make her take it," Granny interjected. Pop wrapped her hand in his. "We love her Oliver, and she's part of this family whether or not the two of you end up together."

My heart raced as the room spun around me. I leaned back against the wall. The room filled with voices all agreeing to letting Emery take the restaurant. Ava and Aubrey chattered about their excitement at having a sister-in-law. My parents scolded me for not letting them meet her if I was that serious about her.

I pressed my hands over my eyes, trying to think. She was going to hate this. I knew she was going to throw every excuse at us for her not being able to take it. But the idea of her being part of our family, of her finally getting to have her dream, filled me with happiness. She had been working so hard on perfecting recipes and policies. The way her face lit up every time she talked about it made me so proud.

The one perfect thing I'd managed to have was going to blow up in my face.

"Okay," I finally shouted over everyone. "We can try to give it to her, but we're doing this with my lead. We can't just drop this on her; it'll scare her away. Let's get the place cleaned out first. Then I'll talk to her about it." I pointed at each one of them. "No one else says a word to her about it."

Nine heads nodded at me as the room exploded with more chatter. I swiped my jacket from the coatrack and walked out the front door.

Chapter 36

Emery

December Then

"Dear, can you watch the front for a few minutes?" Granny asked. "I need to run to the bank. If anyone comes up just tell them you'll get someone to help them and then grab one of the boys." Aubrey had called out sick this morning so it was just the two of us up front.

"Sure, I can handle it, Granny." I gave her a bright smile. I had been hanging out with her enough now that I knew how things worked. I could probably write up a ticket if I needed to. Pops had been joking lately about putting me on the payroll. She patted me on the shoulder and then left.

I focused on the recipe idea I was scribbling down in my notebook, jotting down a few different measurements to toy with. The bell over the front door jingled and I heard soft steps on the linoleum. I looked up to see a woman in her fifties with straight salt and pepper hair. Her eyes were a deep forest green. When she smiled at me one side lifted a little higher than the other.

"Hi, welcome to Franklin Auto shop, how can I help you today?"

Her eyes shifted around. "I'm looking for Oliver," she said.

"Oh, he's out on a test drive right now. Do you want to have a seat, and I'll let him know you're here when he gets back?" I squinted at her smile. It reminded me of Oliver's but nothing else about this woman looked like him. I always thought he looked like a carbon copy of Pop, except for that smile.

She sighed. "No, you probably shouldn't. I was just hoping to catch him." Her eyes scanned over me. "I didn't know they hired anyone to help up here," she said.

The wheels in my brain were turning fast and something gnawed at the pit of my stomach. Something about this didn't feel right. "Oh, I don't work here, Granny just had to step out in the shop for the moment, and I said I'd watch the counter for her." I gave her the brightest smile I could muster. "I'm just a friend of the family."

She nodded and chewed on the inside of her cheek. "Well, will you tell Oliver to call his mom?"

I widened my eyes. "Yeah, I'll tell him. So, I guess you're his mom?" I stuck out my hand to shake her hand. "I'm Emery."

Her shake was timid, her fingers barely gripping my hand. "It's nice to finally meet you. I'm Jodi. I can't believe Oliver's been hiding his girlfriend from us."

Girlfriend.

I took a deep breath, remembering that he had been private about his parents, only saying that I wouldn't want to meet them. She could just be saying that to start something.

None of his family had asked me what was going on between the two of us, they had just accepted me hanging around the shop like it was normal. Had they asked him? Had he told them all that I was his girlfriend?

She dropped her hand to her side. "Anyway, just tell him to call me, please."

I nodded, speechless as she left. A few minutes later the door to the shop opened and then Oliver's arms wrapped around me. He rested his head against my back. "Did Granny abandon you?" he asked in a teasing tone.

"She said she needed to run to the bank." His arms released me, and he spun my stool around until I faced him. He pushed my legs apart, stepping between them. "What are you doing?" I asked.

"You just look so perfect up here, like you belong here." He brushed his thumb over the corner of my mouth. "Can I kiss you?"

"No PDA," I reminded him.

He stuck out his bottom lip in a pout. "There's no one else up here to see us right now."

I leaned forward and caught his full bottom lip between mine, sucking it into my mouth and running my tongue over it. I dragged my teeth over his lip as I pulled away slowly, releasing it with a pop.

"Mhhm," he hummed, "quick and dirty just like I'm going to do you tonight."

I hooked my fingers on his belt loops, pulling him closer. "I need to ask you a question," I said, dodging as he leaned in for another kiss. "What are we?"

He smirked. "Friends with benefits, why? Are you wanting something else?" He waggled his brows at me, lifting his cap and spinning it backwards on his head.

"Are you wanting something else?" I didn't answer his question. I always wanted something else; I just couldn't have it. There was a difference between the two.

"Whatever you need, baby," he said, catching my mouth with his. I relaxed into his kiss for a moment, then pushed him away again, swatting the hand climbing up my thigh. "Fine, no PDA," he grumbled, pulling away. His eyes lifted to mine, widening with concern. "Is everything okay?"

I nodded, lifting my mouth in a fake smile. "Everything is great, Ollie," I lied. We were somehow on the same page while also being so completely confused about what we were. I was terrified.

Chapter 37

Oliver

Christmas Now

Ava

Are you home? I need a favor.

Oliver

What's wrong?

Are you okay?

Is it Drew?

Sweat prickled my palms, and my pulse thundered in my ears. Ava didn't just ask for favors. She damn sure didn't say something like that and just stop responding unless something was wrong. My sister fixed other people's problems, not the other way around.

My apartment felt cold and empty around me. After spending every free moment, every night, at Emery's the past five days I didn't know what to do with myself. I kept waiting for her to change her mind and ask me to come to her parents' house for Christmas.

She never did.

Mom and Dad went out of town for Christmas this year for some church thing. I was thankful they made the choice to skip the awkward family dinner this year. Without Pop and Granny to hold us all together, holidays just weren't the same. Matt invited all of us to join his family later today like we did for Thanksgiving this year.

Three dots appeared on my phone screen indicating Ava was typing. I sucked in a deep breath and held it waiting for the bad news.

What if it was our parents? I didn't even know where they were traveling to. Oh god, I hadn't even responded the last time my mom told me she loved me.

My emotions around my parents were rawer than ever now that I was in therapy. I knew I had trauma, I knew my parents sucked, but I had no idea how deep it ran. Part of me still tried to push all the resentment away with the reminder that they did the best they could.

Ava

everyone is okay. i'll be there in 5

Five minutes later Ava burst through my door with a cloth baby carrier twisted around her torso holding a cat. An empty cat carrier hung from one shoulder, and she pulled a collapsible wagon piled with cat supplies behind her. The tabby cat twisted its head around to face me. Its mouth stretched open in a wide yawn that revealed it was missing half its teeth. I wish I could say this was the first time I'd ever seen my sister carry a cat strapped to her chest.

"Can you babysit for a couple days?" Her fingers worked quickly to free the cat from the cloth.

Her little sleepy face filled with rage and her ears flattened against her head. Yowls of distress filled my apartment. Ava shushed the cat and muttered admonishment like she was speaking to a child.

Ava and Aubrey volunteered as fosters for our local animal shelter which meant they had a revolving door of new animals in their care. Their only foster fail was their dog, Thyme. I was used to the chaos that often filled their home especially during kitten season. I wasn't used to that chaos showing up at my door.

Ava cradled the cat in her arms on its back like a baby, rocking it slightly. The yowls stopped as suddenly as they started. I half expected Ava to pull out a pacifier for it.

"This is Rosie. She's part of a hoarding case that was discovered after her owner passed away last week," Ava explained. She crossed my living room and sat on the couch, still rocking the cat. She relaxed against the cushions and blew out a breath. "She has to be held at all times, or she screams bloody murder. Brie and I haven't slept in two days. She has Thyme so stressed out that she won't come inside."

Without thinking I scooped Rosie from my sister's arms. The cat's face tilted up to me and I braced myself for her screams. She blinked at me with large green eyes and an expression that would put the famous grumpy cat to shame. "What am I supposed to do with her?" She twisted in my arms until she could rest her little head against my chest.

Something in my heart settled, like a missing piece falling into place.

"I just need you to keep her for a couple days until we can find a better foster for her. We're trying to track down the fosters with the other animals and see if she might do better being back with them. I ended up with her because she has some medical issues." Ava's voice sounded far away. The ball of fur in my arms was vibrating, the soft sounds of her purrs drowning out everything. "One of the rescuers said there was a dog there that they had trouble separating her from. Would have made everyone's life so much easier if they'd just kept them together. There were so many animals it's going to be hard to figure out which one it was."

Emery was going to love this cat. She had mentioned just yesterday that she was thinking about getting a pet. Something about Rosie reminded me of her.

"Find the dog. I'll take them both." I clutched Rosie tighter in my arms. Her purrs grew louder against my chest. I looked up at my sister to find her rubbing her forehead. Dark shadows were smudged under her eyes and her normally perfect eyeliner was lopsided today.

"This is a big commitment, Oliver. I don't even know what kind of dog it is. What if it's too big for your apartment? And Rosie needs to be fed a special diet because she has food allergies and is missing so many teeth. I think she may be deaf in her right ear."

My apartment didn't matter in this discussion. Emery had a fenced in yard. It was on the smaller side but still big enough for a dog of any size to be happy. Fuck, I was getting ahead of myself. I should talk to her first before committing to adopting a pet together.

"Just let me know when you find the dog. I'll, um..." I forced myself to swallow the words on my tongue. I almost said that I would talk to Emery about it in the meantime.

"You'll ask your girlfriend?" Ava finished for me.

Rosie's eyes popped open and blinked slowly at me. No doubt about it. This cat was mine.

I cleared my throat and leveled my gaze on my smirking sister. "Yeah, I need to talk to my girlfriend." My face heated when the word left my mouth.

Ava cocked a brow and crossed her arms over her chest. "Like for real this time?"

"For real this time."

"She's not going to break your heart this time? You've been through enough as it, Oliver. I don't want to see her hurt you again."

I hated that everyone was still holding that against her. If I'd forgiven her for then they all needed to too.

Rosie sat up in my arms. I glanced down at her just as her little head bumped against my chin.

"Alright, send her that if you really want to convince her." Ava tapped her phone screen and seconds later my phone dinged in my pocket. "By the way, Mom wants to have a family dinner next month for yours and Dad's birthdays. I told her we would all be there. Bring Emery."

Rosie's purrs couldn't drown out the dread that settled over my body.

Chapter 38

Oliver

December Then

I UNCOVERED EMERY'S EYES. "You can look now, Em." Her brows knitted as she looked at the empty restaurant in front of us. We had been keeping the building cleaned up, even though it had been closed for a couple of years now, so aside from obviously being empty there wasn't anything to make her concerned. Last week Pop, Drew, and I had all worked to take down the old signage and dining room furniture so it would be a blank slate when she saw it. I pulled her against my side. "What are you thinking?"

"I'm trying to figure out why you brought me to an abandoned building. It's a little weird."

I pulled my keys out of my pocket and took her hand, pulling her to the front door. "Let's go inside."

She shifted uncomfortably beside me while I unlocked the door, tugging at her skirt and looking over her shoulder. "What if we get caught?" She bit her lip.

I laughed and swiped my thumb over her lip to free it from her teeth. "I know the owner." I swung the front door open and motioned for her to come inside.

She looked around the empty dining room. I flipped on the light switch next to the door. "What happened to the restaurant that used to be here? Wasn't it here for a long time?"

"Forty-years," I said, sweeping my eyes over the space, still seeing how it had looked for my entire life. "It shut down during the pandemic. We had been thinking about reopening soon, but everyone had already moved on."

She turned back to me, her face scrunching up as she silently repeated my word to herself, trying to work out what I was saying. "Who is we?" she finally asked.

I smiled and pulled her toward me. "My family. Do you remember the name of this place?" I cupped her face in my hands, holding her eyes on me while she thought.

Her hands went to my wrists as her eyes widened. "Darlene's Dinner. Granny's name is..." her words drifted off as her fingers flexed around my wrists.

I nodded, waiting for a smile to spread across her face. A smile that never came. "Darlene," I finished for her. "This was hers for a while. All of their kids worked here at one point." I pointed to the counter. "Right there is where my parents met." She followed where I pointed, her face still in shock. "My aunt was running it for a while, but when we had to shut down during the pandemic she was ready to retire from the restaurant business. Granny and Pop weren't ready to sell the building, so it's just been sitting here empty for the past two years."

I caught her face in my hands again and turned her focus back to me. "Emery, they want to use it for your restaurant."

She frowned and stepped away from me, gesturing around with her arm. "You can't give me a restaurant, Oliver."

"I'm not giving it to you, Emery. We all want you to use it. Once you get established, we can talk about that part, but for now think of it as borrowing it. We had a family meeting; everyone wants to do this."

She covered her face with her hands, peeking at me between her fingers, and backed away from me another couple of steps. Her shoulders were shaking. "Why?"

"Because they all see you as family, Emery. You're perfect for carrying on the legacy of this place, for making something new out of it. It's the perfect chance for you to test out your dreams."

She shook her head as she uncovered her face and gestured between us. "Friends with benefits, Oliver, that's what we said this was."

I shrugged. "So, think of this as a benefit." I held up my hands in surrender. "It's not just me doing this, baby. It was Granny's idea. You know how much she loves you."

She spun around in a circle, one hand over her mouth pinching her lips, as her brows furrowed and her forehead creased. "I can't," she whispered.

I wrapped my arms around her and pulled us both to the floor. She settled on my lap, not fighting as I held her and encouraged her to rest her head against my shoulder. "I know it's a lot, Em. We can call Granny and Pop if you want. They're going to tell you the same thing I am right now. Having you as part of our lives for the past few months has been such a gift for all of us. You fit in like this piece we didn't even know was missing." I squeezed her tighter against me, stroking a hand over her face so she couldn't see me. I looked up at the ceiling, wondering if now was the time to tell her the truth.

All of this had never been a friends with benefits situation, she had to have known that this whole time. She had stumbled into my life on that hot July day when I had been having a shitty day and fit herself in like she had always been there. I didn't know what I was going to do when she decided to leave.

"Ollie," she said shyly against my neck.

"Yes, baby?" I looked down to see her eyes were closed. Her forehead was still creased with worry lines. I smoothed a finger over them.

"I need to ask you a question." The corners of her eyes creased as she squeezed them tighter. I smoothed a finger over those too. "Why do you never talk about your parents?"

I lifted my face back up to the ceiling like I was looking for the words I needed there. "It's complicated."

"Will you tell me? You know all about my complicated stuff." Her head lifted from my shoulder as her hand cupped my cheek. She pressed my face back down, so my eyes met hers. "Please?"

I struggled to push the images that were already clouding my thoughts away. The man that used to tell me it was wrong to ever hit someone slamming his fist into the wall next to my mother's face nightly. Angry words filling our house while I held pillows over Drew's ears hoping he wouldn't hear. Ava and I learned to judge how the night would go based on the smell of his drink.

A nine-year-old shouldn't be able to recognize different types of alcohol by smell.

That night huddled in the neighbor's living room holding my five-year-old brother while my sister stared out the window at the flashing blue lights. Hearing my mother tell us we just needed to pray for him to get better when she tucked us into bed.

"I haven't been close with them for a long time. My dad isn't a bad person, I need you to know that. He just has some problems.

His problems bring out bad things in both of them. He got help a long time ago, but even after that things were never smooth."

I knew I was downplaying things, but I didn't need her to think that my dad was the same as her ex. Growing up, I used to defend my dad, even in the aftermath, because he was still my dad, my superhero. It took me a long time to come to terms with just how fucked up my childhood had been.

My dad was abusive but I'd never been able to say the words. My mom was too even if her abuse was only emotional. Our house was a constant war between two people that lived like we were in a soap opera.

"When was the last time you saw them?"

"They were at Thanksgiving – Granny always makes sure we're all there for the holidays. Before that? I'm not sure. We go months without seeing each other, it's better for everyone." It was too easy to lie to her about my dad showing up at the shop anniversary party. I wanted to forget how close she had been to meeting him. In my memories Emery's face replaced my mom's just when the dry wall cracked and caved under a fist.

My fist? His fist? It didn't matter. I was just as likely to turn out like him as I was to turn out like Pop. Maybe more likely. All that anger was in my blood, wasn't it?

My arms tightened around Emery. She was mine to protect from any of that. For her I could be better, make the choices he didn't.

Was I really that much better when I could lie to her without blinking an eye?

"But you're so close with the rest of your family."

I rolled my lips against my teeth and took a deep breath. "Yeah, my brother and sister are basically my best friends aside from Matt.

I used to be close with my cousin Wade but not as much now. Sometimes I feel like Granny and Pop are my parents more so than my grandparents. All the good parts of my childhood were with them."

My thoughts started to cloud again. The pungent odor of alcohol stung my nose. Years have passed since I last smelled it but in memories it was always just as strong as it was then.

"My dad is an alcoholic. He's sober now, but things were pretty bad for most of my childhood." I took a deep breath to steady myself. "He was a mean drunk." Emery's eyes widened as she took in my words. I didn't know if it was pity or fear that filled her face. "Usually, it was always directed at my mom."

Until it wasn't. Those memories were foggier, like something I may have only dreamed. His words were sharp and clear, the glint of malice in his eyes. It was his hands and the objects in them that were harder to make out. Did he really throw that bottle at Ava for begging them to stop arguing? Did he really slap my little brother for crying?

Emery's eyes studied mine. I could see the thoughts flashing through her head, the questions she was too scared to ask. "How does that translate to you not being close to them now, if everything is better?"

Wasn't it obvious? The drinking may have stopped but the anger was always there simmering under the surface. His fist may have stopped flying but the words didn't.

Because now I wasn't in the house to know if it was really better. Behind closed doors the nightmare could still be happening and we would never know.

I closed my eyes and swallowed. "Because when I was twenty-one, I realized that I was afraid to drink because of him. I went to therapy for a little while and started unpacking all my trauma around the situation. Part of me always knew things were bad when I was a kid, but I didn't realize how fucked up it all was until I was in therapy. I felt like someone took off the blindfold I had been walking around with my whole life. I have so much hate for them. My dad, for everything he put us through, and my mom for keeping us in that situation." Emery turned in my lap to straddle me. Her hands cupped my face, but I couldn't look at her. "I also realized how much responsibility they put on Ava to take care of me and Drew during that time. She never got to have a childhood. I couldn't look them in the eye anymore. So here I am, five years later and I still can't."

"What about Ava and Drew?" she asked softly.

"Ava keeps them at arms length. She talks about cutting them out of her life but then she doesn't. Aubrey says that she still hasn't worked through the trauma, that she might not ever, but I know she hates them. Even at the holiday dinners she only speaks to them if it's necessary. Ava and I thought we had protected Drew, that he was young enough when it all happened that he might not have known what was going on. Turns out we were wrong. He's, um, he's getting help now."

I decided not to tell her about Drew's struggles, about how I found him last year. His demons weren't mine to talk about. He was a good kid, and he was getting the help he needed. Drew may have inherited our dad's addiction, but he didn't inherit his temper. Of the three of us he would probably turn out to be the most well-adjusted.

Emery's thumbs swiped over my cheeks bringing me back to reality. "You're safe now," she whispered against my tear stained skin.

I wrapped one of my hands around her throat and the other cupped her chin, guiding her mouth to mine. Emery was my drug of choice. Her lips parted letting me in and I drowned myself in her. With every move against her I pushed away the voice in my head telling me I would never be safe.

Not as long as I kept lying to myself.

Chapter 39

Emery

Christmas Now

Oliver

Did you mean what you said about getting a cat?

Emery

Are we at the point in our relationship to get a cat?

Babe we're past that point.

Say the word and I'll get a full zoo with you.

I think that's the most romantic thing anyone has ever said to me.

What if we just start with a cat and a dog?

Good. Because I may have gotten us into a situation.

If that's the most romantic thing I've ever said to you it sounds like I need to step up my game.

A PHOTO OF OLIVER cradling a fat tabby cat in his arms filled my screen. I've never seen him look so lovingly at anything. The adoration in his gaze was reminiscent of a father holding his child for the first time. A lump formed in my throat.

We still hadn't talked about my PCOS. After I told him about Levi being abusive, we never discussed my past again, meaning he didn't know about my infertility struggles.

Oliver would be an amazing dad. I didn't even know if that was what he wanted.

Next to me on the couch Matt and Riley huddled together. Matt's finger rubbed around the new engagement ring on her finger. Riley beamed at him and whispered in his ear. My heart twisted in my chest watching them. After months of scheming my sister was getting her happily ever after.

Having Oliver back in my life, saying that we were doing this for real even if we were still figuring it out, made me think I was finally getting my turn. What if my PCOS was the dealbreaker? What if he wanted someone that could give him kids with ease, not after months or years of expensive medical treatment?

Milo was on the floor with Aaron opening the new remote controlled car my parents got him for Christmas. Jenna proudly showed my mom all her ultrasound photos from her new pregnancy. The news of my new nibling made my heart twist even more.

I couldn't wait to have a new nibling. In the back of my mind a voice nagged.

When would it be my turn?

> Her name is Rosie.

> She has to be held or in my lap at all times. But under no circumstances am I allowed to pet her.

A photo of the cat loafed in his lap followed his messages. She glared over her shoulder and one of Oliver's hands rested on his leg next to her with two fresh scratches on his skin. Rosie almost looked proud of herself behind the grumpy expression.

> I love her already. Do I want to know where you found a cat on Christmas day?

> Ava

> She comes with a dog but Ava is still trying to find it.

> Ready to jump in and be pet parents with me?

> I don't know how I'm going to break the news to Rosie if not.

Pet parents. The words tumbled around in my brain, mixing with the fresh doubts about kids. We needed to have the conversation before either of us were too attached.

Too late, we were both attached. We were in the deep end clutching to each other before we ever realized what happened.

Maybe I should have brought it up that first time.

> Meet me at my house? I'm leaving my parents now. We need to talk.

***

The scent of cranberries and citrus wafted through the air when I entered my house. I kicked my shoes off next to the front door and dropped my purse on the coffee table on my way into the kitchen. Nothing could have prepared me for the sight in my kitchen.

Oliver stood in front of the stove stirring something in a saucepan. One of those cloth baby carries was wrapped around him holding a sleeping tabby cat against his chest. He wore the green button down I loved so much with the sleeves rolled up showing off his toned forearms. His lips lifted in the crooked smile that disarmed me so easily a lifetime ago in the shop.

"Hi beautiful," he said. He poured the contents of the saucepan into the dutch oven sitting on the stove eye and then put it in the oven, tucking one arm protectively over Rosie as he moved.

My heart grew three sizes in my chest only to immediately cave in on itself. Hot tears that I'd been holding back during the drive home spilled over. I wrapped my arms around myself, my shaking hands clutching at my sweater.

"You're broken, Emery."

"No one else is going to want you."

All those years fighting to silence his voice in my head and all it took was one thing to unravel it all. The work I put in disappeared in the blink of an eye.

Loud yowls stabbed into my ears. The thoughts in my head grew louder to drown it out.

"You can't expect me to stick around for someone like you."

"You've let yourself go. It's only fair that I get to look at other girls."

"You're not my boss. I don't care if you've got my ring on your finger, I'm still going to do whatever I want."

"I know, babygirl, but mom needs me right now," Oliver's voice broke through the thunder of my thoughts.

Mom. Fuck, that word carved through me like a sharp blade and left a hole where my crushed heart used to be. Rough hands closed around mine and gently worked the sweater free from my fingers. Oliver guided my hands to rest against his chest right over his hammering heart.

"Talk to me, baby. Tell me how to fix it."

I sucked in a deep breath. "You can't fix it, Ollie. No one can fix it," I answered in a broken voice. A sob broke free from somewhere deep inside me.

"Do you remember what I told you two years ago?"

I shook my head. I barely remembered that night when I broke his heart, when I broke my own heart. I remembered the pain. It felt like the pain radiating in my chest right now. The look on his face was etched in my brain in excruciating detail.

I couldn't remember a thing he said after those three words.

"I will love you endlessly through it all, Emery. I don't care what it is. I don't care what you need to do, I'm going to be by your side loving you through it all."

His arms wrapped around me holding all the shattering pieces together. The pressure of his arms triggered something in the back of my mind.

Remember this. When the voices in my head try to tell me the opposite, remember this.

The words I had told myself that day in the park with his hand on my thigh, a coloring book open on a picnic table between us, pushed past the voice of my ex.

With Oliver I wasn't broken, no matter how much I insisted I was. He was the only person that smiled when I was too much and encouraged me to be more. The only one who had ever made me feel brave when I told him my dreams.

The hole in my chest shrank.

"I can't have kids. Not easily. Even with fertility treatments there's no guarantee." I sucked in a deep breath and stared into the only eyes that had ever truly seen all of me. "I have this thing called polycystic ovarian syndrome. It's a chronic illness that affects my endocrine system."

Oliver's hand rubbed small circles on my back. Each pass shrank the hole a little more.

"My body doesn't do a lot of things that it's supposed to and does some things that it shouldn't." I cringed thinking about the hair that grew all over my body in places that weren't normal. The stubborn weight my body held onto even when I starved myself.

Something soft knocked against my leg. I looked down to see Rosie rubbing her head against my calf. Her eyes were closed, and faint vibrations tickled my skin.

"She's not yelling," Oliver said in disbelief. "That's the first time she's been quiet without me holding her."

Rosie blinked up at us and twisted her tail around my ankle. "Hi honey, were you giving daddy a hard time today?" The words felt so natural to say but there was a pang in my chest knowing that I might only ever get to say them to an animal. I wanted to be cooing at a brown eyed baby with a crooked smile.

Oliver tucked my hair behind one ear drawing my attention back to him. I braced myself for the consequences of the last secret I kept from him, for him to finally agree that I was too broken. There was only safety in his eyes. "I don't know if I want kids. It's not really been something I've ever thought about."

The hole in my chest gaped, the shattered pieces spilling free. Oliver never wanted a relationship before me. It made sense that kids were also never on his radar. With a childhood like his I should have expected him to be completely against him.

It caught me by surprise. For a long time I convinced myself that not being able to have kids would be the thing that shattered his idea of a future with me, not that him not wanting them would be the dealbreaker. Because I desperately wanted to be a mom. The idea of letting go of that felt like giving up the one piece of myself I'd held onto even after losing everything else.

"Come back to me, baby. Tell me what lies your brain is spouting." Oliver's hands cradled my face and blocked out the world around us. Just the two of us against it all like it always should have been.

"I want kids. I would do anything to have them, Ollie. If being with you means giving up the tiny chance of me being a mom, I can't do that."

Tears gathered in his eyes. My vision blurred and his face melted into the man whose heart I broke two years ago. All our lies crashed around us and the hope that maybe this time things would stick slipped from my fingers.

Chapter 40

Emery

December Then

OLIVER BROKE OUR KISS and threaded his fingers through my hair. "Emery, I need to tell you something."

My knees ached from the hard floor of the restaurant. My brain was full of static, every muscle in my body on edge. What else could he have to tell me? Trying to get me to take over the restaurant and then unloading all that about his parents was already so much. I couldn't handle anything else.

He ran his other hand up my arm, grazed my shoulders with his fingers, and then combed his fingers into the back of my hair. His thumb stroked along my hair line at the back of my neck. "I can't keep doing this friends with benefits thing with you."

My back stiffened. The restaurant tilted around me. How had we gone from him trusting me with all that to him breaking things off? "What did I do? Whatever it is, I'm sorry. I can fix it," the words poured out of me in one breath.

He shook his head and widened his brown eyes as he drew his brows down so low they almost touched his eyelashes. "You didn't do anything, baby."

I jumped up and shook his hands off trying to pull me back into his lap. I wrapped my arms around myself and tried to think. Outside cars sped by and the lights of nearby businesses shut off for the night. All those people were just going about their day with no idea that my world was falling apart. Stupid Emery always putting herself in situations guaranteed to break her heart.

It's your fault I'm like this, Emery.

If you were a better girlfriend I wouldn't have to be like this.

I thought he was different. The past few months felt like I stumbled into a romance movie. But this wasn't fiction. There was no happily ever after in real life. I chewed on my thumb nail and blinked my eyes. Oliver stood from the floor. With gentle hands he unwrapped my arms from my torso and held them. His thumbs drew soft circles over my knuckles.

"I'll do better, Ollie. Just tell me what I did. Is it because I didn't want to take the building?" I pleaded with him. Maybe if I apologized for the right thing he would change his mind.

His eyes filled with fresh tears and his mouth pulled down in a frown. Then we were back on the floor with me perched across his lap. "I love you, Emery. I can't keep doing this because I love you."

"You love me." I stumbled over the words slowly. He loved me. The words felt wrong. I fixed my eyes on the wall above his head and my vision blurred. The pendulum of panic in my brain shifted. I couldn't keep up. "You weren't supposed to fall in love with me. You promised."

Who was I? I promised myself freedom and then I fell into whatever this twisted arrangement was with Oliver. The thought of him ending things sent me into a scramble to hang onto him. I wasn't supposed to be that girl anymore.

He loved me. Fuck, this was all going wrong. I wasn't ready. God, I was so far from ready. He deserved someone that didn't turn into a sobbing mess begging him to stay. Someone that healed enough to be the support he would need navigating a relationship.

He deserved someone that wouldn't lead him straight into the relationship his parents had.

I wasn't that person.

"I never promised not to fall in love with you, I promised to give you whatever you needed. I know you need room to heal. I want to be here for you while you do, however you need that to look."

"Oliver," I said.

His hands stroked my face but didn't force me to look at him. "Let me love you, Emery. Let me love you right here in this storm and come out the other side with you." His hand gripped my chin and urged my face down. I dragged my eyes down to meet his.

My vision sharpened, focusing on his eyes. I tilted my face until his hand dropped from my chin. "You just want to save me. I told you I'm not here to be saved, Oliver. I'm not ready for more. I can't be more than what I am right now."

"Baby, I love you exactly how you are right now. The past six months with you have been the best my life has ever been." His hands skated over my legs, the callouses catching on my tights.

"I'm not me right now. I don't know who I am anymore."

"I love you, Emery. I've never been more certain about anything else in my life. That day you walked into the shop I knew you were supposed to be someone important to me."

"Love isn't always enough." I moved from his lap to sit beside him. He thought he loved me now, but in a few months he would need more. He would need more and more of me until I had nothing left to give.

I already had nothing left to give.

"It's a start. Let me love you. Let's figure it out together. I'm not asking you to commit to anything more than that." His voice was low, but it crashed through my thoughts. "Tell me you don't love me, Emery."

"I do love you, that's the problem. I love you so much I would give you anything you ask me for," I answered. As the words tumbled from my mouth, I knew it was true. I may have nothing left to give, but I would still give him the pieces that remained. I would fight the fights. Play the games. Give. Give. Give. "I wish I had met you in the future when I was a better version of myself. I'm too broken for this right now. I need to figure out my shit before this can be anything."

Oliver's hand dropped to where my hands were tugging at the bottom of my dress. "What does that mean?"

"You're my right person, Ollie, but the timing is all wrong. I'm not who I need to be for you. I'm broken and toxic right now." The memory of the jealousy I felt seeing him talk to Aubrey flashed through me. The ghost of the anger I felt every time he had to work late steamed in my veins. Every moment I decided not to trust him and itched to pick a fight.

"We can make the timing right."

I shook my head and stood up. Oliver followed me but this time his hands stayed by his sides. I cupped his face with my hands and ran my thumbs over the tears that were streaking down his face. "Some person out there is going to be very lucky to get to have you, Oliver. I wish I could be them." I brushed a kiss over his lips and gathered my things. It took the last of my strength to not look over my shoulder as I left. I opened the door and cold outside air felt harsh against my tearstained skin.

Oliver's arm blocked my path out. "Take all the time you need. Be who you need to be. Do what you need to do. I don't care if you need to do it next to me or somewhere far away. Just know that no matter what, I will love you endlessly through it all."

Maybe in another life those were the words I needed to hear. Right now, it felt like the twist of a knife where my heart used to be. I didn't deserve a love like that.

"Ollie, please don't hate me. You need to let me go."

His arm fell away. The last words I heard as the door closed behind me were, "I could never hate you, Emery."

Chapter 41

Oliver

December Now

EMERY TREMBLED IN MY arms. My chest ached and the kitchen closed in around us. I thought we were doing things right this time. I thought we were both doing better. How did we end up right back here again?

Not this time. It wasn't fucking happening again. I wasn't going down without a fight this time.

In a matter of months my world had expanded to include this beautiful woman again. To include the cat circling around our feet. Somewhere along the way my heart knitted itself back together.

Everyone knew she was going to break me again and I told myself that I would be okay if she did. But I wouldn't.

My molars popped under the pressure of my clenched jaw.

"I'm not asking you to give up anything," I said in the calmest voice I could manage. My fingers clutched Emery's hand and pressed her palm against my racing heart. "This belongs to you, has since the day I met you. And one day it's going to belong to our kids. Anything you want, I'm going to give you."

"But you don't want kids."

"I said I didn't know because I'd never thought about it. Before you I told myself I couldn't have any of this, but I want everything with you, Emery. I want to be your boyfriend and someday your husband. I want the kids and the white picket fence."

When she walked out that door with my heart two years ago, I never thought I'd have another chance at any of it. I never thought I deserved another chance. Someone like me that could lie so easily to the love of my life instead of fighting for her shouldn't get another chance. It was better for everyone that I accepted it. I was saving everyone the pain of me one day becoming my father.

Emery made me remember that I could be Pop, not my dad. I wanted to be better for her.

"Oliver, you don't have to keep lying to me. I'm so sick of you lying to me because you think it's what I need to hear." She tried to tug her hand away and I clutched it tighter to my chest.

Her words were a low blow. I did it then and I did it now. I was a liar when it came to keeping her in my life. It had to end. If we were doing this for real, if this was going to last I knew I had to start being honest with her.

"I'm done lying. I promise you I'll never lie to you again." I sucked in a deep breath. "I think we should go to therapy."

"I'm in therapy," she said.

I shook my head. "Me too, but I think we should go together. We've both got a lot of baggage to work out and I want to do whatever it takes to make sure we make it this time."

Emery blinked at me, the wheels behind her eyes coming to a complete stop. I braced myself for her to tell me to leave. Time stood still while I waited for the words.

Just when I thought my heart might stop she blew out a breath. Her mouth lifted in the smallest smile I'd ever seen. "I think that's the most romantic thing anyone has ever said to me."

Somewhere deep inside me the scared child healed just a little bit. Years of hearing my parents argue about going to therapy together made it feel like throwing in the towel. Couples counseling was wrong, and people only did it so they could get divorced. The right answer was to just pray a little harder and study the bible a little more so God would make everything better.

For us it could be a new beginning, the best chance we could give each other. Choosing therapy meant choosing us. I was ready to choose Emery every day for the rest of my life and now I had the hope she wanted to choose me too.

Chapter 42

Emery

January Now

OLIVER'S CHILDHOOD HOME WAS a small white farmhouse with a large porch at the end of a cul-de-sac. The neighborhood was full of houses that looked almost identical but were all painted different muted colors. I parked my car behind Ava's in the driveway. One of Oliver's hands clutched my thigh and the other rested over top of the rings under his shirt.

"Are you sure you want to stay? I can do this on my own if you're not ready." His thumb smoothed over my tights.

I twisted my fingers with his and lifted his palm to mouth. His eyes met mine when I pressed my lips against his skin. "You and me, remember? If you go in there, I'm going to be right by your side. If you want to skip it, we can go back home and eat this cake by ourselves."

Oliver's mom promised dinner wouldn't have any of my allergens, but he convinced her to let me make the birthday cake. Ava came over early to confirm that all the food was safe for me to eat. I felt uneasy all day about trusting them. Ava settled my nerves by sending constant updates and pictures of all the ingredients.

Now I was more worried about the way Oliver closed in on himself a little more the closer we got to the house. We had our first couple's counseling session earlier in the week. We didn't cover anything we hadn't discussed before, mostly just filling the therapist in on why we were there. Since then, we'd both felt extra vulnerable from rehashing all our secrets.

He'd been telling me every day that we could skip today if I wanted to. I wished he would just tell me that he wanted to skip it. I could meet his parents another day when he was ready.

Drew's car pulled up behind us. Determination settled over Oliver's face seeing his little brother. He slipped into his role as Drew's protector with ease.

"If they do or say anything that makes you uncomfortable we can leave immediately. We don't owe anyone an explanation," I reminded him. Tonight my job was protecting him.

***

Jodi frowned at her husband's back as he disappeared into the kitchen. It was the third time he had excused himself from the table and we were only halfway through dinner. Her eyes returned to all of us around the dinner table and she forced a bright smile.

Across the table Ava's eyes met Oliver's and they exchanged a few unspoken words. I rubbed my hand over his thigh under the table. We all knew why David kept disappearing, but no one was calling him out.

David returned to his seat on the other side of Oliver, the sweet smell of wine wafting through the room. He leaned forward to look at me. Oliver shifted uncomfortably next to me and I braced myself to pull him away.

"How's Rosie doing? She isn't giving y'all too many problems?" Ava asked.

Oliver beamed at her and fished his phone out of his pocket. He opened the photo album that was quickly taking up most of his camera roll space. "She's doing great. She really likes Emery and is getting better about being on her own."

Aubrey rested her chin on her wife's shoulder and while they looked through all the pictures. "She has the cutest little grumpy face," she cooed.

Even when Rosie was happy, she always looked like she was in a bad mood. I loved her little face so much. She had us both wrapped around her little paws. Oliver came home with a cat tree and more toys than she could ever need the day after Christmas. Over the past three weeks I think he had bought one of everything from the cat aisle at the pet store.

At night Oliver had to fight her to be able to cuddle with me because she always wanted to sleep curled up on my stomach. My favorite part of the day was curling up with the two of them on the couch and watching another episode of *Andromeda Portal*.

"I think they finally tracked down the dog she's bonded to," Ava said. "I'm going to set up a meeting with the foster to pick him up this week. Do you want to bring Rosie to my house to meet him?"

"So, any wedding bells in the future for the two of you? I'm really excited to have a daughter-in-law," Jodi said, interrupting Ava.

Ava and Oliver both went rigid. We had discussed the possibility of his mom saying something about grandkids or marriage, but I didn't expect her to insult Aubrey in the process. Even after everyone warned me that she wasn't supportive of her daughter's marriage I thought she would at least be a little more subtle about it.

"Mom, you have a daughter-in-law," Ava said through clenched teeth.

"Any grandkids coming soon? We're all not getting any younger," David said ignoring his daughter. "You need to start getting established in a church so you can make sure to raise those kids right."

My eyes bulged and I choked on my spit.

Drew's fork clattered onto his plate. "Didn't do us much good," he muttered. Every head turned his direction. I still wasn't used to hearing him speak, much less saying something like that.

Laughter boomed from David. I wasn't prepared for how similar his laugh was to Oliver's. Something about it made my stomach twist.

"Oh, I have pictures of the dog that I meant to send to you," Ava interjected. She swiped frantically through her phone with shaking hands. She turned the screen around to show me a photo of a dog that was so ugly it was adorable. His head was too big for his small body and made him look like a bobble head. "You need to have one of those DNA tests done on him," she said with a laugh.

"The three of you just lost your way a little. There's still time for you to get right with the Lord," David continued. "Your mom and I pray every day that you'll find your way back."

Aubrey's face flamed red and she stretched an arm around Ava. "No thank you, David. My wife and I are better off staying away from that place."

"I better off staying away too. I don't think they would be very accepting once they hear I'm bi," Oliver added.

"Oliver, you're not bi. You were just confused, but you're with a woman now so it's all okay," Jodi chided him.

My pulse thundered in my ears. I couldn't believe that his parents would say something so terrible. I believed every word Oliver told me about his childhood, but witnessing it was a whole other thing. How was this man someone raised by Granny and Pop? They wouldn't stand for a single word their son and daughter-in-law were uttering.

"Can we at least try to be on our best behavior tonight? We have a guest," Ava pleaded.

Oliver pushed his chair back from the table and clutched my hand. "Nah, don't worry about it. We're leaving," he announced.

I let him lead me through the house, squeezing his hand as hard as I could to try to ground him until we could make it to the car. He swiped my purse and our jackets from the coat rack on our way out the front door. Someone pulled the door open when I tried to close it behind me. Aubrey pulled her wife behind her; both their jackets tossed over her shoulder. She jutted her chin in the direction of the house next door.

Oliver followed her lead to a backyard with an above ground pool and deck taking up most of the space. A trampoline was tucked into the corner of the yard. Ava opened the net around it and ushered us all to climb on.

"What's the weight limit on that thing?" I asked nervously. It didn't seem safe for four grown adults to pile onto something meant for kids, especially not when three of us were bigger people.

"It'll be fine as long as we don't jump," Aubrey reassured me.

Oliver put my jacket around my shoulders and helped hold down my skirt so I could climb on. The four of us rested on our backs looking up at the sky.

"Anyone going to tell me whose property we're trespassing on?" I asked after a few minutes.

"My parents," Aubrey answered. "Welcome to where we used to hide as kids to get away from Jodi and David."

"The Garretts are pretty cool," Oliver added. His hand found mine again, clutching me like a lifeline. He moved our joined hands to rest on his chest. "Should someone check on Drew?"

The net around the trampoline opened again drawing all of our attention. Drew's arms were braced around the cake carrier with forks and paper plates balanced on top. We all sat up and adjusted positions so he could join us. The cake bounced in the center of the circle we formed.

"I can't believe you just came out and left like that," Drew said, passing out the plates.

Oliver shrugged his shoulders. "Mom's always known. Seemed like a good time to remind her." He recounted the story about the time she caught him writing fan fiction. "I probably should have told all of you before."

Ava threw her head back in a laugh so loud a few dogs somewhere in the neighborhood started barking. The light next to the backdoor of the Garrett's house flashed on and the blinds parted enough for someone to peek out.

"We knew, Oliver. No teenage boy has that many posters of a shirtless man in his room without being at least a little queer. It's nice to not be the only sibling out of the closet now."

"I'm ace-spec," Drew said quietly. "I'm still working out the label that works best for me." He blushed and looked down at his phone.

Ava let out another loud laugh. "Oh this is rich. I can't believe Jodi and David managed to produce three queer kids. Guess that 'raising them right' really didn't turn out how they expected did it?"

Aubrey's phone lit up next to her. She smiled down at the screen while typing something. "My mom said we can come in when we get tired of freezing our asses off."

Oliver shook his head. "I'm going to need a little longer. I think my blood is still boiling."

Ava stretched her arms out behind her and lifted her face to the sky. "What do you think, Emery, you still want to be part of this family?"

A blush heated my cold cheeks. Oliver and I had been dancing around the subject since Christmas. We still hadn't even said the big three words out loud. Obviously, marriage was the end goal – we wouldn't be bothering with therapy if it wasn't – but it felt weird to talk about so soon. We'd only been in a relationship for a month technically even if we'd sort of been together much longer.

Oliver's hand squeezed mine. Maybe it was wrong to be talking to his sister about this when we hadn't discussed things privately yet, but I knew he needed to hear it. I gestured vaguely toward the Franklins' house. "That family, nah, I'm good." I turned toward Oliver and smiled. "The family out here, absolutely."

I cupped his cheek with one hand and watched one corner of his mouth lift with a small smile. Mentally I tried to convey the words I took far too long to say to him. The first time I said them was not going to be in front of his siblings. He blinked slowly at me the same way that Rosie did while purring.

My heart swelled in my chest.

"Hell yes, I'm finally getting a sister!" Ava's voice ruined the moment between us.

Oliver leaned his face into my hand. "We're leaving," he announced. "You guys enjoy the cake."

Chapter 43

Oliver

I T TOOK ALL MY will power to keep my hands to myself during the drive back to Emery's house. She kept glancing at me out of the corner of her eyes. We still played by the rule that we set all that time ago about not having serious conversations in the car. Even happy conversations couldn't happen in the car if they were serious.

Hearing her say she wanted to be part of my family was serious as fuck.

I wanted to go all caveman on her right now. Mine. She was mine.

Her little skirt was pushed up to the top of her thighs. When she got dressed earlier all I thought about was pushing that skirt up and pulling those tights down just enough to fuck her against the wall the second we got home.

Hearing her say that she wanted to be part of my family changed my plans. I wanted her splayed out under me while I told her how much I loved her with my words and body. No more holding back.

Normally I would keep my hand on her soft thigh while she drove. I couldn't touch her right now, not if we were going to make it all the way home. Her eyes kept drifting to my hands and then to her leg, the question clear in her expression. My fists clenched in my lap.

"Ollie, are you okay?" Emery asked at a red light.

"I'm fine. Just really want to be home," I forced myself to say. My hand went to the chain around my neck without thinking. Anything to keep from reaching over to rip her tights open.

Emery flipped on the blinker to make a right turn instead of going straight. Another right turn and we were on the road with the restaurant. We hadn't been here in weeks, both of us agreeing that we should work through our problems before trying to put this place back together. The restaurant came into view and my heart skipped a beat. She had her seatbelt undone before she finished parking.

"I don't want to wait until we get home," she whispered. Both her hands cupped my face pulling me towards her. "I'm sorry I said that in front of your siblings. I know we should have talked about it first, but I meant it, Ollie. I want to be part of your family. You're my future. We both still have so much to figure out and I want you by my side for it this time. I want you to love me endlessly through it all just like you promised me you would." Her eyes scanned my face searching for my reaction. My heart thumped painfully against my ribs. "I love you," she finally said.

I forgot how to speak. My hands bracketed her face and pulled her forward closing the distance between us. The kiss was frantic and clumsy. Her tongue pressed into my mouth the moment our lips connected. Our noses bummed and our teeth knocked together like two inexperienced teens. The words I needed to say to her were caught up in the whirlwind of finally hearing her say she loved me. "Need you," I growled into her mouth. It was the best I could manage in this cramped car where she was so close and too far away at the same time.

I wanted to drag her inside. It would be freezing and there was no furniture, so I knew it was a terrible idea. I also didn't have a condom with me. Emery made it clear she wanted kids and she might have difficulty getting pregnant, but I'd rather not test that right now. We weren't ready to risk the possibility of an accidental pregnancy.

"Need you too," she panted.

I pulled back, putting as much space between as was physically possible. "You need to get us home right now."

She poked her bottom lip out in a pout. I pressed my thumb against it and let out a groan when the tip of her tongue flicked over my skin. Her eyes flicked down to my lap. Her lips stretched into a grin when she saw my erection pressing against my pants.

I reached around to grab her seatbelt and pulled it back around her body. She shifted back to facing the windshield. The movement made her skirt ride up more. This woman was trying to kill me. "Drive safe, baby," I told her, clicking her seatbelt into place.

***

Rosie yowled on when I placed her in the hallway and closed the bedroom door. Emery sat on the edge of the bed to tug down the zippers on her knee-high boots. My knees hit the carpet before I made it all the way to her. I crawled to her, closing the remaining distance and knocked her hand away from the zipper. She gazed down at me with heavy lidded eyes.

"Say it again," I growled.

"I love you." The words made my heart swell too big for my chest, but it wasn't what I wanted.

I shook my head. Knowing she loved me was great, amazing even. This whole time it wasn't what she was fighting against, it wasn't what I needed.

"I want you to love me," she answered.

Fuck, there it was. No more telling me I couldn't fall in love with her. No more running away because I did. "I love you too," I breathed out. I pinched the zipper on one boot and pulled it down. My fingers scraped against the fabric of her tights. I pressed my lips against the rough fabric over her ankle.

"Hurry up," she pleaded.

I smirked up at her, undoing the other zipper even slower. We had the rest of our lives for rushing. I wanted to savor tonight.

I wanted to finally make love to her.

With both her boots off I kissed my way up one leg and back down the other. Then I pulled her tights down and repeated the process, not leaving an inch of skin untouched. Emery reclined back on her elbows watching me. My teeth sank into her inner thigh hard enough to leave a mark behind, and I followed it with a brush of my tongue to soothe the sting. Emery let out a moan and I hadn't even touched her pussy yet. My fingers sank into her dimpled thighs, the sight so erotic I was teetering on the edge already.

Her sweater went next. I repeated the same process over her upper body. By the time I had her naked she was writhing, legs clenched together searching for any friction she could find. "Need you," she begged over and over.

"How do you want it?" I asked. I swiped my tongue over one pebbled nipple. "Do you want me eat that needy pussy until you're screaming my name?"

"Your cock...please...fuck...make me come on your cock." She looked up at me with dark eyes and her fingers clawed at my pants. A frustrated grumble vibrated through her body while she struggled to get her hands between us. "I swear if you don't take your fucking clothes off right now..." she muttered.

That was all it took to have me scrambling off her to strip my clothes off at lighting speed. I opened the nightstand drawer open with too much force and her collection of toys jostled around. It felt like it took me an eternity to roll the condom on and slicked myself with lube. Emery moved the center of the bed. Her nails scraped lightly down my back while she watched me. The pink clit suction and vibrator she loved for us to use together caught my eye. I pulled it out too.

Once I was between her legs, she wrapped them around my hips and pulled me against her. She plucked the toy from my hand and moved it between us. She sucked in a deep breath when I pushed the tip of my cock into her. I paused for her to adjust around me wishing I had gotten her more ready than this. I wrapped my arms around her back and pulled her against my chest. This was must be what heaven feels like, the love of my life in my arms pressed against me as close as possible. My face dropped to the space between her neck and shoulder.

She relaxed around me and her heels dug into my back. "Please," she begged, "I can't wait." She urged me to push all the way in. One hand wrapped around the back of my neck pulling my face to hers. Our mouths met in an all consuming kiss that had me almost coming too soon.

The moment I pressed completely inside her the vibrator between us buzzed to life. So much for taking our time. I moved my hips in a few slow thrusts to warm her up. Fuck, she was so warm and wet wrapped around me. Mine, she was finally mine. "You feel so good, baby."

"Don't hold back. I want to come together," she panted.

"Are you going to come for me already?"

Her hips lifted to meet my every thrust. I watched her lips for every muttered plea of "harder" or "faster" between her moans.

"That's my girl. Fuck, you feel so good," I praised. My mouth captured hers in another messy kiss. Her pussy fluttered around me, and I felt her increase the intensity of the vibrator. "Are you close?"

Her moan into my mouth was the only answer I needed. Seconds later she clenched around me. My name tumbled from her lips pushing me over the edge.

Emery tossed the vibrator onto the mattress beside us, still buzzing. Her arms wrapped back around me and held me close while we came down. She stared up at me with hazy eyes and a soft smile. Her cheeks were flushed a pretty pink. "I love you," I told her again.

"I love you too."

Outside the door Rosie yowled again. Emery chuckled and buried her face against my neck.

"You're going to have to have a talk with her about privacy," I laughed.

Epilogue

Emery

Ten Months Later

I CLICKED THE LOCK on the door of the restaurant and pressed my forehead against the glass. Oliver crowded behind me and flipped the sign on the door. "I'm so proud of you," he whispered in my ear. His hand rubbed small circles between my shoulder blades.

"We did it," I whispered back. We survived the soft opening of Safe Haven, the place I'd spent my whole life dreaming of.

The process to get here hadn't been easy. I was more grateful than ever that we chose to go to therapy together because trying to get this place open had been a true test on our budding relationship. Without the communication tools we worked so hard to learn I didn't think we would have survived it.

These four walls were where we fell apart all that time ago, and they were also where we learned to love each other in the ways we needed.

Every day Oliver was more like the man I first met over three years ago. He was getting better about delegating at work and even let Shelby start learning mechanic work to help around the shop. Our relationship was more about us taking care of each other and less of him just trying to take care of me.

I let myself sink back against him, forgetting for a moment that our employees were working on cleaning up. Oliver's arms wrapped around me, and he rested his head on my shoulder. "I can't fucking believe this is real," I laughed. I'd barely slept all week from the excitement and anxiety over today. The sleep deprivation was starting to get to me.

"I'm so proud of you, baby," he said again.

His heat disappeared from my back. I turned around ready to pull him back against me. My eyes landed on the dining room still filled with our families and employees. They were all standing around with wide smiles watching us.

Oliver's callused hand wrapped around mine pulling my attention down to where he was bent down on one knee. My eyes widened.

We'd been discussing marriage openly all year. He even let me see some of the rings he was looking at. He moved into my house officially in February when his lease ended but we hadn't spent the night apart since that night in December. We couldn't separate Rosie and her best friend Brownie, so it made sense for him to move in despite us not being together for very long. I wasn't too thrilled at the idea of not sleeping next to him even for just a night.

"Three years ago, you walked into the shop and swept me off my feet by telling off a rude customer. I'll never forget the way you blushed after when I talked to you. Or the way you smiled and made the rest of the world disappear. Our journey to get here wasn't easy but there's no one else I'd rather have by myself through all of life's challenges. Emery Harrison, would you do me the honor of letting me continue loving you through it all by making me your husband?"

Tears clouded my eyes and a lump formed in my throat. I nodded my head hard enough to make my neck hurt.

"Words, baby, use your words," he reminded me with a squeeze of my hands.

"Yes, oh my god, yes. I want to marry you."

My knees hit the laminate floor with a thud. The pain was overshadowed by my need to get my mouth against his. With shaky hands I grabbed his face and pulled him towards me for a kiss that was probably a little more than our families should be seeing. The ring box tumbled from his hand and the ring clattered against the floor.

Oliver broke our kiss. He scrambled after the ring, holding it up triumphantly once he found it under a table.

"You two go home. We'll take care of closing up tonight," Ava offered.

Oliver whisked me away before I could decline the offer. Outside he slipped the ring onto my left hand. "I love you," he said and pressed another kiss to my lips.

"I love you too." I looked down at the car keys he dangled between us. "Can you drive tonight? I'm really tired."

His face brightened the way it did each time I trusted him to drive. Letting go of that control was still difficult for me but he made me feel safe enough to let go sometimes. The same way I made him feel safe enough to open up about when he needed help. We were a far cry from the two people we were both times we met and I couldn't wait to see how we continued to grow together.

"I would be honored," he answered.

Acknowledgments

HOLY SHIT, I CAN'T believe we made it to this point. Writing Emery and Oliver's book turned out to be more of a challenge than I could have ever expected. Writing their story took over a year and lined up with a lot of struggles in my personal life. The first draft of this book took shape while I was working through unpacking a lot of childhood trauma that I had never spoken to anyone about. During the process my grandfather's slowly declining health reached the point of him being place on hospice care and eventually passing during my final months of editing. To be frank, this book simultaneously wrecked my mental health and healed parts of me.

I owe the biggest thank you to my amazing husband for holding me together while I navigated all the struggles that surfaced while writing this book. Thank you for being the only person to tell me that I didn't need to be strong for anyone and that it was okay to grieve how ever I needed to. I'll never be able to put into words how thankful I am for you. Thank you for loving all the broken parts that others made me feel like I need to hide.

I also have to thank my sister. Our childhood tried to drive a wedge between us and I'm forever grateful that we've been able to heal. Thank you for being my built in best friend even when I didn't know it.

Thank you to all of my fellow indie authors. The friendships I've built during my time in the indie space, particularly the space for fat romance books, have been instrumental in keeping me going on the hardest days. Thank you for reminding me that I don't suck at this and for all your encouragement while I navigated grief while finishing the book. I don't know what I would have finished this book if it weren't for all you.

Thank you to all my readers. Everytime I hear from one of you it reminds me why I do this. I can't wait to keep sharing stories with all of you.

Coming Soon

Want more of the Franklin family?

Shelby & Wade's story is next!

Kiss The Girl

Coming April 2026

About the Author

Ellie Harper Smith grew up with her nose always stuck in a book as a way to both escape and process the world around her. As a strong believer that everyone deserves a happy ending Ellie writes romance books featuring characters with neurodivergence, chronic health conditions, and mental health struggles. Ellie's books are set in a small town in the foothills of the north Georgia mountains inspired by the area she lives in.

Also by Ellie Harper Smith

Love Me Softly

Take A Hike: A Copper Ridge Novella

Love Notes & Lattes: A Copper Ridge Novella (March 2026)

Kiss The Girl (April 2026)